Killing Them Again

a novel

Dave Vaughan

blue denim press

Dedication

For those who know the system's broken… and fight anyway.

Dave Vaughan wrote the screenplay of the award-winning film, Hokum, directed by Jared Bratt. Advocate, was another film written by him. His debut novel, *Ballet of Deception,* was published in 2023 and his short story, "Unscheduled Departure" appeared in the Hill Spirits VI anthology in 2024. *Killing Them Again* is the inaugural winner of the first AI-judged writing competition presented by MyPoolitzer, Quantifiction, and Blue Denim Press.

Prologue

The elevator doors whispered open, spilling dim light into the silent corridor. A figure stepped forward, each footfall measured. The air stung of disinfectant mixed with something else. Voices that had once been sharp still lingered in the walls, long after anyone remained to listen.

The highly polished floor gleamed beneath the fluorescent glow, slivers of brightness warping into skewed reflections. A stack of papers trembled slightly in the figure's hand until steady fingers pressed them firmly. At the end of the hall, a door hissed open. The papers hovered midair, a single corner flicking upward like a breath caught in a throat.

Inside, slats of pale light sliced through the dimness, slipping between half-closed blinds onto a polished wooden desk. A miniature American flag stood upright in a pencil holder, its colours dulled in the filtered beams.

The figure paused for a beat, then stepped into the room. The papers landed precisely in the centre of the desk. The top sheet caught the glow, revealing a single letter in delicate, looping ink, framed by a teal border.

It carried the weight of something inevitable.

Sedgewick,

The path ahead is littered with shards: truths and fabrications alike. Each sharp. Each unforgiving.

You think you've unravelled the mystery of Babe Lincoln. However, our past exchanges were mere preludes to the raw truths that were waiting to be revealed.

Do you remember our conversations, Sedgewick? Your piercing questions, disguised as curiosity, still echo through me. You were always present, yet distant. Fully engaged one moment, eerily detached the next.

Were you a shield against the unsettling realities I embody, or something worse?

The story I'm about to tell is not for the faint-hearted. It is a journey where reality entwines with illusion and unrestrained fantasy. This may disturb or offend you, but I trust it will captivate you. Hasn't your insatiable curiosity always drawn you to my flame?

You once likened yourself to an eagle: vast wingspan, sharp talons, precise flight. Strength. Freedom.

But then there's the parrot. A creature dismissed as ornamental, mistaken for something lesser. It chatters endlessly, yet how often do people truly listen?

Perhaps that's why you've always stayed perched, Sedgewick. It is safer to observe from a gilded cage than to risk the sky. After all, an eagle in captivity is just another exhibit.

But some creatures don't have the luxury of flight, do they? Some only repeat what they've been taught. Some must tell stories to be heard.

I offer a tale tangled with ambiguity, a touch of audacious impropriety. Whether you interpret it literally or figuratively is entirely your choice.

This journey will lead you into depths where reality twists and the unexpected prevails.

Decipher my words as you will, but understand this: I won't spoil future surprises. You won't merely understand. You will feel it. And I promise, Sedgewick, it will be the ride of a lifetime.

Cheerios,
Babe Lincoln

Part One

Chapter 1

Trouble didn't start with Moosetown's sludge or the screams. It began with the girl in the yellow cap—and the woman in blue coveralls.

At first glance, Moosetown looked ordinary, the kind of Canadian village where time trickled by, unbothered, basking in the glow of a perfect summer day. Cornfields stretched beyond the square. The forest loomed thick and quiet. The air carried the sweet scents of blooming flowers and freshly baked bread.

Neighbours exchanged easy greetings. Retirees sipped coffee outside Tim Hortons, watching the morning unfold. Children's laughter echoed along pristine sidewalks, unaware they were dancing on the edge of disaster.

A "Free Scoops!" banner fluttered above the new ice cream parlour. The scent of waffle cones tangled with wildflowers and fresh-cut grass.

Above it all, Risqué the parrot perched atop a lamppost, eyeing the crowd with twitchy suspicion.

The world felt unshakable.

Molly Darnell stood outside an art shop, damp from the mist, her yellow cap pulled low. A painting in the window caught her eye, a surreal nightmare of a town square warped beyond recognition. Buildings sagged like melted wax. Windows oozed into twisted shapes beneath a blood-red sky. Streets coiled, crumbling into black voids. Above all, a warped clock floated, its melting hands frozen in meaningless directions.

A chill traced down her spine. *Dalí? Here?*

She leaned in, breath fogging the glass. The image stirred something buried. A photograph of a woman she didn't recognize. She'd found it years ago among her father's things.

When she'd asked, he snatched it away.

Face pale. Lips tight.

Molly shook off the memory, but the unease clung, thick and oily. The scene felt too familiar, like a half-formed nightmare she'd been trying to forget. Or maybe it was nothing. Perhaps she was still clouded from last night's partying.

Then—movement. A flicker at the edge of her vision.

Across the square, partially obscured by a delivery truck, a red-headed woman in blue coveralls stood eerily still.

Watching.

Molly's pulse jumped. The woman tilted her head in a slow, knowing acknowledgment. Then, with careful precision, she reached into her pocket.

Something's wrong.

BOOM.

A thunderous explosion shattered the air.

Not thunder. Not fireworks.

Something worse.

The ground convulsed beneath her feet. A deep shockwave ripped through Moosetown. Molly turned to run when a gloved hand clamped over her mouth. Her scream strangled in her throat. A sharp prick. Cold flooded her veins. Her limbs sagged, muscles turning to useless weight.

Sedative.

She fought, but her body wouldn't listen. The world lurched, vision swimming as the drug dragged her under. Rough hands hauled her backward, sneakers scraping cobblestone.

The sounds of Moosetown warped, stretched and vanished. Laughter. Music. Voices melting into a black void.

The sky shifted. Some swore it turned grey. Others insisted it stayed blue. But no one disputed what happened next.

The ground split open.

A pressurized geyser of reeking sludge exploded from the square, black and boiling, thick with human waste. The impact was biblical, a tidal wave of filth that shattered windows, crushed storefronts, and sent bodies sprawling. The crowd barely had time to scream.

Sewage clawed up throats. Choked noses. Burned eyes.

A woman in a floral dress collapsed, screaming, her grocery bag bursting in the muck. A schoolboy turned to his friend, shit dripping down his face. "My grandpa would call this a turd-fest," he muttered, then puked.

Above the squalor, Risqué shook the slop from his wings and screeched into the sky, banking hard toward the horizon.

Down below, a greenish-blue pickup truck fishtailed out of the square, tires flinging filth, taillights glowing red as it tore past the edge of town.

The engine roared, desperate to outrun the carnage it had unleashed.

Chapter 2

Molly Darnell woke to the wrong kind of silence.

A dead silence.

Her skull throbbed with pressure, her limbs heavy and unresponsive. *Where am I?*

Flashes came in fragments—music pounding, bottles clinking, laughter curling through smoke, the campfire's glow licking her skin. The mingling tang of weed and cold beer.

Then the movement. A shape behind her.

A sting.

Nothing after that.

She forced her eyes open. The room lurched into focus—bleak, colourless, suffocating. A rusted cot. A slanted desk cluttered with a crooked gooseneck lamp, a crumpled paper bag, and a sweating glass of milk. In the corner sat a green plastic pail. A piss bucket.

Her stomach turned. *This can't be happening.*

She swung her legs over the cot, muscles aching. Her fingers trembled as she peeled open the paper bag. Inside, two limp sandwiches of processed orange cheese between slices of waxy white bread. Bile surged. She shoved the bag away and reached for the folded note beneath the lamp.

The handwriting was childish.

Dear Molly,

I hope this food helps you recover.

Tonight's experience will be memorable, and I need you to be rejuvenated for the big event.

Oh yes, the ankle bracelet. Consider it a necessity, not a fashion statement. It is a safeguard against your leaving.

Warmly,

Muncie

Her pulse stuttered. The bracelet was real. Cold metal locked around her ankle.

She lunged for the door. Twisted the handle. Locked. She held her breath. Listening.

Nothing.

But she felt it. The eyes of a camera. She scanned the corners. The ceiling. The vents. Nothing obvious.

Her knees buckled. She dropped. "Not me," she whispered. But the fear passed. Anger settled.

He thinks I'll break. He thinks I won't fight. Wrong.

She'd find a way out. Or die trying.

Chapter 3

The day after Molly's kidnapping, Babe Lincoln stood at the chain-link fence of the police impound yard, her microphone poised like a weapon. Sunlight caught the sharp angles of her face, her spiky blonde hair contrasting with the chaotic scene behind her. Beyond the fence, a forensic team swarmed a red '99 Corvette, its surface gleaming under their scrutiny.

Her cameraman and technician watched, wide-eyed and tense.

"For News Four, this is Babe Lincoln," she declared, her voice steady, though unease tugged at the edge of her composure.

"Bravo, Babe! A masterpiece, as always," her cameraman called, winking.

She smiled, fingers tightening around the mic. "Did we capture the red sports car in all its glory?"

"As requested. But do you really think Molly was kidnapped?" he asked, dropping his voice.

Babe glanced at the Corvette again, her gut churning. The car sat too pristine. The forensic team's latex-covered hands dusted and swabbed, but she already knew they'd find nothing. No scratches. No dents. No struggle.

Her instincts screamed: set-up.

She stepped closer to the fence, knuckles brushing cold steel. The sun flared off the polished hood, sending a sharp glint into her eyes. For a heartbeat, she imagined Molly's reflection there, trapped inside, palms pressed to the glass.

She blinked hard, shaking it off. *Get it together.* "Anonymous tip," Babe said, pulling her attention from the car. "Boss decided to run with it."

He shook his head. "Politics and ratings. Then the cops take your car? That's messed up, Babe."

She forced a smile. "I'll sort that out later."

The black Navigator rolled up, changing everything.

Through the window, Babe spotted a printed sign with her name. The man holding it didn't smile or wave.

The driver's massive frame filled the front seat, a man built to make furniture creak.

Babe hesitated, then opened the door and climbed into the back. The air inside stank of polished leather and stale smoke. The door clicked shut. Final. Like a sealed vault.

"The General's expecting you," the driver said.

Babe met his expression in the mirror. "Let's not keep him waiting." She understood the General was a significant power broker who had people delivered to him, not vice versa. The fact that she was now the package? That didn't sit right.

The city pulsed outside, but time dragged like a weight inside the SUV.

Babe cleared her throat. "Excuse me, driver—"

"Otis," he cut in.

"Otis." She kept her voice polite. "We're barely moving. Is something wrong?"

"A repohta and a backseat drivah?" he muttered.

She didn't bite. "Just surprised by the invitation. Where are you from?"

"Boston."

Nothing more.

The silence stretched. Then he spoke, low and measured. "You got real quiet after gettin' in. Guess I'm not what you pictured."

"I didn't have a picture," she said evenly.

He chuckled darkly. "Yeah, you did." He tapped the wheel softly. "Slick-suit chauffeur? Tight-lipped goon? Instead, you get me."

She stayed quiet.

"You don't have to say it." The SUV slowed at a red light. He turned slightly. "We both know what I am."

Babe met his eyes without blinking.

"That look you gave me when you got in? I've seen it my whole life."

He waited for her to flinch.

She didn't.

"Spiky blonde hair, perfect teeth, size six outfit—got that city-girl polish. It's clear as daylight what you're about."

Babe exhaled slowly. "And what is that, exactly?"

"Denial's cute." His fingers flexed against the wheel, the leather creaking under his grip. "But the straight truth is, people see me and think waste of space. You did. Ain't your fault. World taught you that."

A sharp beat of silence. Babe knew he was waiting for an apology. She didn't give him one. Instead, she reached into her pocket and pulled out a stick of gum, peeling back the foil. "You want one?"

Otis blinked. For the first time, she saw him hesitate. Just a flicker, but it was there.

He let out a low, wheezing chuckle, shaking his head. "You're a sharp one, huh?"

She smiled faintly, tucking the gum between her teeth. Didn't answer. And that was a win. A little one, but a win.

Otis shifted. His tone turned casual. "Soon as I get that new shot, everything changes."

Babe didn't like the way he said that. "Hope you checked the side effects."

"Easy to find out where ya live," he said softly, ignoring her comment. "I hear you live with Daddy while screwin' some two-bit actress."

The gum turned bitter.

She kept her voice cool. "I don't know where you're going with this."

"No secrets in this world," he said. "Just takes a call. Or two. And everything you thought was real? Gone."

The words landed like a slow, deliberate knife to the heart.

The SUV pulled up to the estate. The General's fortress. A bastion of excess and opulence. She tried the handle. Locked.

Her heart thudded. "Otis. Unlock the door."

He let out a laugh, the tension evaporating. "All that talk was bull." He clicked the lock. "Hang tough, Babe. You got the stones for it. Boris will greet ya at the door."

She stepped out, pulse still racing.

The black SUV pulled away, leaving Babe standing at the base of the sprawling fortress of stone and glass. No visible security cameras, but she didn't buy it. A place like this had eyes.

An inexplicable unease prickled at her skin as she climbed the steps. Maybe it was Otis's cocky grin. Maybe it was that offhand comment about "hanging tough," in whatever situation she was about to face. Either way, her instincts screamed caution.

She'd learned to trust that voice—the same instinct honed during years spent working at Pistol Pete's Chicken Emporium. Back then, she'd been the only woman to rise from fryer duty to assistant manager in a male-dominated, grease-slicked circus. She'd learned to spot wandering hands, condescending smiles, and the traps men set with polished charm.

No matter what their stripes were, you stayed wary.

The massive door swung open.

Boris stood there. Tall, marble-still, blind eyes hidden behind dark glasses. He raised a red plastic bucket and emptied it over her.

Warm. Pungent. Piss.

Babe exhaled through her nose. Then, calmly, she blocked him from closing the door with her foot. "Good afternoon, sir," she said, her voice cool. "I'm Babe Lincoln. News Four."

Boris tilted his head. "You're early." He turned and disappeared inside.

She followed, as did the stench clinging to her.

Vaulted ceilings. Chandeliers. Cold grandeur. A place built to remind visitors of their insignificance.

Boris handed her a towel and motioned for her to follow.

They moved through a rear door into a winding courtyard, the tapping of Boris's white cane echoing off high stone walls sealing them in. Ahead, the greenhouse loomed—glass panels streaked with grime, vines clawing at the edges. Something about it felt forgotten, swallowed by time. And Babe had the sickening feeling of foreboding—thick, waiting, and poised.

Inside, rows of terra-cotta pots lined a narrow path, some lush, others withered. The air was thick and humid. The scent of damp soil mixed with the faintest trace of decay. At the centre sat the General, perched in a wheelchair like a king on a crumbling throne.

Boris stepped forward, deftly positioning a red pail beneath the plaid blanket on the General's lap. An act performed with unsettling familiarity. "General," Boris announced, bowing slightly, "may I present Babe Lincoln."

"Please to meet—"

The General lifted a frail, arthritic hand to silence her. Then came the sound—a sharp, vigorous stream hitting the pail.

Babe bit her lower lip. She had expected a commanding presence in a tailored suit. Instead, she was looking at a skeletal figure with sharp, predatory features, oiled-back grey hair, and the eyes of a man whose decisions had shaped many lives, often for the worse.

The piss went on for a long time.

When the stream finally dwindled, paused, then resumed, Babe crossed her legs, shifting in the chair Boris had set out for her. "Yes, General, as I was saying—"

"Your balls okay, sir?" Boris interrupted.

"You've polished them splendidly, Boris," the General replied, his tone dry. He reached for Newton's cradle resting on the table beside him, setting the metallic spheres in motion. *Click-click-click.* The rhythmic tapping filled the greenhouse.

"Are you familiar with Newton's cradle, Ms. Lincoln? Momentum transfers from one moving body to another at rest. A metaphor for life," he mused.

Babe exhaled, watching the spheres swing.

The General flexed his fingers. "Although you're not here to discuss my balls. Shall we proceed?"

"Please do," she said, chest tightening as unease coursed through her veins.

He nudged the cradle again, eyes locked on her. "Momentum transfers from one body to another. What do you call that effect?"

Babe frowned. "I… uh, with all due respect, General, I don't see how—"

"Boris, a drink for Ms. Lincoln," he cut in, ignoring her. "How do you take your whiskey? A girl of your stature probably enjoys an egg with her libation. Am I correct?"

"Sure. Whatever works. Call me Babe, please."

Boris's cane tapped unevenly against the floor as he exited. The General offered the faintest of smiles. "Ms. Lincoln. I've been eager to discuss certain matters with you."

Click-click-click.

Babe hesitated, every instinct telling her this was a test. *Urine? Newton's balls? And now whiskey with an egg? He'd have to do better if he were trying to rattle her.*

The distant crash of Boris colliding with a glass wall broke the silence. "There's no end to this!" he howled from the other side of the greenhouse.

Babe turned sharply. "Is he—?"

"Yes." The General adjusted the golden key around his neck.

"Okay," she muttered. "Just curious." What she wanted to say was that Boris was the kind of blindly obedient lunatic that only men like the General kept around.

The General silenced the balls. "Curiosity is good. Merely a tweak in his medication. Nothing a few pills can't fix."

Babe wiped her brow with the damp towel Boris had given her. Instant regret. The smell was worse than the piss. She tossed it aside.

The General ignored her disgust. "Please, feel free to smoke."

That, at least, she welcomed. "Thank you, General."

"And thank you for coming straight from your assignment."

Boris returned, tray in hand—a crystal glass, a whiskey bottle, a damp tea towel draped over his arm. As he set the tray down, Babe ducked his wildly swinging cane and lit a match. The cigarette flared to life between her lips.

The General watched Boris pour. Slow. Measured. "Come, man!" he barked. "Let the girl live a little!"

Boris grunted and tilted the bottle further, whiskey sloshing near the rim. Then, from his pocket, he pulled an egg. And a handful of ice cubes. The cubes tumbled into the glass, displacing liquid over the edge.

Babe snatched the tea towel from Boris's arm, dabbing at the spill.

The General tapped a crooked finger against the glass.

Boris cracked the egg into the whiskey and slid the drink toward her. A thin film of albumen stretched across the amber liquid.

Babe didn't hesitate. She lifted the glass and knocked it back in one swallow. The whiskey hit first, sharp, burning. Then the egg—a cold, gelatinous slide down her throat. She set the empty glass down with deliberate ease.

Silence stretched.

The General studied her, then leaned back in his wheelchair, steepling his fingers. "Shall we begin?"

Babe set the cigarette between her lips and inhaled. *If this were a test, I'd say I passed.* She exhaled slowly, watching the smoke rise. "By all means."

"Tell me, Ms. Lincoln, what do you know about my life?"

"Not much beyond your political ties, General. I'm more curious about why you requested to see me."

"Our city thrives on the unspoken," he said, his voice carrying weight. "It's not the words, but the silence between them, that shapes us."

Babe narrowed her eyes. "And what are we not saying today?"

A sly grin spread across his face. "Many things, Ms. Lincoln, starting with your recent reporting."

"Part of the job. Does it worry you?"

He leaned back, his wheelchair creaking. "You might be walking a fine line with the disappearance of that young lady."

"The mayor's daughter," Babe corrected, letting him know she wasn't some rookie. "I think you should know—"

"Dickie Darnell isn't the mayor; he's pro tempore," the General interrupted smoothly.

Babe peeked at her watch, frustration edging in. *This man liked the theatrics.* "I have another commitment. If we can wrap this up…"

"Of course." The General clasped his hands over the plaid blanket draped across his lap. "Ms. Lincoln, do you know what separates great journalists from the insignificant?"

She flicked ash into the tray. "I'm sure you're about to tell me."

"The answer is access," the General said. "Power is worthless unless you can get close to it. You… are close to it."

Babe let the words settle before responding. "That's an interesting observation, General. I'm more curious about why you requested to see me."

He pulled a slim grey envelope from beneath the blanket and slid it across the table. "Inside, you'll find an address and a name. You'll also find a story no one else has. Consider it a gift."

Babe didn't reach for it. "And what do you expect in return?"

"Loyalty."

She let out a short laugh. "That's a big ask."

"Oh, I don't expect immediate devotion." His face darkened. "But I expect you to recognize when to choose sides."

Babe leaned back. "If this is such a big scoop, why hand it to me?"

"Because I admire talent. And because, quite frankly, you are the type to take things over the top!"

Babe arched an eyebrow. Something about how he said it—his tone, the certainty—itched at the back of her mind. A half-formed memory, just out of reach.

"You're an outsider in a world that eats outsiders for breakfast." The General gestured toward the envelope. "And that, Ms. Lincoln, is your invitation to the main event."

Babe picked it up, turning it over in her hands. She had a choice: open it and follow the trail. Or toss it and walk away. Her fingers hovered at the seam. She stood. "Thank you for the drink, General."

"Shall I summon Boris?"

She lifted her bag onto her shoulder, her face unreadable. "I'll find my way." Without another word, she stepped into the foliage, vanishing into the shifting greenery. Then, with a decisive flick, she ripped the envelope in half and tossed it into a bush.

Behind her, through the dense leaves, it came again. *Click-click-click.* The sound echoed after her. But Babe didn't flinch, nor did she turn back.

Chapter 4

Babe Lincoln sat in the dim, cramped waiting area of police headquarters, her phone resting on the chipped table beside her. It had taken a soaking at the General's mansion, but to her relief, it still worked. She'd swung home to change, tossed her stinking clothes in the trash, and checked on her daddy. Now, here she sat, waiting.

The Corvette was another matter. Seized by the cops. And she wanted it back. Filing a complaint was a trap. Paperwork only made targets bigger.

She exhaled slowly, forcing herself to focus on the real problem. Molly Darnell. Something about the disappearance felt off. Last she heard, Molly was at a campsite. Probably drinking. Partying. Acting like nothing could touch her. Had she pulled some reckless stunt? Or something worse? It was probably just a misunderstanding. These things usually were.

She ran a hand through her hair, restless. A half-folded newspaper on the chipped table beside her caught her eye. The headline read, "Local Film Director Killed."

Babe skimmed the article. Grim. Brutal. What people could do to one another intrigued her, but it always carried the same reminder: life was fragile. She tossed the paper aside. Her mind circled back to Molly. *Where the hell are you?*

What she didn't know was that just down the marble-floored corridor, behind a heavy wooden door etched with Lieutenant Abbie Choi, her name was being bandied about by the chief of police.

Chief Brisk stood beside an oak desk, speaking into the phone, his voice smooth but clipped. "We're doing all we can."

But Acting Mayor Dickie Darnell was never satisfied. His face burned red inside his limousine as he barked into his phone. "Why is this on the noon news?"

His assistant, Miss Horn, scribbled furiously on her tablet, her blazer pulled taut across her shoulders. The balding fifty-year-old shrugged at her, a silent apology for his tantrum.

Brisk pinched the bridge of his nose. "That's a question for News Four."

Darnell wasn't having it. "I need those surveillance tapes. Where are they?"

Brisk knew it was a ridiculous request. Those tapes didn't exist. "We're looking into it."

Darnell slumped back, a vein pulsing in his temple. "For Christ's sake, get this sorted out. I'm coming down there."

Brisk slammed the receiver down. The sharp motion betrayed a crack in his usual composure.

The door opened. Lieutenant Abbie Choi, a striking Asian-African American, stepped inside. Her office bore the marks of mid-renovation: a tarp draped over a ladder, paint rollers drying beside open cans. The air still carried a faint chemical bite, but the high ceilings and wide windows softened the disarray, casting a warm, tranquil glow across her features as she made a direct line for the chief.

Brisk knew Choi was adaptable, professionally and otherwise. But ambition made loyalty disposable. She was the type to sniff out advantage in every room, which worked to his benefit. For now. Better to end things on his terms—clean and quiet.

Still, the temptation lingered. He'd love to pull out his sizable endowment, the prodigal son, as he liked to call it, and give her a quick workout. But that would be begging for disaster, and Brisk preferred to stay in the control seat.

In his prime, it had been all about youth—smooth skin, tight bodies—the gold standard. But those days were over. Now they ignored him, or worse, told him to fuck off. Political correctness had wrecked the game.

So he adapted.

He'd met a stunner in her mid-thirties not long ago. Called it mentorship. Called it mutual growth. But it was the same endgame, just wrapped in better branding. He knew the odds were long, but Brisk never left any stone unturned for what he called a gorgeous piece of trim.

Choi reached for Molly Darnell's photo and slid it across the desk. The image showed an attractive young woman in a yellow baseball cap, long dark hair spilling over her shoulders. "Molly Darnell's disappearance is about to land in our lap."

Brisk exhaled through his nose. "I just spoke with her old man. I'd call him a stooge, but that'd be unfair to Moe, Larry, and Curly."

Choi had no idea who he was talking about, nor did she care. She set another photo in his meaty hand. "Babe Lincoln. Word is she's asking too many damn questions."

"Reporters tend to," Brisk said dryly. His tone cooled as his thumb grazed his jaw. "You've read her file?"

"Resourceful. Reckless. But not stupid."

Brisk nodded, tapping the photo's corner against the desk. "Let's make sure she doesn't get any bolder."

"She's in the waiting area."

"You speak to her?"

"Not yet."

Detective Slim Meekins sauntered in. Slicked-back hair. Bright red sunglasses. The kind of guy you'd see running a ring toss at the county fair—and pocketing your wallet while laughing about it. "Files you asked for, Chief," Slim said, holding a box labelled Evidence: Molly Darnell.

Brisk pointed to the desk. "You're off for a few days now, aren't you, Slim?"

"Yes, sir," he replied, setting the box down.

"Got plans?"

Slim grinned. "Figured I'd grab some candy, hit the dog park, mess with the soccer moms."

Brisk deadpanned. "Just don't end up on a leash."

Slim chuckled. "Thanks for the tip, Chief." He disappeared down the corridor.

Choi crossed her arms. "You think he's serious?"

Brisk rubbed his temples. "I hope not. Last thing we need is footage of one of ours creeping around a dog park like it's a singles bar." He handed her the photographs. "Get on with it."

Choi set the photos on the desk. She couldn't shake the chief's reaction to Babe Lincoln's photograph. Amusement? Interest? Or something else entirely? She shook off the thought, stepped into the hall, and called, "Lincoln!"

Babe entered with the kind of calm that irritated certain types of authority. Not flippant. Just unbothered. She slid into the seat across from Choi, arms relaxed, expression unreadable.

Choi wasted no time. She placed a photograph of Molly on the desk beside her badge and let it sit. "I've read your statement. Here's my take," she said. "Molly's missing. I'm guessing you wanted revenge. She stole your boyfriend. Sound about right?"

Babe focused on the ceiling, debating whether this was worth her energy. She looked at Choi. "Boyfriend? I don't even have a boyfriend," she shot back.

"This isn't about your tragic love life, sweetheart. This is bigger than boys playing stink-finger in the backseat of your fancy red car. Capiche?"

"They found a backseat? Those forensic boys must be real pros," she muttered.

Choi leaned back, flipping through Babe's file and clicking her tongue. "Impressive résumé, Lincoln." She glanced up. "Not in the traditional sense, of course."

Babe leaned back. "I get by."

Choi tilted her head, studying her. "That's the thing, isn't it? You always 'get by.'" A pause, measured. "No credentials, no degree. But here you are, front and centre." She lifted a folder from the desk, tapped its edge against her palm, and then set it down with deliberate care. Just as deliberately, she lifted her badge and placed it neatly on top of the folder, tapping it with a well-manicured fingernail.

Babe didn't look at the photo. She glimpsed at the desk—scattered papers, neatly stacked folders—before shifting to the tarp-draped corner of the room. "Renovating?" Her voice stayed light, almost curious. "Looks like you've been busy." A calculated pivot—an invitation to underestimate her. She reached out, her fingertips brushing the badge. It was not a dramatic move, just a quiet, precise turn, enough to make it noticeable.

Choi's pen stilled between her fingers. A flicker of something in her expression. She let the moment stretch past before sliding the photo of Molly a fraction closer to Babe. "People like you don't usually land in places like this." A measured pause. "Unless they're real unlucky. Or dirty."

Babe didn't respond right away. She let her eyes drop to the badge again, her expression unreadable. Then, with a barely perceptible flick of her fingers, she nudged it another fraction out of place. She didn't look up. Didn't smile. Just let it sit.

Choi exhaled sharply through her nose, then lifted the badge, set it back on top of the folder, and tapped it again. A small thing. But Babe already saw what she needed. This cop liked control.

And Babe had just poked a hole in it.

Choi's lips pressed together, but the office door swung open before she could reply. Chief Brisk stepped inside, a pair of well-polished shoes in hand.

Babe's eyes dropped to the shoes, then back up to the top cop.

Brisk swapped the shoes for Molly's photograph and studied Babe with narrowed eyes. "So, you camped with the acting mayor's daughter at Bear Lake. That correct?"

"For her birthday," Babe said, her patience fraying at the edges. "She won a contest. Prize included a trailer." She felt a prickle of heat creep up her neck, but forced herself to stay still.

The chief eyed the thick tape sealing the Molly Darnell evidence box on the desk. "So, you two are a pair of…" His voice dripped with disdain. "What do they call college girls engaging in wild antics? Liberals?"

Babe's stomach tightened. *Breathe.* She forced a tight smile, careful not to let her irritation show. "You mean people who think for themselves? Sure. We're dangerous like that."

Choi scoffed under her breath. "Woke yahoos," Choi muttered, like the words tasted sour.

Babe didn't take the bait. She let the silence hang, its weight pressing against Choi like a stone.

Brisk shrugged. "Don't mind Choi; she's a pit bull. Depending on her mood, she might rip out your heart for breakfast or lunch."

He scrutinized Babe's photograph, then glanced at Choi. "Nice outfit. Maybe a softer colour would suit her better. Don't you agree, Lieutenant?"

Choi's mouth twisted into something resembling a smile. "Absolutely, Chief," she said, glancing at Babe. "Had his colours analyzed last month. Took it real serious."

Babe noted Choi pluck a piece of lint from Brisk's sleeve. A small gesture, but combined with the lieutenant's shift in body language, it spoke volumes. Babe exhaled slowly like she was bored rather than irritated. "We all have our priorities."

Brisk studied her, his expression unreadable. "Yes, we do." He set the photographs aside. "We'll work this case backward, forward, inside out until we find the kid."

Babe's fingers tightened around her phone. Her pulse ticked faster, but she kept her hand steady. Unbeknownst to the chief, she'd hit record.

Brisk's tone darkened. "Where do we begin?"

Babe felt her voice catch for half a second, but she pushed through, aiming for casual, not challenging. "How about a cup of coffee?" She gave Choi a small, sly smile that could be read as friendly or just slightly needling. "I'll take a cappuccino, Choi-ski. Skim milk. Just a titch of cinnamon."

Choi's stance stiffened, and Babe's pulse kicked up a notch. *Was that a mistake?*

Before Choi could respond, the chief stepped between them. He'd seen enough to know when things were about to go south.

Chapter 5

Dickie Darnell sat rigid in the back of his sleek limousine, tilting a compact mirror under his chin. He examined his eyebrows, plucking a single defector with meticulous care. The city's cacophony throbbed outside—sirens wailing, horns blaring, pedestrians shouting over one another. Even through tinted glass, he could feel the city pressing in, loud, messy, disobedient. A reminder of how thin his grip on power was.

Being the acting mayor was a balancing act, and today, Chief Brisk was the tightrope. Miss Horn, as always, was the counterweight. Her sharp insight cut through the murky waters of city politics, keeping him from drowning in it.

The limousine slowed to a stop in front of police headquarters. Dickie snapped the mirror shut, inhaling sharply, holding the breath as if it might fortify him. He needed to control this meeting.

Miss Horn stepped out first, heels clicking against the pavement with practiced grace. He couldn't help but glance at the sweep of her elegant legs before wrenching his focus back where it belonged. He adjusted his waistband and cleared his throat. "Miss Horn, this requires the utmost discretion regarding… let's call her The Remedy."

"Understood." Calm, detached. Her green eyes barely flicked toward him, sharp behind horn-rims, sharper without.

Dickie quickened his pace to match hers. "We need Chief Brisk on our side."

Miss Horn tapped her stylus against her tablet. "Start with subtle influence. Shape the narrative. Protect the office's reputation."

Dickie let out a tight laugh. "Remember, shit flows downhill. We can't afford to get our hands dirty."

She glanced up just long enough to offer a small, knowing smile. "You're uniquely suited for this. Perhaps the most decisive leader I've ever supported."

Her words, smooth as silk, slid under his skin and tightened his spine. He straightened his tie and squared his shoulders. "That's why I'm here." He said it steadily. Almost presidential, if no one looked too hard.

Miss Horn barely glanced up from her tablet at the entrance, already plotting their next move. Their routine was seamless. Each morning, he picked her up from her condo, and together they strategized the day's headlines. Gossip about their relationship buzzed behind closed doors, but no one doubted her role as the gatekeeper to his administration. She even insisted that staff, who privately mocked him as Dopey Darnell, refer to him as The Honourable Richard Darnell.

"You'll end up the hero, MD," she murmured, just loud enough for his ego to catch it.

His chest swelled at her use of his initials. Few people enjoyed the privilege. His second ex-wife had called him shit-for-brains, so Miss Horn's insistence on respect felt like salve on an old wound. He held the door for Miss Horn and stole another glance. With her hair down and glasses off, she could pass for a supermodel. He shoved the thought aside. Focus. Control.

Brisk was a bulldog, unpredictable at best. Securing his cooperation was everything.

Winners find a way, Dickie reminded himself. *Losers find excuses.*

Inside, the scent of stale coffee and disinfectant hung thick in the air. Neither Dickie nor Miss Horn noticed Lieutenant Choi slipping out of the building through a side exit.

Choi pulled out her phone, voice low and clipped. "Chief. Darnell's here with his handler."

Chapter 6

Wynns wasn't just a restaurant; it towered as an oasis of sophistication in the city's heart, frequented by the elite. The maître d', dressed impeccably in a black jacket with gleaming silver buttons, ushered guests through the polished brass doors with a gentle push into a world where soft light made diamonds glitter and champagne flutes shimmer.

Babe stared down at her cappuccino, a blotchy, symmetrical pattern spreading across the foam—something between a Rorschach test and a hallucination. Wings? A face? Something darker? She tilted her head, trying to make sense of it, then ran her spoon through the design, watching it dissolve into nothing. "This is… a bit much," she murmured, looking up at Chief Brisk across the table. "We could've just gone to a coffee shop."

Brisk leaned back, his eyes steady. He reminded her of a predator indulging in patience for sport. "First, let's confirm this conversation is off the record."

Babe nodded, forcing a small smile. "Of course. Discretion's my middle name."

"The staff prides itself on treating every customer like royalty. They opened early as a professional courtesy."

"Oh." Babe fumbled in her pocket, pulled out a business card, and handed it to him.

Brisk glanced at it briefly. "I already have one," he said.

"Now you've got two," she replied, offering another faint smile. Her eyes dropped to her cup. "About the scene back at headquarters—"

"Justice follows its own pace." Brisk slipped the card into his jacket pocket.

Babe's eyes locked onto his. "Like what's happening with your lieutenant… the one with the mixed heritage?"

He hesitated, lowering his voice. "Father's African American. Mother's Chinese."

Babe bit her lip, eyes fixed on the polished table. She could see her reflection, warped and ghostly. "Right. That tracks." She shifted in her seat, fingers knotting in her lap.

Brisk raised an eyebrow. "Something on your mind?"

"Not really. It's just… I don't know. Your lieutenant seems a bit…"

Brisk leaned forward, his voice sharp. "What are you trying to say? Spit it out."

"Her forefathers helped build the transcontinental railroad. They worked brutal hours, faced harsh terrain, and endured relentless discrimination to leave a mark. I'd hope she respects that."

"I didn't ask for a history lesson," Brisk said, scowling.

"You're right, sorry. I'm here to listen to what you have to say."

Before Brisk could respond, a man approached the table, his demeanour warm and confident. "Chief Brisk, welcome again," he said, extending a hand. "I trust everything meets your satisfaction?"

Brisk shook his hand firmly. "As always, Diego. Everything's perfect."

Diego leaned closer, lowering his voice. "The gentleman we discussed has arrived." He nodded toward the back of the restaurant.

Babe noted an arresting brunette leading a middle-aged man with a clipboard toward the kitchen.

Diego added, "Lucia will keep him occupied until you're ready."

Brisk stood. "Excuse me a moment."

He left Babe with Diego, who turned to her with a curious smile. "Are you a friend of the Chief's… or perhaps his granddaughter?"

Babe blinked, caught off guard. "Oh, um… just a colleague," she said quickly, focus shifting back to her cappuccino.

"Ah, understood," Diego said with a nod. "Chief Brisk has been a great friend to us here at Wynns. Always looking out for us." He signalled to a passing waiter. "Mateo, bring this young lady anything she needs."

"I'm fine, thank you," Babe replied, uneasy under the attention.

"Excellent. It was my pleasure to meet you. If you'll excuse me, the Roberts have arrived." Diego turned to escort an elegantly dressed couple to a private dining room.

Alone again, Babe stared at the polished silverware, her curiosity gnawing at her. The man with the clipboard stormed out of the kitchen, face flushed, eyes darting like a cornered animal sizing up escape routes. Behind him, Lucia's hand lingered on Brisk's arm as they trailed behind. Something twisted, sharp, and cold in Babe's gut.

Brisk returned, his expression unreadable but his eyes glinting. "Did you look at the menu?"

"I'll stick with coffee. How about you? Find anything tasty in the kitchen?"

"I might go for a salad," he said. "Wouldn't want to overdo it. I have a delicate matter to attend to later."

Babe forced a smile, uncertain how to respond. The silence between them grew thick, heavy with unspoken history. His tone carried something unreadable, but she chose not to pry.

Brisk leaned in, his voice dropping low. "News 4 will drop all coverage of Molly Darnell's disappearance. Understand?"

Babe swirled the coffee in her cup, letting the silence stretch. She could feel Brisk watching her, waiting. She tilted her head slightly, her voice smooth. "Of course, Chief. Just one thing."

Brisk's brow lifted, wary. "What's that?"

Babe leaned forward, lowering her voice. "That 'anonymous tip' about Molly?" A beat. "Wasn't so anonymous."

Brisk's fingers flexed against the table. She saw the tension in his face, subtle but lethal. But he was a pro. If he knew she was bluffing, he wasn't giving it away.

Babe smiled, soft but knowing. "So, if I drop the story now, well… wouldn't that look a little odd? A little too… convenient?"

Brisk's expression hardened. "You're playing with fire." He leaned in a little closer, his voice dropping into something gravelly. "Play smart, Babe. Smart's the only currency that doesn't run out."

Babe laughed lightly. "Then I hope you brought a fire extinguisher." She reached into her bag and pulled out a small pink gift bag.

Brisk studied her for a moment before placing a hand on her arm. "You're good at what you do, Babe. You could do much better if you wanted to."

She glanced at his hand but didn't pull away. "Like you've ever cared about that."

His expression darkened. "Don't push me," he said quietly. Glancing around the room, he lowered his voice. "Remember, *Grand Theft Auto* isn't just a video game."

Babe paled. The memory knifed through her, sharp and sudden, stealing her breath. "Oh, now we're pretending it was some game? How old was I when you made me do it? Do you even remember?"

A flicker of discomfort crossed Brisk's face. "You were willing. Or have you forgotten?"

"Willing?" Her voice dropped to a whisper. "I had no choice." She pulled a perfume bottle from the gift bag and placed it on the table. "There was always some twisted quid pro quo, wasn't there?"

"You could handle it," he muttered. "Listen to me. You're gifted. Use that for something meaningful. You're practically a savant with schematics."

"I'm done. Save your flattery."

Brisk watched her momentarily, then slid an envelope from his coat across the table.

She opened it cautiously, revealing a crisp hundred-dollar bill. Her brow furrowed. "What's this?"

Brisk nodded toward the man with the clipboard, who was furiously scribbling at a table near the back wall. "County health inspector. He's extorting Diego and Lucia with fake violations."

"What's he writing?"

"A confession, 'I've been a naughty boy,' a hundred times. After that, he'll scrub dishes and mop floors. If he refuses, I'll hold onto that bill with his fingerprints. By morning, he'll explain why he's unemployed to his wife."

Babe shifted in her chair. "Is that necessary?"

"He earned it."

She glanced down, fidgeting with the perfume bottle. "If you say so," she muttered. She spritzed her wrist and extended it toward him.

The perfume wasn't even hers, just a favour for a friend. But the scent crawled under her skin uninvited, too familiar.

Brisk leaned in, his sleeve brushing the bottle as he inhaled the scent. "Lovely," he murmured. Then he straightened, his tone sharpening. "Back to Molly. Officially, we're not on the case."

"Then give me back my car." She didn't mention the slick looking detective and the evidence box in Choi's office. Not yet.

"Lieutenant Choi handles that. Trust me, Babe, Molly is missing."

"If I believed that, I'd already be searching, with or without your permission, or help."

Brisk pulled out a Number 10 pencil, scribbled on a smaller envelope, and slid it across the table. "Take this," he said. "Choi's cell number is inside. Read the message."

Babe's eyes widened as she read it. "You're serious?"

Before he could respond, the inspector let out a sharp breath. Then, with a sudden roar, he shoved back his chair and lunged across the room at Brisk, the pen clenched in his fist like a blade.

Brisk's revolver barked. One shot, clean and final.

Babe flinched, her fingers clawing the edge of the table.

The inspector staggered mid-stride, his body twisting as the pen clattered at her feet. He crumpled. Blood bloomed across the marble floor.

Babe's breath caught. Her hands shook as she backed from the table. "I… I wasn't here," she whispered. Then she turned and ran.

The problem wasn't what she'd just witnessed. The real danger was still ahead. And there might be no going back.

Chapter 7

The doors of police headquarters slammed shut behind him, but Acting Mayor Dickie Darnell didn't flinch. His exaggerated storm-out had been for effect. Public theatre. A well-rehearsed tantrum for the cameras that weren't even there. "Stir the hornet's nest, expect stings." He turned to Miss Horn as she caught up. "Too much?"

Miss Horn offered a faint smile, the kind that barely curled her lips. "Not in the least, MD. Old clichés still draw blood."

Dickie wasn't convinced. His pulse thumped louder than the city's hum around them. "He skipped our meeting on The Remedy? Unacceptable!" He smoothed his silk tie, fingertips lingering as if grasping for control. "Stir the hornet's nest, expect stings."

Miss Horn closed her tablet. "Skate on thin ice, you drown."

"Mess with the bull, get the horns."

"Exactly." She looked at him now, green eyes gleaming behind horn-rimmed glasses. "Unmatched nerve. Rare vision. You lead with poise that few possess."

Dickie squared his shoulders. "We do what's necessary."

They reached the limousine. The scent of leather and polished wood drifted from the open car door, mingling with exhaust fumes and city grime. Pedestrians passed by, some stealing glances at Miss Horn, none at him. Dickie exhaled slowly. Good. Let them gawk at her instead. He knew the truth. Their indifference wasn't because he was forgettable—no, no, no. He was camouflaged. A king in plain sight. They'd beg for autographs, advice, or a second of his time if they recognized him.

Fame, after all, was best wielded selectively.

He opened the door for Miss Horn but blocked her entry. His voice dipped, the veneer of civility barely holding its shape. "Do we review the chief's performance?"

Miss Horn tapped her stylus once, twice, measured as a heartbeat. "Not yet. The current's swift. Let it carry us."

He traced the faint curl of her smile. "You know, Miss Horn," he said, his voice unsteady, "your loyalty keeps me anchored."

Her fingers gently pressed his shoulder. "You don't sit on your hands, MD. You grip the wheel." Her voice dripped patience, masking power. "The tide surges, the rocks threaten, but you steer through."

"Yeah, that's right."

She let him bask in it. Just long enough. Then her voice softened, silk threaded with something dangerous and intimate. "There was a time when assistants wore less fabric and more temptation."

Dickie straightened, his tone ragged but warming. "And just hinting at my oral presentation skills could derail an entire meeting."

"Your delivery still disarms."

He exhaled. "Pressure's building. I'm not sure how long I can keep it up."

Her hand remained on his shoulder. Her smile never touched her eyes. "You will, MD. And when the moment comes, you'll finish strong." She slipped past and slid into the limo, her grace precise.

Dickie watched her for a moment, gathering himself.

Miss Horn glanced up at him, voice light but sharp enough to cut. "And Miss Lincoln?"

Dickie's lips twitched. "She's already halfway buried."

Chapter 8

The bedroom stank of rot and despair. Peeling wallpaper, yellowed with age, clung to cracked plaster walls. A thin, stained mattress sagged on a corroded frame, while a chipped nightstand sat beside it like a defeated relic.

For Ariana Barbeau, a five-foot-six blend of seduction and grit in her mid-twenties, the squalor of the room meant nothing compared to the will to survive.

Jet-black hair hung in tousled waves over her bare shoulders, damp with sweat and tension. Her crimson dress clung to every curve, slit high to reveal long legs that moved with purpose, indifferent to the dirt beneath them. The neckline dipped low, framed with black lace, drawing the eye to the soft rise of her chest. Her breasts lifted with each breath, full and flushed, exposed just enough to distract but not disarm. Vulnerability was suggested, but not offered.

Her face was pink from exertion, her lips parted, her gaze sharp and unflinching. The blue in her eyes seemed deeper in the dim light, not just filled with fear, but with focus. She wasn't waiting to be saved. She was already calculating her next move.

Ariana's breaths came in harsh gasps. Her bound wrists twisted against the rope. Muffled footsteps echoed beyond the door. A shadow crossed the sliver of light beneath the frame.

She froze. Every muscle locked. Her breath caught.

Panic gave way to defiance as the footsteps resumed. Silence pressed down on her like a lead weight as the sound faded. Ariana bent forward, biting into the rope with perfect teeth. Sweat slicked her brow as her chest heaved with each pull. The coarse fibers scratched her lips, her jaw ached, but she didn't stop until the ropes dropped to the floor. Red, raw wrists flexed as she rose. Every movement, deliberate.

She eased to the window. Dirty plastic curtains hung limp over the warped frame, filtering the light. A narrow gap, barely an inch between the sill and rusted metal. Not much, but enough.

Ariana pressed her palms against the frame and shoved. The sharp edge bit into her hands as the window rose. She squeezed through the frame and tumbled outside.

Pain shot up her ankle as she landed, but she bit her lip to stifle the cry. Sunlight seared her eyes, too bright after the dim prison she left behind. For a moment, she lay still, the grass cool beneath her, the sun's warmth mocking her with its reminder of freedom. Her chest heaved, her pulse racing, but she wasn't safe yet.

Gritting her teeth, Ariana forced herself upright. Each step sent a sharp jolt through her ankle, but stopping wasn't an option. Her head snapped around every few paces, searching for any sign of pursuit.

A low, guttural growl cut through the air.

Her pulse spiked. A guard dog? No weapon. No cover except for a rickety garden shed leaning precariously in the distance. Its warped walls wouldn't hold for long, but it was all she had. She hobbled toward it, the sun beating down on her slick skin.

Then she saw him.

A figure stepped from the shadows. His pristine white lab coat gleamed in the sunlight. In one gloved hand, he held a syringe, the needle glinting like a fang. In the other, a three-foot sword, its polished blade flashing with cruel precision. He moved slowly, deliberately, as if savouring the chase.

Panic flooded her veins. Her ankle buckled, but she caught herself and stumbled to the shed. Her fingers curled around the handle, wrenched the door open and slammed it shut behind her.

The dim interior reeked of dampness. Crooked tools lined the walls, junk littered the floor. Her hands closed on a garden rake, its wooden handle splintered beyond repair. She crouched low and peered through a crack in the wall. The glare outside made it hard to see his silhouette.

A violent thud rattled the shed. Ariana flinched as a blade pierced the wall, stopping inches from her ear. Splinters rained down. The door flew open. The sight of his hooded face sent a shiver up her spine. Fear tipped into desperation. Ariana swung the rake, missing his chest by inches. The force threw her off balance and to the floor.

The figure loomed large and plunged the sword downward, then stopped in mid-air. A beat passed. Then—

"Cut! Thank you, Ariana," the director's voice rang out, shattering the tension. The shed dissolved into the edges of a film set, the danger fading into illusion. The sword, dulled and harmless under the lights, dropped to the floor as the hooded man walked away.

Ariana stayed on the floor, her chest heaving. The line between story and reality blurred. She couldn't tell if the trembling in her hands belonged to her or the victim she'd become.

Gomsie, the prop master, wheeled in a mannequin, a flawless replica of Ariana, complete with a torn crimson dress and dirt-streaked legs. Crew members moved with clinical efficiency.

She stood slowly and saw Babe waiting in the distance. Ariana's flushed face softened at the sight of her, the noise and hubbub surrounding her blurred into nothing.

The craft services lady leaned toward Babe, whispering, "With Ariana's short blonde hair in *The Big Reveal* and your eyes, you two could be twins."

Babe brushed off the comment with a faint smile. "Perhaps," she said, unwilling to fuel the crew's gossip.

Ariana approached. Babe handed her a small pink gift bag. "You deserve a better future, my love," Babe said softly, her tone gentle but weighted. "I got you something to celebrate your last day on set. And that perfume you've been eyeing for the director."

Ariana pulled a pair of red-handled scissors from the bag, but paused mid-motion when she saw Babe freeze, just for a second, eyes flicking toward the shadows near the house.

Babe's fingers tightened on her bag strap, thumb stroking the leather. Her shoulders, usually full of swagger, now slumped, drawn and wary.

"What's wrong?" Ariana asked. "Babe. Talk to me."

Babe didn't look at her. She focused on the set—corners, exits, shadows.

Ariana wondered if she was expecting someone to show up.

"Later," Babe said.

Ariana adjusted her grip on the scissors. The air felt heavier now. Like the breath before a scream. The set should've felt safe. But Babe's silence said otherwise.

That night, their bedroom held the quiet they couldn't find on set. A map on the wall, pins marking places they swore they'd go. Plans for tomorrow, in a world where tomorrow wasn't promised. Ariana stood before the floor-to-ceiling mirror wrapped in a towel. Behind her, Babe ran a brush through her damp hair.

Her eyes met Babe's in the mirror. "Do you think Molly is really missing?"

Babe set the brush down, the image of Chief Brisk shooting the health inspector gnawing at her thoughts. "Maybe. I called her cell, but that doesn't mean much. She's out in bum-fuck nowhere."

Ariana adjusted the towel. "Maybe she's just being her usual secretive self. You know how Molly gets after meeting someone new. Remember that rich guy? The one who thought breakfast in bed meant she owed him a blow job for giving her walking-around money?"

A reluctant smile tugged at Babe's mouth. "She told him she was vegan to get out of it."

Ariana laughed. "Girl's got nerve, no doubt. What do you think we should do?"

"I want to believe she's fine. But let's give it the night. Rushing in without more information might piss her off."

Ariana turned, brushing her lips against Babe's. "We'll figure it out."

Babe loved Ariana. She had become Babe's anchor in a world that often tilted sideways. Ariana never let her sink into doubt. She saw Babe's on-air persona not as a mask, but as a foundation. "You're building something solid," Ariana would say. "Decide how far you're willing to go."

But that was the problem.

Babe had spent years fading into the background, where safety beat ambition. Ariana made her question that instinct, suggesting there was more waiting, if only she reached for it.

Ariana, with all her fire and drive, could have gone anywhere. But she stayed. She chose Babe. Not out of obligation, but because she saw something Babe struggled to see in herself.

It wasn't a transformation. Not yet.

But it was a beginning.

Ariana's voice pulled her back. "Let's think about something else for now," she whispered, letting the towel fall. The glow from the globe-shaped lamp lit every curve, flawless in ways that had nothing to do with luck.

They moved toward the bed, their sanctuary where words became unnecessary. As Ariana's arms wrapped around her, grounding her in the moment, she felt a flicker of tension, like something hadn't fully come home. She didn't say anything. She just held her tighter.

Outside the bedroom, the air was still. But not quite. Something was coming.

And it wouldn't knock.

Chapter 9

The Cape Cod-style cottage, known locally as the American Embassy, sat tucked in the woods along Bear Lake's glassy shore near Moosetown. Across the grounds stood the bunkie—a squat, utilitarian structure that looked like a budget motel cabin, divided into two cramped rooms—one of them Molly's. Two Muskoka chairs faced the lake from its narrow porch, and crescent moons stencilled on the steel doors echoed the motif on the nearby outhouse, a half-hearted nod to charm.

Molly sat on the bunkie's steps, lacing her sneakers. Sunlight caught the gleam of her ankle bracelet, a cold reminder that her freedom wasn't real; it just looked that way from a distance.

Ginger Shepard leaned against the porch railing, red ponytail swaying in the breeze. Wiry and sharp-featured, she wore the same unflattering blue coveralls as Molly, her frame appearing even leaner in the morning light. "What a lovely day," she said, irony sharp in her tone.

Molly didn't look up. "Sure it is."

"How'd you sleep?"

"Like an angel in heaven."

Ginger rolled her eyes. "Sarcasm won't make this easier."

"And pretending it's a lovely day won't either."

Risqué—the bright green parrot—perched on Muncie's arm as he stepped out of the cottage. Clad in weathered overalls and well into his fifties, Muncie looked every bit the caricature of a rural eccentric: wiry energy, a too-wide grin, and eyes that sparkled with some private joke no one else found funny. His banty-rooster strut oozed puffed-up pride and zero self-awareness. He adjusted a crooked cap emblazoned with a faded Sentinels Mall logo, the bill casting a shadow over his smirking face. A well-used axe rested on his shoulder. He drew in a deep breath, savouring the scent of pine needles and freshly chopped wood like it nourished him.

Molly adjusted her yellow cap and stepped off the porch. The grass was damp beneath her shoes. Ginger followed.

Then, without warning, pain tore through Molly's calf, locking every muscle in violent spasm. She crumpled, fingers clawing at the grass as she gasped for breath.

Beside her, Ginger collapsed, knees buckling with a strangled cry.

Molly's leg twitched. She forced herself upright, jaw tight against the burn. Jesus. She refused to rub it. Refused to give him the satisfaction.

Ginger, still working her calf, spat toward the cottage. "Knock it off, asswipe!"

Muncie's laughter boomed across the yard. "Just testing the battery!" He waved a small red controller in the air, grinning like he'd won something as he swaggered toward the woodpile.

Molly and Ginger trudged toward the stacked logs wedged between Muncie's pickup truck and the woodshed. They passed an inflatable pool and a garden hose. Both felt like mockery dressed up as normalcy.

Ginger had once suggested they strip down in the pool and rinse off with the hose after finishing the day's assignment. "The soap even floats," she'd said, her grin sharp enough to make Molly's teeth grind.

Molly hadn't missed the way Ginger watched her, eyes cool and clinical, like she was a specimen under glass. And she didn't doubt others would be watching, too.

At the woodpile, Ginger grabbed a burlap sack and held it open. "I'll hold this while you load. Then we'll switch."

"Can't wait," Molly muttered, hefting the first slab of wood. The rough bark bit into her palms, and a dull ache settled between her shoulders, not just from exhaustion but from something deeper.

Above, Risqué fluttered between branches, green feathers catching the light. His beady black eyes locked onto Molly, tracking her every move.

"Don't pull a hammy, Molly!" Muncie hollered, splitting another log with one clean swing. "I need to drop a deuce. You ladies carry on." He strolled off, the axe balanced on his shoulder, while Risqué hopped onto his arm with eerie precision.

"Where's that slug next door?" Ginger yelled after him. "Why are we stuck doing his work? This is bullshit."

"Don't worry about things that don't concern you," Muncie called back, entering the cottage. "Klarence, with a K, is indisposed."

Molly leaned against the pickup, exhaustion grinding her down. The sleepless night had drained her, making the chore feel like an uphill battle. She rolled her shoulders, but the ache refused to leave.

Ginger's voice dropped into that fake-sweet register she used when laying out her best lies. "Sweetie, it's normal to feel overwhelmed. It helps to believe Muncie has our best interests at heart, even if he doesn't always show it."

Molly shot her a sidelong glance, lowering her voice. "Didn't seem like that was his priority last night during his… big event."

Ginger's attention shifted to the tree line. "Muncie battles his demons. The best thing you can do is soak up the sun and fresh air. That's how you survive this."

Molly's fingers twitched. Ginger always had a way of saying things that sounded like wisdom but felt like excuses. "What's the point of this, anyway?" she muttered.

"Delivering these logs to some old hag in the bush has something to do with Muncie's buddy next door," Ginger replied.

The explanation felt hollow. Every answer only deepened the absurdity of her situation. Expecting truth from Ginger was a waste of time.

Molly resumed stacking. Her muscles burned. "Let's just finish before Muncie gets back with more commentary."

Ginger shrugged. "Relax. He's probably fussing over his wardrobe."

Molly's chest tightened. *Wardrobe? No. He plays dress-up with other people's dignity.*

Chapter 10

Babe's cherry-red '99 Corvette sat caged behind chain-link, gleaming like defiance in the grey sprawl of the impound yard. Around it, rows of dead machines boxed in like prisoners—faded paint, shattered mirrors, scrawled numbers on cracked windshields. Broken promises no one planned to fix. A busted security camera dangled from a pole above the gate, its lens fractured and blind. Rusted signage warned: Entrance Only-City Impound Lot. Below it: No Entry Without Authorization.

Lieutenant Choi circled the Corvette, snapping photos with her phone before sliding behind the wheel and firing up the engine.

Out on the street, a taxi screeched to the curb. Ariana stepped out, crisp, composed against the rusted sprawl. Babe followed, cigarette already lit, smoke curling from her lips like a curse.

Ariana adjusted the collar of Babe's blazer. "You're carrying the world in those eyes. Maybe a laugh would lift it better than a cigarette."

Babe flicked ash into the gutter. "Honey, not now."

A convertible roared past, packed with college boys. Laughter spilled out, sharp and mean. One leaned out, his grin slick as oil. "Bet you'd look better on your knees, sweetheart!"

"Up yours," Ariana yelled, giving them the finger.

The car peeled around the corner. Babe caught the tremble in Ariana's hands. "Don't waste your fire," she said. "They're garbage."

"I'd tear their smug little faces off," Ariana sneered.

Babe crushed the cigarette under her heel. "Let it go."

They stepped into the impound yard. Rows of rusting cars stretched out like tombstones. Babe's red Corvette was nowhere in sight. She stopped, scanned the lot again, slower this time. Was it hiding, waiting to be found? It wasn't. Her stomach twisted. She muttered a curse, then pulled out her phone and called Choi's number Brisk had scrawled on the envelope at the restaurant—voicemail.

Off to the left sat an ATCO trailer, squat and grimy, tilted slightly on cinder blocks. A uniformed officer leaned against a white unmarked cruiser, chatting with a woman in heels who laughed too easily. The service garage behind them looked idle, like everything else in the yard—except Babe's rising temper.

Then she moved fast. Her boots struck the asphalt with sharp, angry steps as she crossed the yard, shoulders set, pace hard. She yanked the trailer door open like it had something to confess.

The room stank of stale coffee and grease. Papers spilled across a battered metal desk. Faded policy sheets peeled from the walls. Boxes were stacked everywhere. The washroom door hung ajar. Behind the counter, a man in dreadlocks wearing a bright dashiki took a deep pull from a plastic evidence bag, eyes half-closed in bliss.

"I need my car," Babe rasped. "Red '99 Corvette coupe."

The man waved her off. "Not here. Try da bus stop."

"Why would my car be at a bus stop?"

He shrugged. "Ask de city planner."

Ariana stepped up, voice like cut steel. "Where's her car?"

The man grabbed another evidence bag and inhaled. "Police matter. You're shit outta luck."

Babe turned on her heel and stalked outside, boots scuffing the asphalt. Ariana followed close behind.

Behind them, the washroom door banged open. A short man in a crooked bow tie stormed out. Beady eyes locked on the stoner. "What the hell are you doing? Get behind the counter!"

The Rastafarian rolled his eyes and shuffled back.

Outside, Ariana tried to break the tension. "Did you know Costco hands out free samples?"

Babe didn't react.

Ariana's smile wilted. "Okay, okay, I get it. You're pissed."

Babe's phone buzzed. A message: Emergency meeting at News 4. Attendance required. She exhaled slowly. "How long for a cab?"

Ariana contemplated the unmarked white Charger still parked at the service garage. The uniformed officer and the woman in heels were nowhere to be seen.

Moments later, tires shrieked as the Charger shot out of the lot, fishtailing onto the street. Ariana clutched the armrest, knuckles white. She glanced over. Babe's face was stone behind the wheel. "You go, girlfriend," she muttered. "Unleash the beast."

Babe's foot sank deeper. The Charger surged. Horns blared. The speedometer climbed.

"Jesus, Babe. I was kidding!"

They blew a red light. Tires screamed. The car fishtailed, then snapped straight. Ariana slammed into the door. "Never giving you ideas again."

Babe's eyes stayed locked on the road. "You're still breathing, aren't you?"

"Barely."

The city blurred past in streaks of steel and concrete.

Ariana watched her, pulse still racing. Something cold curled in her gut.

Babe was burning the brakes off restraint.

And there was no going back.

Chapter 11

The tension in the News 4 boardroom went deeper than business. It stank of quiet chauvinism, thick and metallic as blood in the air. Miss Horn sat with perfect poise. One manicured hand rested on her iPad, the other twirled a silver stylus with effortless grace. Her red silk blouse dipped low, clinging like liquid fire—the line of her cleavage deep and deliberate. A weapon disguised as invitation.

Around the long, polished table, every man gawked at what she offered—just enough to tempt, but never allowed to touch.

Miss Horn wasn't blind to it. She wielded it. She adjusted her neckline, not to reveal more, but to remind them she was the one in control.

Across the room, near the back wall, Babe sat apart. Her spine was straight as scaffolding, one hand gripping her bag strap so tightly her knuckles had gone bloodless. The leers behind fake smiles, the glossed-over rot beneath custom suits made her skin crawl. They didn't look like executives. They looked like wax figures, already starting to melt.

Her focus landed on Miss Horn. If the woman felt the weight of the room, she didn't show it. But that silence, that stillness—it didn't read as strength but as strategy. The calculated calm of someone who'd been diminished so often, she'd learned to turn objectification into power.

At the head of the table, Cecil Carleton, Acting Mayor Dickie's lawyer, spoke in the easy drone of a man used to hearing himself echoed back. His critique of the media's handling of Molly's disappearance was barbed, each phrase sharpened like a dart.

Richard Eaton, head of News 4, lounged beside him, arms crossed, a faint curl of amusement tugging at his mouth. Dickie Darnell sat to his left, watching Carleton perform like he was admiring a trained seal.

Then came the proposal.

Halt all coverage of Molly's disappearance, for national security reasons.

The words didn't land so much as crawl. Heads nodded around the table—mechanical, unthinking. Not even a token question was raised. Not even a pretense of discomfort. The silence wasn't awkward. It was orchestrated.

Babe clenched her teeth until the pressure rang in her ears. This wasn't about silk necklines or corporate optics. It was about control. About what got buried—and who was paid to keep the dirt packed tight. *What are they hiding? Who are they protecting? Why does no one care that a woman is missing?*

She scrutinized Eaton. His apathetic sneer poured gas on the fire already eating its way up her spine. Her nails bit into her palm, carving crescent moons into the skin. She stood. The scrape of her chair sliced through the silence.

Heads turned. Their collective attention hit like a wave, but she didn't flinch.

"If this is really a federal issue," she said, her voice low and clear, "where's the proof? We owe the community an explanation. Why are we killing this story?"

No response. Just stillness, like the room was holding its breath.

Eaton exhaled with a little puff of amusement, like she'd told a mildly inappropriate joke. His expression sharpened. "The particulars of national security aren't for you, or anyone else here, to validate," he said. "The directive is simple. Cease all reporting. Understood?"

Her stomach coiled. "With all due respect," she said, voice measured but hardening, "our job is to pursue truth. Not to fall in line. If Molly's missing, how do we justify looking the other way?"

Eaton leaned forward, elbows on the table. "Spare me the ethics speech. You think you're the only one who cares about the truth?" His smile shifted, slow and serrated. "Where were you when we needed someone to cover the health inspector's suicide at Wynns' restaurant?"

Babe blinked. "What suicide?"

Eaton's eyes narrowed. "You didn't know?" He leaned back, smug and slow. "Maybe you need a break. Some comfort food. A vacation. Get your head on straight."

Heat rose beneath her skin, but this wasn't the kind that made her angry—it was the kind that made her ashamed. She wanted to bite back, but nothing came. The silence was a vacuum, sucking the air right out of her lungs. In the back of her mind, Ariana's voice surfaced, quiet but insistent: *Decide how far you're willing to go.*

Babe unclipped her press badge, tossed it onto the table, and walked out. Each step echoed down the corridor like a dare. Her body moved like steel forged for war.

Outside, the sun flared too bright, and the concrete scorched through Ariana's shoes. She leaned against the unmarked cruiser, coffee in hand, one ankle crossed over the other. The breeze tugged at her jacket, but she remained still, watching the building's entrance from behind tinted lenses.

Babe appeared, lighting a cigarette with unsteady hands. The flame shivered. From Ariana's vantage, Babe radiated tension, a powder keg waiting for a spark.

Ariana kept her silence, studying her. The way her shoulders stiffened, how her gaze skated across the parking lot like she was hunting for a target. "So?" she finally asked, "Was your meeting wonderfully fulfilling?"

Babe exhaled. "If they think I'm one of their peons, they're in for a rude awakening."

Ariana tracked the subtle shifts: Babe's jaw tightening, her fingers fidgeting around the cigarette like they couldn't decide whether to hold on or let go. The story spilled out—a shutdown, a silence, a suicide. Ariana let the words fill the space, but her focus stayed on Babe: the restless posture, the narrowed mouth, the barely contained flicker in her eyes. Every word sounded like it had been dragged through barbed wire.

Ariana's gaze drifted to the street. Cars slid past, slow and indifferent. The world outside didn't care. Or maybe it knew—and that was worse. "Maybe the cops should handle it," she finally said. "Talk to the chief again."

Babe's mouth twisted. "I didn't tell you before," she said. "The chief shot someone."

Ariana froze mid-sip. "Come again?"

Babe flicked the cigarette into the gutter. "He dropped the man like it was nothing."

Ariana stared, considering everything she had heard.

"We need to figure out what to do about Molly," Babe continued.

Ariana opened the passenger door. "Jesus, Babe. We're in over our heads."

Babe slid behind the wheel. "There's someone I need to talk to. He'll know what to do."

Chapter 12

The steel door in Lieutenant Choi's basement sealed shut behind her with a click. Inside, her sanctuary held its breath—part armoury, part confessional.

Low pot lights carved hard shadows across the walls. Old training photos hung in neat rows. Choi at twenty-five, younger, sharper-eyed, cradling an AR-15 like it was a birthright. Another print, styled like a retro Abercrombie ad, showcased polished Smith & Wesson revolvers. Grit pretending to be glamour. Nostalgia for a world that never existed.

She didn't move. Just stood there, breathing, letting the stillness press into her bones.

Molly Darnell was gone, and the story didn't track. Brisk's claim of black-budget money and national security reeked of theatre. The knot in her gut twisted tighter. She clenched her jaw until her molars ached. Brisk. Obsessed. Weak. *Keep your theories locked down. Play the long game.*

The Wynns' shooting had cracked the surface. Brisk's sudden leave spoke louder than any press release. And Babe Lincoln?

Jesus.

That girl was a stray dog in lipstick and a fast car. Brisk chasing after her was almost sad. Almost. But power made men stupid. Made them believe they could see through walls.

Choi pictured that candy-apple Corvette. Could almost hear it purr. Could almost smell the trouble pouring out of the exhaust. She spat on the concrete floor. Perfect mascot for this goddamn carnival.

She turned to the wall. Rifles gleamed—honest steel. The AR-15. The Marlin 336. These didn't lie. They didn't grandstand or beg for understanding. Pistols sat cradled in velvet, Colt 1911, Ruger Mark IV. Lessons earned in blood. Shotguns and long-range rifles waited silently along the far wall, patient and absolute.

She stepped to the safe, spun the dial, and let it swing open. Cold air kissed her face. The scent of oil, brass, and sweat drifted up like incense. Her fingers found the Desert Eagle. Sandra. Heavy. Certain. "You never flinched," she whispered. There had been nights when everything hinged on one shot. Sandra had never blinked.

These weren't tools. They were verdicts. And every verdict came with a cost.

She stepped back, taking in the room. Pride? Maybe. Or maybe just proof that the world could be kept at arm's length if your aim was good enough. Or a reminder that trust was for fools and corpses.

Balancing business ambition with her badge had always felt like navigating a minefield. Public safety remained her sacred charge—one she guarded with unflinching rigour. Racism. Sexism. Relentless scrutiny. She'd absorbed it all like body armour. Years in the military and SWAT had forged her discipline, scorched hesitation out of her system, and sharpened her instincts into something closer to prophecy. She'd earned this room. Every weapon. Every whisper in the dark.

Her hand found the derringer. Light. Deceptive. She kissed the smooth grip. "Allie Oops," she murmured. "My last laugh."

Inside the safe, Charlton Heston stared out from a framed black-and-white photo—steady eyes, jaw like a mountain. She tapped the glass. "They can have it," she said. "But they'll choke on the barrel."

She let the safe click shut, turned off the light, and stood in the dark just long enough to remember the glory of winning.

Chapter 13

The ornate dining room of the Lincoln residence glowed, but not warmly. It shimmered with a hollow, polished brilliance that masked old truths. Crystal teardrops dangled from the brass chandelier like frozen grief. The oak table stretched the length of the room, its shine nearly blinding beneath the light—a stage too pristine for the quiet tensions that pulsed beneath. Plush chairs circled it like witnesses to secrets too bitter to spill.

Babe sat between her father, Daddy Lincoln, and Father Johnson.

Daddy Lincoln wore his eccentric charm like camouflage. Outsiders mistook it for whimsy; Babe knew it as defence. His thick-framed glasses, high-waisted pants, and constant fidgeting spoke of a man fraying at the edges, barely holding the line. Behind his smile lived scars she could trace by feel.

Father Johnson sat straight-backed, his diminutive frame, barely four-foot-eight, nearly swallowed by the oversized chair. His black suit gleamed. Clipped grey hair sat perfect, untouched by disorder. But his eyes flickered—quick, calculating—beneath a practiced serenity. He was a man who'd heard confessions that curdled blood.

Daddy Lincoln dangled a platter of cookies just out of the priest's reach, his laughter thin and sharp. Father Johnson stretched, fingertips grazing the edge, only for Daddy to jerk it away.

Babe shot her father a look sharp enough to draw blood. She slid the platter closer. "Please, Father. Take one."

Daddy seemed oblivious. "Remember the circus, Babe? The midgets running under the big top." His voice cracked with nostalgia's acid edge.

Father Johnson took a cookie, his smile soft but his eyes darting. "Laughter can soothe—or sting."

Babe's stomach twisted. Her voice turned flint. "We don't use that word anymore, Daddy. It's cruel." She forced warmth, nodding to the priest. "Have another cookie, Father."

She fixed her father with a hard stare. "Little person. Or person with dwarfism. It's basic respect."

"Yes, dear," he muttered, eyes falling.

Babe pivoted. "Father Jay, does scripture still hold weight in a world tearing at the seams?"

He chewed slowly. "Faith bends but doesn't break. Compassion. Courage. Action. We're called to stand in the storm, not cower from it."

Babe's mouth twitched. "These days, people care more about the Kardashians' next post than Christ's return."

Father Johnson allowed a thin smile. "The church could use better PR." The priest's eyes flicked toward the window. "Did you see the police cruiser outside?"

Babe's smile thinned. "City's new loaner program. All good."

He raised an eyebrow but let it go, reaching for another cookie.

Daddy Lincoln poured tea, the china rattling. "Father Johnson's eyeing the Colon property. His flock needs a new sanctuary."

"If you boys want to talk shop," Babe said, rising slightly, "I'll slip outside for a smoke."

Father Johnson's mouth tightened. "My dear, that's a fast road to an early grave."

Babe's grin turned wicked. "Jesus was a chain-smoker. Rolled away the stone, still puffing."

Father Johnson's breath caught between a laugh and a rebuke. "Where did you hear that?"

"Probably fake news."

The hallway door burst open. Ariana sauntered in wearing nothing but a bra and thong, red-handled scissors flashing in her hand. Her grin was pure mischief, but her eyes hinted at knowing far too much. "Sweetheart!" she purred. "Henckels makes the best scissors."

Daddy Lincoln's face lit up. "There you are, honey. Join us for a little treat."

Father Johnson's eyes widened as he took her in, a flicker of raw lust flashing across his face before shame surged and he looked away, too fast.

Ariana snapped the scissors in the air. "Got a wild beaver to tame."
She twirled the blades, winked over her shoulder. "Later, maybe I'll
have a... potato chip."

Babe pressed her fingers to her temple.

Daddy Lincoln dropped to the floor and barked—harsh, guttural.
The sound ripped through the room like a warning shot.

Father Johnson flinched, "Good God. Is he barking?"

Babe's voice dropped to ice. "Daddy Doggie, no!"

He growled, low and feral.

She leaned in, scratched behind his ear. "Who's a good boy? Is
Daddy Doggie a good boy?"

Father Johnson sat frozen. Decades of confessions had not
prepared him for this.

Babe crumpled a napkin and lobbed it down the hall. "Fetch. To
your room."

Daddy bit the napkin and bolted, shoes scraping hardwood.

Father Johnson's composure cracked. "What on earth is
happening?"

Babe exhaled slowly. "One of his episodes. We manage."

His voice trembled. "Why does he do that? How long has this
been happening?"

"My mother ran off with a potato chip salesman when I was a
kid. Not long after, the gypsy whore came back demanding support
money. Daddy didn't handle it well. He started obsessing, potato chips
this, potato chips that. Scared me so much, I wouldn't bring a bag into
the house." She reached for her tea. "Then I went to a hypnotist's
show. Had Daddy put under. Now, whenever he hears the words
potato chip, he becomes a dog."

Father Johnson stared at her. "You... did this on purpose?"

"I wanted him to understand what humiliation feels like," she said.
"The good news is, he wasn't turned into a monkey."

"I'm sorry—what?"

"Well," Babe said, "the hypnotist came back to town. I took
Daddy, hoping he could reverse it. But we hit traffic. By the time we
arrived, he was already onstage, turning some poor bastard into a
monkey. The guy's screeching, pulling these ridiculous faces, wide eyes,

twitchy fingers. The audience loved it." She shook her head. "Then, mid-act, he drops his pants and starts stroking his… well, you get it. Nature documentary stuff."

Father Johnson blinked. "And?"

"The hypnotist snapped him out of it fast. But degradation cuts deep. So the guy shot the hypnotist. Had a concealed carry permit. What can you do?"

Father Johnson rubbed his temples. "Your life is… something else."

Babe barely smiled. "Reminds me of 2 Corinthians 4:8-9: 'We are hard-pressed on every side, but not crushed; perplexed, but not in despair.' You taught me that."

He nodded, but his composure was cracking. "But aren't you afraid he'll bite someone?"

"We've planned." She tapped her phone. Metal shades slid down with a hum that felt like finality. "If Ariana and I aren't home, he's contained. If the fire alarm triggers, they rise—but then, all bets are off."

He raised his brows. "Impressive. I imagine the noise would alert the neighbours."

"No. We had to disconnect the clangour. The ringing drives Daddy berserk. Learned that the hard way—he tore apart the sofa and piddled on the floor."

"And Ariana? Is she safe?"

Babe's lips curved. "You saw how deferential he was. Offered her treats. He's terrified of her."

"Why is that?" he asked. "Or do I even want to know?"

Babe leaned forward, voice darkening. "You know how dogs love peanut butter?"

Father Johnson blinked. "Oh dear."

"One day, during an episode, Daddy Doggie got a little too friendly with Ariana's leg. She locked herself in our room till it passed. Later, when he snapped out of it, she… taught him a lesson."

He hesitated. "What kind of lesson?"

"She waited until he finished his shower, then yelled, 'Potato chip.'"

Father Johnson closed his eyes. "I don't want to hear this."

"She smeared peanut butter all over his scrotum."

His eyes snapped open. "My God."

"He spun in circles, trying to lick it off. Hours of barking, howling—until he pulled a tendon."

The priest tugged at his collar. "I've heard of dogs chasing their tails, but this is… something else. Ariana sounds formidable."

"She's steel."

He shifted, searching for safer ground. "What's she do between acting gigs?"

"Cleans a federal building downtown. Polishes the head honcho's private elevator. Chrome and mirrors everywhere."

Father Johnson sighed. "Life's cruel poetry. Imagine someone telling you this story ten years ago."

"I'd have laughed," she said softly. "Father, if someone is missing, someone who needs help, how far would you go to find them?"

His voice lowered. "James 4:17: 'To know the right thing to do and not do it is sin.' We are called to find the lost. Bring them home."

She hesitated. "Are we talking about…"

"Eternal damnation, Babe," Father Johnson whispered. "And it has your name all over it."

Chapter 14

Skyscrapers loomed over the downtown intersection, their glass facades slicing sunlight into shards of brilliance. Neon signs hummed, bleeding streaks of red, green, and gold across passing vehicles. Pedestrians drifted in steady streams, footsteps clattering against concrete, faces lit by their phones, blind to the glittering traps in storefront windows. Horns blared. Engines snarled. Taxis, buses, and rust-bitten sedans fought for inches.

Ariana gripped the wheel of the stolen white Charger. The engine thrummed beneath her palm, a caged animal itching to run. She scanned the dashboard and mirrors. Any second, traffic cams could ping the plate. Alarms would shriek back at the station.

The red light dragged on, thick, suffocating. A horn shredded the air behind her, a jagged blade across already frayed nerves. Ariana's jaw clenched. She forced her fingers to loosen their grip. She didn't look in the mirror. Weakness invited pursuit.

Beside her, Babe sat cross-legged, manicured nails tapping her phone screen—each stroke calm, precise.

"Listen to this," Babe said, holding the phone like evidence. "My email to Dopey D, our ever-incompetent temp mayor. Patron saint of clueless toads."

"Impress me."

Babe read it aloud. Outrage and threat, polished into elegance. Venom disguised as civic concern. She wove in Molly's disappearance, the impounded Corvette, and a fabricated cousin—ex-U.S. Marshal with a nasty habit of digging where he wasn't wanted.

"You have a cousin who's a Marshal?"

"It's called hyperbole."

"So now we're leaning on bullshit?"

"Bullshit's won more fights than truth ever has."

The light flicked green. Ariana hesitated. Another horn stabbed the air—shrill, impatient. She raised a hand and gave the driver behind them a cheery wave.

"Fans," she murmured. "Love it."

"Move it, superstar," Babe said, tapping the phone off.

Ariana hit the gas. The Charger surged forward, swallowed by the crush of downtown. Her pulse pounded. Consequences circled like wolves—sirens, cameras, a grainy match on a screen.

"You forgive me for the potato chip fiasco?" Ariana asked.

"Father Jay was going to find out eventually."

"You didn't have to cover for me."

"I know."

Ariana checked her mirrors. "I'm still nervous about this trip. They call it Bear Lake for a reason. Canada's crawling with grizzlies."

"I didn't see any."

"And snowstorms? Did you even check the weather?"

Babe waved it off. "Sweetheart, you worry too much."

Ariana's voice came quieter. "Maybe Molly would've stayed home if you hadn't gone with her."

Babe exhaled. "She won a free camping trip and a ticket to some ice cream shop's grand opening. No one else to go with, and you were still filming *Everyone Has One*. It made sense at the time."

Silence settled, taut and heavy.

Babe folded her arms. "Nothing lines up. I get a text to cover Dickie's press conference. I leave Molly and come back—conference cancelled. No reason, no warning. Like someone didn't want me near her. My boss is dodging questions. Now I'm suspended. I saw an evidence box with her name on it. If that doesn't reek, I don't know what does." Her voice hardened. "And don't get me started on that meeting with the General."

"The guy with the little balls?"

"It's called Newton's cradle."

"What about him?"

"Powerful people are hiding something," Babe said. "I just don't know if Molly's the key, or the sacrifice."

"If that blind prick had thrown piss on me, I'd have kicked his ass."

"We should be so lucky if that's the worst we face."

Ariana tapped the wheel. "What about those liquor bottles Molly posted? You said they don't even sell that brand in Canada."

"Exactly. I keep thinking about the stuff we talked about as kids. Survival tricks. She used to joke about hiding lockpicks in her bum in case we got kidnapped. Maybe she still remembers."

Ariana wrinkled her nose. "That's vile."

"Forget I said it. The point is, something's off." She turned to Ariana. "Talking about the General reminded me."

Ariana groaned. "Enough with the freak and his tiny silver balls."

"No, listen. Remember that day we came home and Molly was out in the yard, yapping into her phone? Doing her phone-sex thing with a client?"

"Oh God." Ariana dropped into a ridiculous accent. "Mon chérie, eet eez so hard, like ze granite stone."

"Stop." Babe bit back a grin.

"And Daddy Lincoln," Ariana went on, "hiding in the bushes in that hideous lime-green pantsuit and floppy purple hat, pretending to prune roses while she moaned like—"

"Enough," Babe said, but she was laughing now.

"The sounds of pure rapture. Probably the closest that poor man's ever come to hearing an orgasm."

Babe wiped her eyes. "My point: she had him on speaker. The General told her to go all in, said she was the type to take things over the top." She paused. "He told me the same thing."

"You think that douche is behind all this?"

"I'm not ruling anyone out."

The city peeled back in layers. Chrome and glass gave way to rust, splintered fences, yards strangled by weeds that didn't bother hiding what had been left behind—bicycles without chains, dreams without owners.

"What about our little troublemaker?" Ariana asked. "Think he'll be okay alone?"

"I asked the reverend to check Daddy's water, let him out," Babe said. "He asked about you, by the way."

"I bet." Ariana snorted. "His little legs probably gave out from chasing choir boys."

"Father Jay's not like that."

"No? Then why did his eyes light up like a Christmas tree when he ogled me? Not a big one—a little window display job."

Babe groaned. "Stop. I'm sure the good reverend meant no harm."

"If you say so."

Ariana slowed near the end of a battered street. A sagging house crouched behind a chain-link fence barely hanging on. In the yard: a leaning shed, roof patched with whatever hadn't rotted. She pulled into the driveway, killed the engine, and climbed out.

Babe joined her at the fender, arms crossed, scanning the wreck of a yard. "So... now what?"

"We wait."

"For what?"

"For him to notice." A smile tugged at her lips. "Gomsie always notices."

They stood without speaking. A breeze stirred dust. Dogs barked in the distance. Glass shattered somewhere unseen.

Amid the noise, Babe found a rare edge of focus. She ran through the plan again, stripping it to the bones. There could be no mistakes. She hoped the man responsible for props on Ariana's film was as useful as promised.

This was where it would begin. And from here, there'd be no clean exits.

Chapter 15

Lieutenant Choi stepped out of her unmarked cruiser, its black paint veiled in dust, and stared out at Bear Lake's shimmering expanse. The afternoon sun fractured the water into shards of light against the jagged Canadian wilderness. The crisp, pine-sweet air cut through the city smog still ghosting her lungs. For a moment, it almost felt clean. Almost.

But the silence pressed against her chest—heavy, expectant, and false. Answers waited out there. So did danger.

She passed the weathered Bear Lake Boat Rental sign, her boots grinding gravel, breaking the illusion of peace. The building sagged under years of neglect. Paint peeled like dead skin. The flower baskets were limp and rotting. A red ATV, crusted with dried mud and missing a mirror, sat near a path leading into the adjacent forest, keys still dangling in the ignition. The porch groaned beneath her weight as she pushed open the door.

The stink hit hard—damp wood, motor oil, and something gone bad beneath it all. Empty display cases lined the room, their glass fronts streaked with grime. A rack of dusty brochures whispered promises of adventures no one believed in anymore.

A faint shuffle from the back. Her hand hovered near her holster as a man stepped into view. Greasy boots scraped the floor. Khaki shorts hung low. A T-shirt stretched tight across a soft belly. His red hair teased into a ridiculous bouffant that didn't belong in this ruin. "Afternoon!" His grin was too wide, too bright. "I'm Rusty. Welcome to paradise. Here for the views? The mystical allure of the lake?"

Choi didn't blink. "I'm headed to Moosetown. Care to explain why the road sign pointed me here?"

The grin cracked. His eyes darted toward the door, calculating. "Vandals," he muttered. "Kids think it's funny. I reported it."

"Fix the sign." She flipped her badge open. "Lieutenant Choi. Official business. What can you tell me about the campground on Bear Lake?"

"We cut ties. The owner's... proud."

"Proud?"

He fidgeted. "Call it whatever you want." His hands wouldn't stay still.

Choi leaned in. "How's business?"

He let out a thin laugh and gestured toward a heap of junk in the corner. "You're my first visitor since the remodel, sister. Antique fishing net, a priceless history."

"You're a real preservationist," she grunted, sweeping the crumbling displays with a glance. She didn't wait for more lies.

Outside, the dock stretched into the lake, its boards warped and splintered. A cool breeze swept across the water, but didn't touch the tension coiled in Choi's gut. The view looked like a postcard. The place felt like a grave.

Behind her, boots thudded on the porch. She turned as Rusty hefted a wooden oar, nodding toward an aluminum boat half-submerged near the shore. "If you're crossing, this beauty'll get you there."

She eyed the dented hull. "Who rents this trash?"

He shrugged, grin tight and empty. "That's just how it is, sister."

One more sister, and she might forget her manners. "Anything strange across the lake?"

Rusty hesitated, just long enough. "Heard a woman last night. Screaming something about a bone doctor. Spooked me."

Choi's pulse jumped. "A bone doctor?"

He nodded. "Sound carries."

She locked eyes with him. He looked away, fingers twitching. He knew more. But pressing him now would make him run.

Choi turned back toward the water. Calm. Pretty. Lying through its teeth. Every ripple whispered secrets just out of reach. She hadn't driven this far to be brushed off by a twitchy boat-rental clown. Whatever Bear Lake was hiding, it would crawl out on its own. And if not, she'd drag it screaming.

Chapter 16

The grounds of the Embassy sprawled beneath a cloudless sky, the silence broken by the restless whisper of leaves and the faint creak of an old saw blade swinging from a nail. Near the woodpile, Ginger snapped open a frayed blue tarp with slow, deliberate movements, stalling for time.

From the back of the house, Muncie appeared, boots crushing the gravel. His scowl deepened as he stalked toward the pickup half loaded with bags of firewood, muttering curses under his breath. He yanked open the truck door and shoved an arm beneath the seat, rifling through the shadows. "Damn it," he snarled. "Where are my wires?"

Ginger shrugged as she gnawed on a jagged fingernail, bracing for the next outburst.

"Where's the girl?" he growled.

Without looking up, Ginger lifted an arm and pointed toward the outhouse. She focused on the dirt beneath her nails as though it mattered more than the heat radiating off Muncie.

The outhouse door creaked open. Molly stepped into the sunlight, dragging the coveralls like dead weight. Her legs caught the light, long and bare above scuffed sneakers.

Muncie's eyes dragged over her, slow and greedy. A muscle jumped in his jaw. He drew in a long, controlled breath, holding something darker in check. "She's an odd one," he muttered, tongue flicking across his lower lip. "Still looks like an angel. Fallen, maybe. But pure enough to break."

Ginger stiffened. "Don't start, Muncie. It's too early for your crap."

He chuckled, slow and syrupy. "Just admiring those legs. Stairway to Heaven."

"Enough." Ginger's voice snapped.

Muncie's grin widened, filth radiating from him like heat off asphalt as he tapped his temple. "You thought it too, cupcake. I'll grab the bungees," he said.

Ginger folded her arms. "Why bother covering the wood? We're not going far."

"Rules," Muncie shot back. "It's about appearances." He waved toward the pile. "Can't have things looking sloppy. People start asking questions."

Molly stopped a few paces from the woodpile. "Can we eat? I'm starving."

"Me too," Ginger added.

"Maybe we'll have chicken wings," Muncie said.

He glanced up at Risqué, who let out a strangled squawk, part birdcall, part something else entirely. A single feather drifted down, landing in the dust like a warning.

Muncie turned back to the women. "Focus. Life's harsh realities don't include worrying about food."

"Self-care matters," Molly said, voice steady. "Neglect it, and there are consequences."

His smile stayed frozen, but something twisted in his eyes. "Drop the attitude. Losing the coveralls is a privilege." He jerked his chin at the woodpile. "Finish up."

Ginger trudged toward the stack. Molly followed, adjusting her cap before lifting a log. The rough bark scraped her palms, but she barely felt it. Each movement rehearsed, part of the mask. Her thoughts stretched miles ahead.

Muncie slapped his thigh. "Forgot my hat. Be right back." He stole one last glance at Molly before heading toward the cottage. Risqué flapped after him, settling on his shoulder as they vanished inside.

Molly waited until the door latched. "What's with that pigeon?"

"Parrot," Ginger corrected flatly. "He goes wherever Muncie goes. Some… connection."

"A connection with a bird?" Molly raised a brow.

"If the bird shows up without him… it means he's dead."

Molly snorted, a bitter laugh escaping before she could stop it. "That's the craziest thing I've heard in forever."

Ginger gave a nervous smile, adjusting the rolled-up sleeve of her coveralls. "Welcome to Bear Lake."

Molly stepped in close. "We need an escape plan."

Ginger's eyes flicked to the forest, scanning shadows between the trees. "I know. But we need to be smart. He's always watching."

Molly nodded, but inside, distrust simmered. Last night had told her everything—Ginger was tangled in Muncie's world deeper than she let on. She'd play along. For now. "Tonight," she whispered. "When it's dark. We run."

"Tonight," Ginger echoed, but her voice trembled.

Molly turned back to the pile, tossing another log into a sack. Her hands moved automatically. Her mind was already gone. Movement inside the cottage caught her eye.

Risqué perched on the windowsill. The bird cocked its head—just slightly. Watching. Waiting.

Molly could've sworn the damn thing smiled.

Chapter 17

Moosetown Campground was a faded relic. Yellowed grass and scarred picnic tables marked the sites, while weeds and wild grasses crept in unchecked. Fallen branches choked the trails. A broken swing groaned on rusted chains, like the place had given up. Once a haven for budget campers, it now whispered of vanished summers and a lost sense of community.

Lieutenant Choi crouched by a fire pit, prodding charred wood with a stick. The air was thick with the acrid scent of ash and damp earth. The deserted campground confirmed her suspicion—it only came to life on weekends.

She considered a rusted minivan parked beside a trailer, beer cans strewn across the ground like confetti from a forgotten party. The scene matched the photos Molly had posted. A mosquito buzzed near her ear—high-pitched, relentless.

A shout tore through the stillness. "Hey, you fuckin' nip. What are you doin'?"

Choi's hand slid to the grip of her sidearm as she locked eyes on the gaunt man leaning from the trailer doorway. "Why don't you get back inside and save me the trouble of shooting your pathetic ass?"

He spat on the ground, then slammed the door.

Whiteside emerged from the campground office, a Styrofoam cup in hand. The modest building sat at the lake's edge, its windows reflecting the shimmer of Bear Lake. His plaid shirt was neatly pressed but hung awkwardly on his wiry frame, like someone trying too hard to look respectable. Sandy hair, clean-shaven cheeks. Boyish, almost. But the fine lines around his hazel eyes told another story: long hours, low pay, and a life that never quite took. The screen door creaked behind him, hinges rasping like an old man's breath. "Hey there!"

Choi turned.

His smile flared too fast, off-key and overcompensating. "Name's Whiteside, but most folks call me Whitey. How you doin'?"

Her assessment was quick. Too eager. Too rehearsed. "Lieutenant Abbie Choi," she said, extending a hand.

His grip was light, hesitant. Canadians were supposed to be laid-back, but the man shouting slurs earlier had reminded her to never lower her guard.

"You look like someone needing directions," Whiteside said, glancing at her cruiser.

"Do I look lost to you?"

He leaned in, voice dropping to a hush. "You're not from around here. Either that, or you're lookin' for work. And honestly, we don't need any coolies."

The word landed hard. She didn't blink. "Excuse me?"

"Domestics," he said. "We're full up. You might try the Chinese restaurant in Moosetown. Some of your people hang out there."

Her fingers curled into a fist at her side. She exhaled slowly. "Maybe I'm interested in a campsite. What do you think about that?"

His confidence stuttered. "Well… okay. You're not pulling a trailer, so I guess you're looking to tent. Or maybe you're into cowboy camping?"

"Cowboy camping? What's that, your attempt at matchmaking?"

"No, I don't think I'd have much luck with that around here. It's sleeping under the stars. Just a bag. No shelter. For people who enjoy roughing it. Do you enjoy roughing it, Miss Chang?"

"It's Choi," she said, voice flat. "Do I look like someone who enjoys roughing it?"

He shrugged, his laugh brittle. "Not for me to say. I could give you a park overview, but, uh… we don't have ping-pong tables. If we did, they'd be for everyone, naturally."

Her patience thinned. "Does my ethnicity make you nervous, Mr. Whiteside?"

"No, no. Nothing like that. I don't see colour."

She slipped off her aviators. Her eyes locked onto his. "My race shapes my identity and how the world treats me. Ignoring it doesn't erase the problem."

He shifted, confidence unravelling. His hand trembled slightly as he raised the cup. "I'll try to do better."

"Maybe another time," Choi said. "Right now, I need information about two girls. They drove this car." She held up her phone—Babe's red Corvette gleamed on the screen.

Whiteside's face darkened. "You should talk to Constable Karl in town. I can't just hand out information to any Tom, Dick, or Harry. You've got one uppity attitude for a coloured woman."

Choi took the Styrofoam cup from his hand and drove a knee into his gut. He collapsed, gasping. Her boot pinned his face to the dirt as she took a sip, then spat it out. "At least you like your java black," she muttered. "Could use more sugar. Good for the disposition." Her eyes swept the campground. "What have you got here, thirty trailers or so?"

"I suppose," Whiteside wheezed.

"Supposing's not how you run a business. What about kids wanting to party? Young, single women. You get many?"

"I… I guess…"

"You guess?" Her voice dropped to a low, dangerous pitch. "You don't know?"

He groaned. "Huh? I, well—"

"Do you have a library in the village?" She stepped back, lifting her boot.

He stayed on the ground, gasping.

"Get up," she snapped. "What is wrong with you?"

He scrambled to his feet, dazed and apprehensive. "Huh?"

"Library! Big building, full of books."

Whiteside grunted as he clutched himself, his eyes pleading. "I, um, yeah."

"Take your carcass to the library and look up the meaning of insertion."

"In… insertion?"

Choi stepped closer. "You do know how to read, correct?"

Whiteside's face contorted as he nodded in agreement. It was a look that spoke of inner turmoil, a man caught in the web of a situation he never expected.

"If you fail to pony up full cooperation, I'll take the shotgun from the trunk of my fine automobile and jam it up your ass. Then you'll have expanded your vocabulary. Capiche?" She shoved the cup into his hands. "Now go make some fresh coffee. Use real sugar."

"Artificial sweetener okay?"

"I don't remember saying a good goddamn thing about artificial. Borrow some sugar from that trailer rat if you have to. I don't care how you get it."

Whiteside scrambled upright, shaky on his feet, and stumbled backward. "Got it. I think we got off on the wrong foot—"

"I'm dying to hear your thoughts," Choi said. "Head back to your office. Reflect on your life. And when I'm done poking around this little Shangri-La, you're gonna tell me everything about the girls who showed up in that flashy red car." Her eyes flicked to the dark stain spreading down his pant leg. "And another thing," she added. "You might want to invest in some diapers."

Neither noticed Muncie's truck barreling down Nine Mile Road, the blue tarp flapping wildly behind it.

Chapter 18

The black limousine slid through downtown traffic, its polished exterior mirroring the pulse of city life. For Acting Mayor Dickie Darnell, the vehicle was more than transportation—it was a fortress. For Miss Horn, it was a mobile theatre. A place where men like Dickie could pretend they were in control, while she quietly set the stage.

Inside, tension gathered in the silence. Dickie reclined against the cool leather seat, the smooth surface brushing his bare skin where his silk boxer shorts ended. His composure was a performance she'd seen countless times—entitled bravado wrapped around thinly veiled panic.

Across from him, Miss Horn worked with methodical precision, makeup brush in hand. She dusted foundation and powder across his face, each stroke erasing sharp lines into something unrecognizable and disarmingly real. Her fingers adjusted his blonde bouffant wig next, settling it with the care of someone crowning a monarch, or a saboteur.

She didn't rush. Dickie needed the illusion of beauty, of control. And she? She needed the illusion that she still respected him.

Dickie's eyes fell on the cobalt-blue sequined dress beside him, its fabric catching the low cabin light in shimmering waves. His fingers traced the hem.

Miss Horn watched him touch the garment like it held magic. It didn't. What it held was her advantage, because she'd picked it. Measured it. Pressed it into his grasp like a mirror.

"Have you decided on the bra?" she asked, her voice cool.

Dickie's hand glided across the lace. "Perhaps we skip it."

"No? That's bold, even for you."

"Sometimes boldness is required," he replied, a faint smile pulling at his lips.

"Ever the adventurer, MD," she said, setting the brassiere aside. Her hands moved with the efficiency of a tailor and the intimacy of a confidante as she helped him into the dress.

As the zipper found its place, Dickie's expression tightened. His eyes locked on hers. "That reporter's email," he said. "Reread the last part."

Miss Horn retrieved his phone and scanned the screen. "I'll paraphrase. Babe Lincoln claims you know more about the disappearance of The Remedy. She says she's enlisted a federal marshal to dig for the truth and expose whatever they find."

She handed the phone back, watching how the words sank into him like lead. His vanity couldn't protect him from that kind of pressure. That's why she managed the damage. That's why he needed her.

"We need action," he said at last, voice clipped. "Stress to our contacts delays are no longer tolerable. We expect results, or we withdraw our support."

"I'll handle it," she said, reaching for the champagne bottle nestled in a silver ice bucket. There was no tremor in her hand. There never was. He drank to feel powerful; she drank to remind herself she didn't need to. With a clean twist, she popped the cork and poured the sparkling liquid into two crystal flutes. She passed him one with a measured smile. "Have you decided on Lollypops?" she asked, tone light, but the question carried weight.

Dickie glanced at the drink. "Strip clubs like Lollypops," he said, "represent a moral battleground. A threat to the city's foundation. I've been leaning toward shutting them down."

Miss Horn didn't flinch. But a pointed pause followed. "I've been performing at Lollypops," she said. "Under the name Cassandra."

The flute halted near his lips. She watched his eyes narrow. Watched the wires short-circuit behind them.

She pictured the image blooming in his head: her onstage, sequins and feathers, legs like scaffolding. And she knew it rattled him, not because he disapproved, but because he suddenly couldn't separate command from desire.

"I see," he muttered.

Yes, she thought. *You do now.*

"I think we should take a different approach," she said, smooth and measured. "Instead of shutting them down, advocate for oversight. Regulation. Respect individual liberties while promoting responsibility."

For a moment, Dickie said nothing. Then he nodded. "You're right. Moderation, not prohibition. Thoughtful regulation."

His lips moved, but Miss Horn could see it—the cognitive fog that followed shame. She let him sit in it. Let it reshape him. He'd just given her more than a concession. He'd given her leverage. He wouldn't know what had changed, only that something had. That was how true influence worked. You didn't twist arms, you made people think they twisted their own.

It hadn't escaped her how his gaze lingered on her daily, filled with silent questions and unspoken curiosities. There was always an edge to it, a weight that went beyond professional interest. Let him fantasize. Let him believe that agreeing with her meant access. She'd built her power on that misconception, and she'd continue to let men drown in it.

She leaned forward, voice dropping. "Let's discuss Chief Brisk. You have an opportunity to accomplish much with minimal risk. You visit Lollypops in that wonderful dress, equipped with a recording device. Meet the chief and offer him a sizable bribe for two complete police uniforms. Knowing his character, he'll take the bait. Once the exchange is in our hands, we'll have the city's top cop under control. And, if I might add, it's the perfect payback for his antagonistic attitude toward you."

Dickie's brow furrowed. "You don't think he'll recognize me?"

Her lips lifted, a curve of assurance, not affection. "My confidence in this knows no limits."

"I'll give it consideration," he replied, though his tone wavered.

Miss Horn raised her glass, her smile deepening. "To your continued success, MD."

He hesitated, his hand tightening around the flute. "Wait. How do we know Brisk will even show up?"

Her smile widened—a clear signal of control. "Because I've ensured he will. Trust me, MD, you'll do the right thing for your career."

Dickie clinked his glass against hers, the delicate chime lingering in the air.

She didn't drink. Not yet. She watched. Calculated. His courage tasted like carbonation—quick, bright, and gone in a breath.

Miss Horn's plan hovered between them, potent and charged. It wasn't just strategy, it was a test. Not just of his loyalty, but of his courage. Would he rise to her expectations? Or would she chart a different path, leaving him behind like all the others who mistook proximity for power?

Chapter 19

The log cabin huddled among Bear Lake's ancient trees, its weathered logs dissolving into the wilderness. Each timber bore scars of resilience, etched deep by seasons and silence. The sloped roof followed the land's natural rise, and a wide porch stretched across the front like an open invitation to rest or reconsider.

Lieutenant Choi stepped out of her cruiser, shrugging the tension from her shoulders as she scanned the property. For a fleeting second, the place exhaled serenity. But serenity didn't last. It never did.

She turned toward the adjacent lot Whiteside had dismissed as an American Embassy. Whatever else he knew, he'd been too rattled to say. His intel had come between bouts of dry heaving, his fear so pungent she'd left without the coffee she'd demanded. She had no patience for cowards. But she'd pried loose one lead—the kid next door. Klarence. If anyone had seen or heard something about Molly, it was him.

Through the jagged tree line dividing the properties, a crude wooden placard jutted from a post: No Trespassing. Vienna Convention on International Law.

The attempt at intimidation fell flat. No fence. No guard. Just words on weathered wood. Beyond it, an American flag snapped in the breeze—faded but defiant—above a Cape Cod-style cottage. Where the gravel laneway met Nine Mile Road, a carved eagle clutched another No Trespassing sign like a deranged mascot. Whiteside had probably never even set foot here. His story reeked of gossip passed through too many mouths.

Movement near the shoreline drew her attention. A young man emerged from the water, dragging a kayak up the sandy bank. Sunlight skimmed his bronzed skin as he hauled it onto dry land. Lean and athletic, his frame straddled the line between strength and something more elusive: grace, maybe. Or menace. Water streamed from his blond hair, and his soaked shorts clung to his thighs.

Her glance lingered on the prominent bulge beneath the fabric. Thoughts flickered somewhere unprofessional. She shut it down fast. *Focus.* As she approached, he looked up, smiling easily, almost dopey. "Are you Klarence?" she asked.

He swept back his wet hair with both hands, all charm and laid-back bravado. His rugged features could've belonged to a model if not for the stammer that softened the edges.

"K-K-Klarence, with a K," he said, flashing an awkward grin. "Klarence holds his breath underwater for long-long time."

Choi blinked. *Holds his breath? What the hell does that have to do with anything?*

His stutter and wide-eyed delivery gave her pause. Whiteside had written him off as a simpleton, but Klarence wasn't so easily boxed in. Not just slow, but slippery. Maybe both. Getting anything useful would take finesse. "Whiteside at the campground says kids come here to drink after dark. You see that a lot?"

Klarence tilted his head. "C-come here?"

"Yes," she said. "After curfew."

"C-c-curfew?" He echoed the word like it belonged to a different language.

"Let's keep it simple," she said. "No need to repeat everything I say." Her eyes scanned the quiet stretch of trees. "It's hot out today. Any chance you might have a nice cold glass of water inside your cabin?"

"Mama don't allow beer or nothin'."

"Not beer," Choi said. "Water. Your mother home?"

He shook his head.

"Well then," she said, offering a faint smile, "let's find that drink. Maybe change out of those wet shorts while you're at it. Wouldn't want you catching a cold." Her tone stayed warm, coaxing. But her mind circled him like a shark.

"Uh, okay," Klarence said, trudging up the slope toward the cabin.

She followed, appreciating the curve of his back, and how the damp fabric moulded to his ass. Whiteside hadn't been entirely wrong, but he hadn't been right either. Klarence was something else. "What else are you good at, besides water sports?" she asked.

"I fix stuff around the cabin. Mama says I'm good with my hands."

"I bet you are," she said. "You meet a lot of people out here? Ever see any young girls around?"

Klarence shook his head. "Girls are silly."

"What about women?" she asked. "Not silly girls, real women. Smart women."

He shrugged. "Haven't met one like that."

Choi adjusted her sunglasses, hiding the grin threatening to creep across her face. "Well," she said, voice low and loaded, "maybe today's your lucky day."

Chapter 20

The split-level home, a relic of 1960s suburban architecture, blended into the monotony of its neighbourhood. Neutral-coloured bricks and dark wood accents lent it a timeless yet characterless appearance. A wide porch and brick pathway led to a space where mediocrity ruled every detail.

Chief Brisk parked Babe's red Corvette in the driveway, his lies and deceit weighing on him like an anchor. He stared at the front door, exhaustion carved into his face after a night spent fabricating a narrative for Internal Affairs. His story about a rogue health inspector wielding a steak knife had seemed plausible enough—especially with

Lucia, Diego's wife, backing him up. Rumours spread quickly. The civil servant's death was branded a suicide by cop, a desperate act meant to provoke officers into lethal force. Grim as it was, burying the truth beneath layers of misinformation served his purpose.

But relief was fleeting. His personal life felt like a cage—every lie, every compromise tightening the bars. The affair with Lieutenant Choi had only deepened the pressure, not relieved it. What began as release now felt like an obligation, a tether laced with risk. She was essential to his team, and emotionally invested in ways that made severing ties feel dangerous. Mishandling her could end his career.

A recent text from a dancer at Lollypops offered an unexpected lifeline—a rendezvous at a Holiday Inn after her performance. It whispered of freedom, of being wanted without consequences or emotional weight. For a moment, he allowed himself to imagine it: a night far from his wife's sanctimony, his daughters' judgment, and Choi's scrutiny. Just skin, sweat, and forgetting.

His marriage had become a cold, rigid performance art, devout to the point of cruelty. Forgiveness wasn't even on the table. His daughters hovered like vultures, eager for proof that their father was exactly what they suspected: a fraud.

The dancer's mystery stirred something dormant. Choi had met his needs, but this woman reawakened a different hunger. Something primal. Something unburdened. After years of sacrifice, it didn't feel like betrayal. It felt like inevitability.

You've earned this.

Drawing a deep breath, Brisk sat in the stillness, torn between ruin and relief. Temptation wrapped around him like smoke.

The buzz of his phone broke the spell. Brisk answered quickly, forcing cheer into his voice. "Lieutenant Choi! How's my number one crime fighter holding up in Canada?"

"A girl got drunk and stole booze from this place they call an embassy," Choi replied, flat as pondwater.

"Bad connection, I can barely hear you. Can you hear me?" His tone was edged with frustration.

"I'm here."

"Good. Where are you?" Brisk shifted in the driver's seat, angling for a better signal.

Choi glanced around Klarence's cabin. No stone fireplace, no polished floors, just grease-stained pizza boxes, mismatched beer coolers, and sagging camping chairs stacked like garbage against the wall. A warped plywood shelf held dozens of plush animals and dog-eared comic books. "A cabin beside this place locals call an Embassy."

"An American Embassy up there?" He sounded incredulous.

"There's a sign," Choi said, irritation edging in.

"Maybe it's a covert CIA op. Just… watch your back."

"Want me to come back?"

"No, I said watch your back." His tone softened. "That's an order."

"This is me, Chief."

"Forewarned is forearmed. What else?" Brisk lifted a garment bag and the Molly Darnell evidence box from the Corvette's passenger seat.

"A drunk girl stole booze from this so-called Embassy," Choi said.

"You said that already," Brisk snapped.

"Molly posted about it online. You forget?"

He groaned. "Was she Dickie Darnell's kid? You catching this? Can you hear me?"

"Klarence struggles to keep his story straight."

"Klarence? Who's Klarence?"

"Picture a man with the mind of a child. At first, I thought he was smuggling a Muppet."

Brisk blinked. "What the hell does that mean?"

"He's packing at least three inches on you. Don't ask how I know."

Brisk froze. The image of her with Klarence opened a door. If Choi moved on, maybe their mess would resolve itself. "Goddamn, I'd like to shake his hand."

"You want to shake his *gland?*"

"No, I—never mind. Is he married?"

"Has a Bible-thumping mother that lives in the woods."

"So, a God-fearing soul?"

"Before he tasted the honey, I had to convince him it wasn't poisoned fruit. A slug named Whiteside, who runs the campground where Molly stayed, said that Klarence's place draws teens. Molly might've been one of them."

"She's not exactly a teenager."

"Whiteside doesn't seem interested in women."

"Has a streak of lavender in him?"

"Chief, that's harsh."

"What should I call him? Nancy boy? Gearbox? F—"

"Enough." Choi cut him off. "Whiteside saw the Corvette. That's all. Did you find the key? I barely missed Lincoln spotting me at the impound."

"She's a sweet ride. That Babe, gotta hand it to her."

"I'd hand it to her, all right," Choi muttered.

Brisk ignored her and carried the garment bag and evidence box into the house, unaware of the eyes tracking him from the upstairs window.

Choi turned to Klarence, now edging across the room in nothing but a damp towel clinging to his hips. He leaned in and kissed her cheek. "K-K-Klarence needs to pee-pee before tasting more manna."

She watched him shuffle away, a faint smile tugging at her lips. "Lift the seat this time," she called after him.

"You still there?" Brisk said.

"Yes. I'll check out the so-called embassy," Choi replied.

"Talk to the local sheriff first. I called and got patched through to some pizza joint."

"I'm on it." She ended the call.

Brisk lowered the phone, attention on the mezuzah mounted by the doorframe—a symbol of protection that now felt hollow, its promise of shelter meaningless beneath the weight of his deception. In the hallway mirror, his reflection caught: stubble creeping along his jaw, eyes dulled with fatigue. It was a reminder of the cleanup still ahead: a shave, a hot bath, maybe even a splash of charm before meeting the dancer. Her name, Cassandra, had amused him at first. He didn't believe in omens, but he still hoped this one wasn't trying to prove him wrong.

Upstairs, silence lay heavy, the house cloaked in a museum-like hush. Pale sunlight filtered through the wide windows, glinting off plastic-covered furniture. The pine table in the dining room stood untouched, waiting for a gathering no one planned to host. The adjacent kitchen—its dated appliances and worn linoleum—clung to the past, its promise of convenience long expired.

In the primary bedroom, the en suite featured an oversized bathtub, an indulgence from the only renovation. Tika Brisk perched on the edge of the sagging bed, posture stiff with tension. Her teased 1950s bouffant and oversized hoop earrings framed a face worn thin by years of resentment. She chewed her gum with a metronomic rhythm, eyes locked on the small TV atop the dresser.

Onscreen, Babe Lincoln held a microphone, the vivid red '99 Corvette gleaming behind her in the police impound lot. "We'll bring updates as they become available," Babe said. A chyron scrolled beneath, offering a half-hearted apology for a broadcasting error.

Tika clicked off the TV with a tap of her red-lacquered nail. She studied Brisk entering, garment bag and evidence box in hand. Without a word, he dropped them onto the second twin bed. "Another new suit?" Her voice was tight, barely masking the heat underneath. "How can we afford to retire in Florida if all you do is spend, spend, spend? What happens if you drop dead before your pension kicks in?"

Brisk shrugged off his jacket and tossed it onto a chair. "Your rabbi can wear new threads for a change," he muttered, disappearing into the bathroom.

The bed creaked as she shifted her weight. "What about the acting mayor's daughter? Are you tangled up in that mess?"

Water gushed from the faucet, muffling his response. "Just a dumb kid making dumb choices. She's become a walking migraine, one headline away from scandal. I've got a meeting tonight. Who knows, I might even get lucky."

Tika narrowed her eyes. The late meetings, the excuses—each one harder to ignore. "News 4 mentioned your case," she said. "Babe Lincoln. You know her?"

His voice came flat above the running water. "No. I don't track every reporter in the city."

Tika had heard Brisk outside before stepping into the house. The line from earlier kept looping in her head: *She's a sweet ride.* Too smooth. Too knowing. Like he wasn't just talking about the car. Her eyes shifted to his jacket. A floral scent clung to the fabric. It was unfamiliar. Not hers. She picked it up. Something slipped from the pocket and landed on the floor, a small rectangle facedown. Crouching, she turned it over. The name was bold. Undeniable.

Babe Lincoln.

Chapter 21

Lieutenant Choi slid into the cruiser's driver's seat and glanced back at Klarence, standing on the porch in green leather lederhosen, one hand lifted in an earnest wave. The sight was oddly fitting, an out-of-place relic from a Bavarian postcard planted in the middle of the Canadian wilderness.

"B-bye-bye, Miss Choi!" he called, his voice lilting across the clearing with innocent finality.

She exhaled, a soft laugh slipping out before she could stop it, and lifted two fingers from the wheel—just enough to wave back. His gesture stirred something tender inside her, a place she didn't often let herself feel. What had passed between them hadn't been part of the plan. Her strategy had become intimacy, quiet and unexpected.

Choi turned the key. The engine rumbled to life, its growl slicing through the stillness like a reluctant goodbye. Her phone lay powered down on the passenger seat, one last rebellion to preserve the fragile calm still clinging to her skin. Brisk's crude voice echoed in her mind, dragging bile to her throat. His homophobic jabs and leering sarcasm weren't just off-colour, they were corrosive. Whether born of ignorance or malice, the damage was done.

As the cruiser rolled away, Bear Lake shimmered in the rearview—sky and water fused in stillness. The place called to her, whispered of letting go. Trading everything she'd built for something wild. Wordless. What began as a search for a witness had become something else entirely. Klarence had slipped past her defences, quiet and unexpected. What should've been a detour had become a map— not just to him, but to some version of herself she hadn't known was missing.

Then, like muscle memory, her focus snapped back to the case. Molly—still missing. Bear Lake's stillness was a mask. Beneath it, something was buried. Clues. Lies. Maybe bodies. Even as she drove, the ache of leaving him lingered. But so did the pull forward. She had a job to do. And for the first time in years, the road ahead didn't feel fixed. It felt like a possibility. He'd shown her something brighter. Strange. Joyful. Unplanned. She wasn't there yet. First, she had to find Molly. But as the cruiser carried her farther from the cabin, his memory stayed close. Not just a connection. A possibility. It wasn't just the way he'd looked at her, like she was the smartest, strongest woman alive. It was his raw honesty. No pretense. No angles. Just himself.

The country road stretched ahead, a ribbon of gravel carving through Canada's indifferent wild. Half-collapsed barns and rusting tractors marked the landscape like abandoned thoughts. The silence pressed in, broken only by the wind in the trees. The directions Klarence had given her felt more like a dare than a map. Every mile deepened the question: was she looking for a girl that didn't want to be found? Her grip tightened on the wheel.

Something shifted up ahead at the edge of the road, snapping her back to the present.

A lean, sunburned man embodied rural grit, face weathered like old leather, beard scruffy and unkempt. He wrestled with a stubborn donkey that stood in sharp contrast: sleek, well-fed, its coat shimmering in the afternoon sun. Each tug on the reins only made the animal dig in deeper.

Choi eased the cruiser to a stop and rolled down her window. "Nice pony," she called, deadpan.

The man scowled, eyes flicking to her cruiser's New York plates. "Missy, sweet-talkin' about my ass won't change a damn thing about them communication towers," he muttered. "I know how you government types operate, sneakin' in lobbyists from 'Merica and all."

Choi bit back a laugh. "Relax. I'm not here about towers or lobbyists. I just need directions to Moosetown."

He adjusted his hat, watching her warily. "Town's gone quiet. Like a ghost town. Folks are spooked, but no one's talking."

Choi's instincts sharpened. "What happened?"

He stepped back, eyes shadowed. "Can't say for sure. People are buttoned up, just sayin' it's bad. Something about the lines between what's real and what ain't getting blurred." He scratched his beard, staring into the distance like the answer might be out there in the trees.

Choi sensed the slide into local folklore. "Appreciate the heads-up," she said, keeping her tone even. "Am I at least headed the right way?"

He hesitated, then gave a nod. "You'll turn right on the next road, Lingus Lane. At the stop sign, there's a white church. That's Nine Mile Road. Go right for the nitwit's campground. Left takes you into town." He paused. "Hell, better if I draw it out." He pulled a carpenter's pencil and a scrap of paper from his overalls and scribbled a crude map. "I still say you shouldn't go."

Choi pocketed the map. As she drove on, his words stuck with her. This place was starting to feel like another world. A place where even reality had to fight to hold its ground.

Her cruiser rattled into Moosetown Auto Repairs & Rentals, gravel crunching under the tires. A flat tire added to her mounting frustration. The shop's chipped paint and rust-streaked exterior mirrored the disrepair of the storage yard behind it. Oil-stained dirt and knee-high weeds choked piles of discarded tires and rusted car parts. A green Jeep sat beneath a weathered banner: Special Sale.

The mammoth garage door groaned as it slid open.

Choi braced herself, expecting a grizzled mechanic in greasy coveralls. Instead, a man in his forties strutted into view, tan skin gleaming under the midday sun. Mechanic Joe was stitched on the chest of his shirt. His slicked-back hair, high-water pants, and pink socks tucked into shiny patent leather shoes belonged on a dance floor, not in a repair shop. A dazzling smile stretched across his face.

"Has your magnificent chariot suffered misfortune, my dear?" he purred, tone dripping with theatrical charm.

"Flat tire," Choi said, holding up her phone to display a photo of Babe's red Corvette. "Seen this car around?"

Joe's eyes sparkled with delight. "A vision behind the wheel? Pouty lips, alluring curves, a true showstopper?"

"Was she alone?" Choi pressed, ignoring his theatrics.

"Alas, I'm only guessing. No such goddess has graced our town," he sighed, gesturing to her cruiser. "But speaking of visions, your tire appears to have lost its will to live."

"Can you fix it?"

Joe spread his arms. "My talents lie elsewhere. But I can offer you a delightful discount on this rascal!" He gestured to the green Jeep, giving the fender a quick polish with a lace-trimmed handkerchief.

Choi narrowed her eyes. "Why does your shirt say Mechanic Joe if you don't fix cars?"

Joe placed a hand over his heart. "Appearances can deceive, my dear. A slushie-related incident forced a wardrobe change—"

"Where's the police station?" she interrupted, patience thinning.

Joe executed a flamboyant pirouette, pointing theatrically down the street. He took great pains not to brush against her dusty cruiser, then scrutinized the vehicle like a jeweller assessing a counterfeit diamond. "These petite scoundrels can be elusive," he said, then fumbled with the hood latch. His eyes flicked to the front seat. "Honeybunch, I'm afraid I must place you under citizen's arrest."

Choi flashed her badge. "You have a problem."

"Don't play coy with me, my precious," he said, plucking a baggie of marijuana from the front seat. "Unless you're a Mountie—crimson tunic, majestic steed, giddy-up and all that? And I don't see any oats in this feed bag! I could blow a whistle and summon reinforcements. Now assume the position."

She'd had enough. First, the boat rental jerk, now this doofus in pink socks threatening to blow a whistle?

"You're a day late and a dollar short," she snapped.

"Are you suggesting I'm all hat, no cattle?"

"All sizzle, no steak." She moved to the trunk. "Are you familiar with a Mossberg Shockwave?"

Joe blinked. "Does it involve seismic activity… or climate change?"

Choi pulled the 14-inch shotgun from the trunk and levelled it at his chest.

Joe's confidence evaporated. "Although I'm always open to those discussions."

"Enough, Mechanic Joe, or whoever you are." She exhaled, steeling herself. The shotgun didn't just level the playing field, it gave her the upper hand.

And she planned to use it.

Chapter 22

Babe lived in a world where deception wasn't a tactic—it was the rule. In media circles, FOX News and MSNBC pushed duelling narratives, stoking division while thriving on viewers who claimed to hate the circus but kept buying tickets. Corporations—from tobacco to pharma—had long since mastered the art of lying. The result? A landscape where truth was optional and outrage was currency. Against this backdrop, Babe chose to lean in. If everyone else was playing the game, why not her?

The spin? A mannequin dressed as an old woman, belted into the cruiser's back seat. Ariana had taken one look and muttered, *"Weekend at Bernie's."*

The plan was bold in its simplicity. Babe would pose as an FBI agent extraditing a fugitive. Her justification? An obscure theory from the agency's Behavioural Analysis Unit: escaped prisoners often complied when a familiar face—usually a family member—was present. The dummy, dressed as the fugitive's mother, was the bait.

Gomsie, Ariana's go-to prop guy, had outdone himself. The dummy looked real. The forged FBI credentials could pass a flashlight test. Every detail boosted Babe's confidence, but the real challenge lay ahead: clearing the border inspection without blinking.

The unmarked Charger approached the turnoff for the Canadian border. Babe rehearsed the script in her head, stealing a glance at Ariana, slumped in the passenger seat, eyes closed.

It all depended on precision. One wrong answer, one suspicious glance—prison. She had drilled Ariana relentlessly. Their story: Ariana was an exhausted city cop assigned to assist in federal surveillance. Her job was to say little. Let Babe do the talking.

Then, the phone buzzed. Babe glanced at the screen. One line. Her pulse slowed. She read it twice, then yanked the wheel hard, throwing the Charger into a U-turn. Tires shrieked against the pavement.

"What the hell? Why are we turning around?" Ariana's voice was thick with sleep and panic.

Babe's tone was flat. "Brisk is dead."

"Dead?" Ariana blinked. "Like… *dead* dead?"

"Yes. And he had the evidence box tied to Molly's case. We need to get to it before someone else does."

Ariana sat up straighter, brushing hair from her face. "Where are we going?"

"To pay our respects." Babe flicked on the misery lights. The siren wailed to life as the Charger surged through the hum of traffic.

"You think the evidence is at his house?"

"Brisk stashed it in the trunk before we left for the restaurant. If we're lucky, it's there." She exhaled sharply. "Jews don't waste time. They bury fast."

"So what exactly is the plan?"

The Charger fishtailed as Babe yanked it into a tight turn, tires shrieking through the intersection. "We're doing the chicken."

Ten minutes later, they slid to a stop near the curb where luxury cars—Mercedes, Audis, BMWs—clogged the street. It looked more like an evacuation than a funeral.

Ariana stepped out and caught up to Babe, who was already moving fast, clutching a grease-stained bucket stamped with Pistol Pete's Chicken Emporium.

"This isn't overkill?" Ariana asked.

"No such thing at a Jewish funeral," Babe muttered. "They're grieving, not judging. Bringing food's a mitzvah." She didn't slow her pace. "And it buys us five minutes inside without question."

"How'd he go?"

"Electrocuted. Took a radio into the tub. Real genius move."

"Musical baths? That's a thing now?"

"People die in strange ways. Let's stay on task."

"You don't seem too broken up about this guy biting it."

"It's complicated," Babe said flatly.

What she didn't know: Chief Brisk's death hadn't been an accident. It was Tika. She had found Babe's business card, and a trace of unfamiliar perfume on his coat. She waited until he was in the bath. Plugged in the radio. Stepped inside. Let it drop.

The sidewalk was lined with plastic vases of flowers, beyond a man in a yarmulke whispering into a phone. The hush of grief wrapped the street like cellophane, tense and transparent. They rounded the hedge toward the chief's split-level home and stopped cold.

"The fuck!" Ariana gasped.

There it was—Babe's red Corvette parked in the driveway like it belonged.

"The chief loved his secrets," Babe said. "But he couldn't resist a tight little ride with serious thrust."

They stepped onto the porch. Ariana lowered her voice. "What if his wife answers?"

"Friends and family greet guests. You talk about casseroles while I go for the files." Babe raised a hand to knock. The door opened. "Hi, I'm Babe—"

A fist smashed into her face.

Babe staggered back into Ariana.

Chicken exploded across the porch in a greasy arc. The bucket flew like a failed Olympic discus. A cardboard box labelled Evidence: Molly Darnell hit the porch, Corvette keys skittering beside it.

Tika slammed the door shut.

Ariana scowled. "So not crispy." She tossed a drumstick over the hedge.

From the street: a yowl, screeching brakes, the bone-jarring crunch of metal on metal. Two cars collided in perfect disharmony.

Babe peeled the chicken bucket off her head. "Guess they keep kosher," she mumbled.

They regrouped by the Corvette.

"You good?" Ariana asked.

"She hits like a toddler."

"That widow's lucky I didn't bring my scissors. I'd have turned her into abstract art."

"She's grieving. Let it go," Babe said. "I'll meet you at the cruiser." Babe scooped up the evidence box and slid it onto the Corvette's passenger seat. She removed the Targa roof panels, stored them in the rear, then climbed behind the wheel. The car growled to life.

Halfway down the block, Ariana's voice cut through suburbia. "Go crawl back to your basement, you greasy little incel!"

Babe rolled to a stop beside Ariana. Across the street, a man was flailing beside a wrecked Camaro that had smashed into a parked Cadillac. "What now?" Babe asked.

Ariana popped the cruiser's trunk and yanked out a shotgun. "He said my ass should come with a warning label, so creeps like him don't sprain their wrists."

"And your plan is to what, shoot him?"

"I'm sick of being eye-fucked everywhere I go!" Ariana hissed, raising the shotgun.

Babe stepped out, snatched it from her, and tossed it in the back of the Corvette. "We don't have time for this. No room for luggage, either. Grab your pack, we're moving to Plan B."

Ariana glared at her suitcases. "My designer outfits are in there."

"Are you insane?" Babe yanked out the mannequin and placed it behind the cruiser's steering wheel. "We'll be lucky to make it out alive."

"But you said something about factory outlet stores—"

"Molly's case comes first. Then you shop."

Ariana slung her pack over one shoulder. "You had me worried for a second."

Sunlight bounced off Babe's short blonde hair as they hopped into the Corvette and peeled away.

Ariana twisted sideways in her seat. "What do you think the cops'll do when they get their cruiser back with that mannequin behind the wheel?"

Babe shrugged. "Call for backup, surround it, then wait for some sergeant to show up and chew them out for being meatheads."

"I'd pay money to see that."

Babe nodded toward the evidence box wedged between Ariana's feet. "See what's inside."

Ariana pulled her red-handled scissors from her pack and jabbed at the tape. "Damn thing's sealed tighter than Brisk's lips."

"No stabbings today." Babe snatched the scissors and tucked them into her boot.

"Scissors saved my life," Ariana huffed. "What if your ankles swell? You'll never get them out."

"Don't worry. Just rip it open."

Ariana bit through the tape and yanked the lid. A gust of wind rushed through the car, sending the shredded paper inside into a swirling confetti storm.

"Dammit." Babe barked, spinning the wheel. The Corvette fishtailed as paper plastered the windshield. Tires squealed. The car skidded sideways before straightening.

Ariana peeled paper off her lap. "Well, that was festive. Add a mariachi band and it's a party."

Babe relaxed her grip on the wheel and gave Ariana's hand a quick squeeze.

"The chief's wife must be a piece of work," Ariana muttered. "Who does this?"

"Those papers were already shredded."

"You're not pissed?"

"It says more than you think."

"How?"

"It's like spotting a fin in the water. You see the hint, but the real danger's underneath."

Ariana groaned. "*Jaws*. Big shark. Lots of screaming. Tell me you've seen it."

"Not the time."

"I'm right," Ariana muttered, arms crossed.

Babe shook her head. "Okay, I need a distraction. Time for a smoke." She pulled a cigarette from her shirt pocket.

"Didn't Father Johnson tell you to quit?"

"Any decent man of the cloth would recommend a cigarette after a day like this."

"Your driving was impressive. But cigarettes will kill you like a car crash."

"Are you done? Or should we talk about how you don't own a phone because you think it fries your brain?"

"Fine." Ariana huffed. "Where is it?"

"There." She pointed at the glove box. "And stop making faces."

"I would never," Ariana said with an exaggerated pout. "Shocked you'd suggest such a thing."

"You rolled your eyes when I mentioned silver-plating it."

Undeterred, Ariana retrieved a chrome-plated .45 automatic. "How much did modifying this cost?"

"Forget that."

She pulled the trigger. After a few dry clicks, a butane flame snapped to life. She lit Babe's cigarette with the tricked-out lighter.

Babe exhaled smoke through the open top. "You know I love you, right?"

Ariana leaned in and brushed her lips across Babe's cheek. "Of course, my sweetness. And I love you too."

"I mean it. To the ends of the earth. But you're a pain in the ass."

"Careful, or I'll think you're getting romantic."

Babe laughed. "You're insane."

"You wanted adventure. What can I say?"

"Don't remind me. Hang on, we're almost there."

The Corvette screamed onto the Peace Bridge, slicing through the golden haze of afternoon light. Beyond the border, answers waited.

So did the trouble.

Babe's pulse hammered as the car ahead cleared the inspection kiosk. With both governments cracking down on fentanyl trafficking, heightened security meant more searches, more dogs, more chances for things to go sideways. The wrong agent, the wrong question, one random check, and their entire cover could crumble.

Up ahead, a K9 unit circled a black pickup in secondary inspection. The dog leapt onto the tailgate, paws thudding, nose working overtime. Two border agents popped the truck's toolbox and yanked it open.

Babe swallowed hard. They'd bet everything on simplicity—no aliases, no props, no flashy cons. Just two women on a weekend shopping trip to Toronto. Babe had even explained to Ariana that KISS wasn't a band reference. It stood for Keep It Simple, Stupid. But simplicity didn't mean shit if they got flagged and the shotgun was found.

The Corvette crept forward. The Customs and Immigration officer stood at the checkpoint, uniform crisp, posture rigid. His eyes scanned the car, then locked on them.

"Passports, please."

Babe handed them over. Her fingers didn't tremble, but her gut was coiled tight. The officer flipped through the pages.

"Purpose of your visit?"

"Shopping in Toronto," she said. "Taking advantage of the exchange rate."

"Remove your sunglasses, please," he added.

Ariana pulled off her Serengetis with a smirk. "I don't think they'll fit you," she purred.

Babe stiffened. Her mind raced. One more crack like this, and they'd be in a back room with agents snapping on gloves.

But the officer chuckled. "Just need to match the photos," he said, warming slightly.

Babe exhaled as he continued the routine questions. She told him they were staying at the Hilton by the airport. The lie was plausible, convenient, easy to believe.

Then he paused on her passport. "Are you related to Abraham Lincoln?"

Babe didn't miss a beat. "Distant relative," she said smoothly. "I don't talk about it much. People get weird about politics these days."

The officer lit up. "I love American history. Can't believe how people take their freedoms for granted. We should grab drinks in Toronto."

Babe forced a smile. "Sounds nice. Let's plan on it."

Ariana reapplied her lipstick in the visor mirror, her reflection catching his attention.

Wrong team, buddy. You'd have better luck dating your history books, Babe thought.

"Hotel bar. Nine o'clock?" he suggested, handing back the passports.

"See you then," Babe said.

He winked. "You're good. Have a safe drive."

"Always," she replied. The Corvette rolled forward, and with it came the first clean breath she'd taken in ten minutes.

A mile down the road, red and blue lights flared in the rearview mirror, slicing through the calm.

"Fuck me," Babe muttered, tightening her grip on the wheel.

Ariana twisted in her seat, eyes wide. "Shit. They're onto us." Her eyes darted to the hatch. The shotgun made her stomach drop.

The siren wailed louder, crawling up their spines. Babe's mind scrambled for an excuse.

Then, with a rush, an ambulance blew past them. The siren faded into the distance.

Ariana slumped in relief, hand pressed to her chest. "Jesus. I thought we were about to end up in an *Orange Is the New Black* reboot."

Babe reached over and squeezed her hand. "We're fine."

But the knot in her stomach didn't ease. How long could their luck really last?

The rest of the drive passed in silence. Ariana stayed quiet, her usual sparkle dampened by nerves.

They finally pulled into Bear Lake's Boat Rental. The sun-bleached building sagged with age, its flower boxes hanging on like an afterthought.

Ariana frowned. "I thought we were heading to a campground near Moosetown?"

"We are."

"But the sign says—"

"Forget the sign. Go shopping. I'll meet you at the campground later." Babe could see Ariana was wound tight. Time apart might help her decompress.

Ariana paused. "What about you?"

"I'm talking to boaters. Last time I was here with Molly, the lake was packed. Somebody might've seen something. Background matters."

"How do I get there?"

"Back out to Terminal Road, turn left, keep going. It runs parallel to the highway—you'll see it."

Ariana nodded, then pulled a ball cap from her bag and tugged it over her hair. She climbed behind the wheel, but lingered a moment. "Love you, baby."

"Me too, sweetie. Be good."

Ariana smiled, then hit the gas. Gravel spat from the tires as the Corvette peeled off, leaving a thin cloud in her wake.

Babe turned toward the lake. The shoreline was a quiet mess of empty boat trailers, waterlogged debris, and an aluminum boat half-submerged in the reeds.

Rusty ambled out of the weather-beaten shack, clutching a paddle like a prized heirloom. "Skittle-scaddle, who needs a paddle?" he called, grinning like he'd invented the line. "Though for a lady of your obvious calibre, might I recommend a pontoon? Lounge chair under a cheerful umbrella, champagne, maybe a mint julep. Or, if you're feeling more adventurous, I've got premium marijuana strains. Citrus, kush, berry, you name it. Thank Justin for that."

"Where's this pontoon? I don't see anything remotely looking like a boat," Babe said, her patience thinning.

His grin faltered. "We're fresh out."

"A sign might've saved me some trouble."

Rusty shrugged. "If you'd like to come inside, I can take your information. I'll call when we restock."

"Let's not waste each other's time."

"Be that way, it's your loss, not mine." He hopped onto the red ATV and rumbled down the pathway and into the woods.

Babe scuffed her boot in the sand and nudged a loose rock into the lake. The splash barely registered. Every delay shaved down her resolve. She inhaled, deep and steady, trying to hold focus while everything inside her strained to move.

Near the shoreline, the battered aluminum boat tilted in the reeds, its bow full of water, a metaphor she didn't need spelled out: half-sunk, forgotten, still somehow afloat. Molly's trail was cold. If Babe didn't turn something up soon, it wouldn't just fade, it would be erased.

She stared across the still water, its surface glassy and indifferent. Somewhere out there, someone knew the truth.

And she'd find them before the silence buried it forever.

Chapter 23

A faded wooden sign hung from rusted chains, swaying in the breeze. Stay Chipper. Beneath it sat a battered school bus, once bright yellow, now streaked with white paint. Time had not been kind. Rust bled through chipped metal, creeping along the wheel wells and beneath a bolted-on service window. Most of the glass was covered in warped plywood, duct tape, and sheets of clouded plastic, giving the bus a haphazard, uneasy look. Smoke curled from a steel pipe jutting through the roof, carrying the acrid scent of old grease and something less identifiable.

The menu board, scrawled in uneven lettering, offered the usual artery-clogging fare: burgers, hot dogs, onion rings, fries, and thick-cut fries drowned in gravy and crowned with cheese curds, known as poutine. The business followed a simple motto: build it and they will come. Most weekends, the place swarmed with locals and truckers chasing cheap indulgence.

Today, the lot was empty, except for Risqué, perched like a statue on Muncie's pickup, eyes tracking the gulls overhead.

Molly stared at the charred hamburger on her grease-stained plate, the congealed mess mocking her. Options were bleak, eat or go hungry. The slop offered no comfort for the storm brewing inside her.

Across the picnic table, Muncie and Ginger ate with single-minded focus—cheeseburgers, a mountain of oily onion rings, and a shared poutine, all washed down with loud gulps from jumbo sodas. Their gluttony only deepened her nausea.

Driving miles for this garbage felt absurd. But sulking wouldn't help. She needed strength for what lay ahead. Fighting the wave of disgust, she took a breath and bit into the burger. The overcooked patty crunched like gravel between her teeth, the brittle texture jarring against the soft bun. Every bite felt like a parody of normalcy.

Muncie wiped mustard from his chin with the back of his hand, smiling—a cross between a leer and condescension. "Molly," he began, voice thick with food, "you'll need a tutorial later. Last night was a shortfall of epic proportions. Think of it as friendly advice for finding peace and tranquility. Your success reflects on all of us. And inner calm? That's the key." He punctuated the thought with a belch.

She barely masked her revulsion. Watching him chew and talk at once only added to her growing list of grievances. She glanced at Ginger, who was inhaling her food like a rescued castaway.

Ginger suddenly straightened. "Did you know most people think German Shepherds are the ideal dog? Loyal, courageous, intelligent, steady!"

"Thank you for sharing," Muncie cut in, slurping the last of his drink.

He turned back to Molly. "I can't begin to tell you how excited I am to pick up some eggs."

"Oh, goodie!" Ginger clapped like a preschooler.

"Ginger loves a fresh farm egg," he stated.

"Thanks for sharing," Molly said.

"Don't be like that. The egg is powerful. The yolk represents consciousness. The white part—unconsciousness. It's wholeness. Balance. Completion." He leaned in, voice firmer now. "Think of it as a reminder why your journey matters."

Ginger added, eyes wide, "Muncie says it represents rebirth. A new beginning!"

Molly stared, her frustration rising. Was this satire? Or delusion? Some kind of cult thing? But she bit her tongue. Blowing up would only tighten their grip.

Muncie gestured to the circling gulls. "See those shit hawks? Survivors. Ginger's here to help you adapt. I expect the same intelligence from you. And don't get any wild ideas about the locals."

Molly scoffed. "The birds ask people for help?"

His tone sharpened. "Anxiety's made you delusional. But you'll adjust. The transition will happen."

She eyed a transport truck barreling past the edge of the property. Just yards away. Just.

"Don't get any foolish ideas in that pretty little noggin of yours. You see, Molly, we have the carrot, and we have the stick. Not wearing coveralls? That's the carrot. Need I remind you what the stick is?" He held up the red controller. "Are we clear?"

"Now who's being delusional?" she snapped, hurling the burger across the lawn.

Seagulls descended in a frenzy, tearing the meat apart. Their shrieks shattered the tense silence.

Muncie's eyes stayed locked on her. Cold. Measured. This wasn't just a power trip. Every word he uttered, every move he made, was part of a system designed to isolate her. Strip her down. Break her.

Here, in this godforsaken hamlet, Muncie made the rules. And time was running out.

If she didn't act soon, her chance to escape would vanish for good.

Chapter 24

The red Corvette purred over the two-lane blacktop, its polished surface gleaming under the sun. The endless sky stretched above like a canvas brushed with wisps of white cloud. Cornfields and dilapidated barns broke the monotony, framed by scrubby bushes and scattered patches of forest.

Ariana shifted in her seat, her bladder protesting. A faded sign reading Roadside Diner rose on the horizon, standing like a beacon in the rural emptiness. Babe had mentioned that Terminal Road saw little traffic after the nearby highway opened. The diner's presence surprised her, though she doubted it still operated. The once-vibrant building sagged under the weight of neglect, its sun-bleached paint curling like old parchment. A worn sign offered gas and food, but the neon tubes hung dark and lifeless.

The gravel lot was rimmed with scraggly trees and brittle shrubs, their leaves clinging to dusty branches. A motor home idled by the pumps, the driver just finishing up at the tank. Ariana pulled in and parked near the front of the diner, grateful for the chance to stretch her legs and find a restroom. She spotted a sign pointing around the side of the building. Stepping out of the Corvette, she headed toward the washrooms. Then, the sudden roar of engines shattered the quiet.

A dozen bikers from the Runaway Motorcycle Club thundered into the lot, their motorcycles growling like predators on the hunt. The stench of gasoline and exhaust clung to the air. Polished chrome flashed under the sun as leather-clad riders dismounted, their vests marked with the club's insignia. Bandanas and mirrored sunglasses hid their faces, but their swagger made their intentions clear.

Whistles, catcalls, and obscene jeers cut through the air. "Hey, hot stuff, need a hand?" one biker jeered.

"We'll take you for a special ride," another added, blowing her a kiss as laughter erupted.

Her stomach twisted. She glanced at the Corvette, tempted to flee, but her bladder refused to negotiate. She kept walking.

Inside, the cramped washroom reeked of bleach and mildew. Ariana finished quickly, then washed up at the sink, her reflection in the cracked mirror tight with tension. She splashed water on her face, careful not to smudge her makeup or soak the brim of her cap. After drying her hands on a stiff paper towel, she adjusted her sunglasses.

When she stepped outside, her heart sank.

The bikers had boxed in the Corvette, parking their choppers in neat rows on both sides. The motor home had left, leaving only the bikes grinning behind the diner's greasy windows. Wolves at the edge of the woods.

Panic surged. They wanted her inside. And whatever awaited wouldn't end well.

Ariana squared her shoulders and tugged her cap lower, as if the brim could shield her from their stares. She inhaled slowly, then sprinted toward the Corvette. She hopped onto the hood, grabbed the windshield frame, and vaulted into the driver's seat through the open roof. Pulling off a move she'd only seen in movies gave her a jolt of confidence.

Maybe I could use a stunt like that in my next film. If they ever let me keep my clothes on long enough to perform one.

The engine roared to life. She eased the car into reverse, carefully threading the Corvette between the rows of bikes. Gravel crunched under the tires. Her hands trembled slightly, but she didn't clip a single chrome fender.

Back on Terminal Road, Ariana gripped the wheel, knuckles white. Her mind reeled through past encounters—crudely worded come-ons, lingering stares, the low hum of threat that clung to certain men like a second skin. But this time, anger gave way to action.

She'd always told Babe: Go big or stay home. If ever there was a time to live up to that motto, it was now.

Tires shrieked as she spun the Corvette into a tight U-turn, the rear fishtailing before gripping. The car surged back toward the diner.

She pulled into the parking lot and parked across from the motorcycles. The driver's window lowered and out slid the double-barreled shotgun.

BOOM. BOOM.

The twin blasts cracked the air. Flames leapt from the bikes as gas tanks erupted in fiery plumes. Shrapnel flew. Black smoke curled skyward, thick and fast.

Ariana pulled the weapon back inside and set it beside her. She tugged her cap lower, adjusted her sunglasses, and eased the Corvette out of the lot.

In the rearview mirror, bikers poured out of the diner, with faces twisted in disbelief and rage.

She raised her middle finger through the open roof. Her pulse still thundered, but a smile ghosted her lips. The fear was gone, replaced by heat, resolve, and the undeniable high of a clean shot and a roaring engine.

Ariana's grip tightened on the wheel as the Corvette devoured the blacktop. A hulking biker on a massive Harley roared past in the opposite lane, red bandana snapping in the wind. He turned sharply, eyes locking with hers as their vehicles passed.

Wind whipped through the open roof, tugging loose strands of her hair beneath the cap pulled low over her brow. The premium sound system thumped with bass-heavy beats, each note vibrating in her chest.

Her mind drifted toward Moosetown, where the memory of the diner, the bikers, and their leering grins would soon fade. She smiled at the thought of surprising Babe with a gift, something bold, something guaranteed to make her laugh. After all, hadn't Babe gone out of her way for that perfume and those scissors? Ariana could already picture her face: half a blush, half a grin. That look made everything in the world seem possible.

The road stretched ahead, flanked by swaying cornfields and weathered barns leaning into time. Ariana exhaled, tension bleeding away as the scenery blurred past. Her eyes flicked to the glove box. She remembered the joint Babe had stashed there. Maybe a quick hit would take the edge off. Stretching an arm over the gearshift, she fumbled for the latch while keeping the road in her peripheral vision.

Her fingers grazed the edge of the glove box, and the tires struck a slick, brownish smear across the asphalt, reeking of rot and sewage.

The Corvette swerved. The wheel wrenched in her hands. The car fishtailed. Ariana's breath caught as the car veered, seconds from spinning out. She fought the skid, muscles straining, but the sleek machine had a mind of its own. The screech of rubber tore through the air. The front tires hit the shoulder and launched.

Her world flipped. Gravity abandoned her as sky and earth spun in a violent blur of blue and green. The car slammed back down, fibreglass crunching on impact. Her cap flew off. Sunglasses shattered against the dash, shards scattering like ice.

The Corvette tumbled through underbrush. Tree trunks flashed past. Branches snapped, thudded, tore. Each impact stripped the car of shape, shredding what had once been sleek, powerful, untouchable.

Ariana screamed. Her chest slammed forward. The seatbelt bit into her ribs. The airbag exploded against her face, suffocating, disorienting, sealing her in.

Then stillness.

The wrecked Corvette groaned to a halt, wedged in the forest's teeth. The silence was heavy and absolute.

Ariana slumped forward, body limp against the airbag. Blood trickled from her temple, streaking her jaw, soaking her collar. The engine sputtered once, then died, leaving only the rustle of leaves and the steady drip of fluid pooling below. Gasoline hung in the air, threaded with pine and scorched rubber. Every breath came shallow. Pain pulsed deep in her ribs. Somewhere in the haze, Babe's name surfaced. A lifeline. That spark in her eyes. That brave softness Ariana couldn't stop chasing. She blinked. Vision dimmed. A tear slid down her cheek, carving a clean line through the dirt. Her fingers twitched, seeking contact, and finding none. The void pressed in. Relentless. Quiet.

The last thing she registered was Babe's smile like a beacon in the dark.

Chapter 25

Lieutenant Choi drove the Jeep toward the local police station, Mechanic Joe trussed up in the back seat beneath the garage's faded Special Sale banner. She hoped to gain the constabulary's support for a visit to the so-called American Embassy. Choi doubted the place was legitimate, its very existence seemed absurd, but every angle had to be explored to close the case. The idea of an ambassador detaining an American citizen was laughable, but confirming Molly's absence might bring closure and mean seeing Klarence again.

Before leaving, Choi had rifled through Joe's wallet and discovered his real name: Harry Lickenhouser. Two photographs tucked inside had caught her attention. One showed Whiteside, the campground owner, leaning affectionately toward Joe. The other depicted Rusty, the boat rental operator, standing stiffly between them. Rusty's uneasy smile clashed with the cake he held, which read: Welcome to Bear Lake; Not All Bears Hibernate Alone. Choi chalked it up to small-town eccentricity. Even after learning Joe's real name, she kept calling him Mechanic Joe, shutting down his protests with the barrel of her Glock pressed between his eyes.

The Jeep rattled over potholes. A foul stench drifted through the open windows. It hit the back of her throat and turned her stomach. She breathed through her mouth, trying not to dwell on what it reminded her of. Rot? Garbage? Something worse? Best not to dwell on that.

A heavy silence hung over the streets, amplifying the unease sparked by the old man's earlier warnings. The town looked functional at first glance, though a few storefronts were boarded up with plywood. Many still displayed Open signs, but the sidewalks were empty, except for an elderly couple shuffling past beneath an oversized yellow umbrella, despite the cloudless blue sky.

Choi parked at the curb. A Fresh Pizza sign clung to the police station's window beside a Closed notice on the door. The chief's earlier comment about a confusing call involving a pizza shop made sudden sense. A police station doubling as a pizzeria added yet another layer of absurdity to an already baffling case.

She wouldn't waste more time here. Klarence's mother might be a better lead.

Leaving town, Choi pulled onto the shoulder of a country road and yanked Mechanic Joe upright. She unwrapped just enough of the banner for him to point to a location on the donkey man's crude map. His breath came in ragged gasps as his trembling finger touched the page.

Choi had promised him freedom in exchange for the info, but had no intention of keeping that promise. His sobs echoed through the woods as she shoved his lace-trimmed handkerchief into his mouth, rewrapped him in the banner, and drove off without a second thought for his awkward position in the backseat.

The Jeep bounced along a gravel track twisting into dense woods. Skeletal branches scraped the windshield, their shadows flickering like claws. With every mile, the trees thickened and the air grew heavier. The idea that anyone chose to live in such isolation struck Choi as reckless and alien. She regretted leaving her shotgun behind but took some comfort in the handgun at her side and the derringer, Allie Oops, strapped to her ankle.

The lane opened into a clearing, startling a flock of chickens. Their frantic squawks shattered the quiet as they scattered. Choi wondered how long their freedom would last before someone came swinging a blade.

Ahead, a sagging shack slouched on crumbling cinder blocks. Moss clung to the roof. Dead branches weighted it down. Filthy windows hid the interior. The yard resembled a junk heap with rusted appliances, broken furniture, and weeds thick as waist-high grass. A battered outhouse stood near a rusting hand pump and a dented bucket. Even the chickens moved cautiously, their jerky steps betraying unease, as if they sensed what lingered here.

Choi half-expected a banjo-playing recluse to step out. Instead, a wiry woman emerged from the shack. Her frizzy hair framed a face carved by hardship. Sharp eyes locked onto the Jeep and the barely visible banner in the back seat.

"Afternoon, ma'am. How's it with you?" Choi called, stepping into the yard with care.

"Ain't no need for that ma'am nonsense," the woman snapped, voice rasped from years of smoke. "Young'uns call me Mrs. Broom, but seein' as you and me's about the same age, just call me Mama Kaye."

Choi resisted pointing out their obvious age difference and gave a curt nod. "Quite the place you've got here."

"Thought youse was me beau when I heard ya comin' down the lane," Mama Kaye said, sticking an unlit joint between her lips.

"Your beau?"

"Muncie. Lives next to me Klarence, with his big ol' furry cock-a-doodle-doo."

"Muncie isn't American, is he?"

"Nope. Far as I know, he's got no gun," Mama Kaye replied, lighting the joint. Smoke curled around her face. "I'd offer you a hit, but it might take you places you don't wanna go."

"I'll pass. It's been one of those days," Choi said.

"Ain't it always?" Mama Kaye nodded toward the shack. "C'mon in."

Dim light filtered through grime-streaked windows, casting long shadows across the room. A wood stove simmered with stew, filling the air with a thick mix of broth and marijuana. A basket of eggs sat on the counter beneath shelves lined with jars of chokecherry jelly, pickled beans, and salted venison.

Choi observed a framed photo on the wall. Two young men. One was Klarence. The other wore a police uniform. "Your sons?" she asked.

Mama Kaye's lips pinched the joint tighter, ember glowing as she took a slow drag. "Karl with a K and Klarence with a K. Good boys, both of 'em." Her tone darkened. "Their daddy bled out after gettin' hit with an axe for doin' that which may not be spoken of in polite company. You remind me of him."

Choi tensed. "How so?"

"He carried secrets too heavy to bear," Mama Kaye said, exhaling a thin stream of smoke. "Secrets always got a way of comin' out, don't they?"

The air thickened. Choi didn't like the direction this was going. The words felt less like an observation and more like a warning. "They do," Choi said. "And sometimes they take us places we don't expect."

Mama Kaye's eyes drifted to Choi's hip, where her jacket covered the Glock. A slow smile tugged at her lips. "Let's see if you're as good at keepin' secrets as you are at findin' them."

Choi's fingers brushed the gun.

Mama Kaye didn't flinch. She took another drag, calm as dusk. "Careful, darlin'. You in my house now."

Choi didn't blink. "Then I guess we should get to know each other better."

Chapter 26

Babe trudged along the sun-scorched shoulder of Terminal Road, each step a drag through exhaustion. Heat shimmered off the asphalt, sweat trailing down her back, soaking her shirt. Her fists clenched, frustration coiling in her chest. Her sunglasses were still in the Corvette, one more screw-up to tally, if she made it out of this.

Isolation pressed in. Spotty cell service mocked her attempts at contact, though it hardly mattered, since Ariana had refused to carry a phone. Babe scanned the horizon for any sign of life, but nothing stirred beyond empty fields and rolling heatwaves.

A weathered sign in the distance: Roadside Diner. Faded block letters promised food and gas. Her dry throat urged her forward, but as she neared, relief soured. Motorcycle parts smouldered near the building, the stink of burnt metal thick in the air. A cluster of bikers lingered near the wreckage, their curses drifting with the heat. The reek of char and gasoline clung to the back of Babe's throat.

She pressed on. Fear simmered, but she buried it. Turning back wasn't an option.

"Excuse me, is someone here I can talk to?"

The bikers turned as one, slow and predatory. Two stepped forward, hulking silhouettes blocking out the sun. A rough hand clamped her arm, another gripped her shoulder.

"I don't want any trouble!" Her voice rang out, but it didn't matter.

They yanked her off balance. Pain flared as she twisted, kicking wildly, boots connecting with denim and leather. Buttons popped, scattering in the dust as her shirt tore open. Her camisole clung to sweat-slicked skin, no defence against their leering stares.

One of them laughed. "Bitch got some fight in her."

"I like 'em frisky," another added, grinning.

Panic surged as she reached for the scissors in her boot, but a sharp pull sent her sideways. Her fingers missed the weapon by inches. A scream built in her throat.

"Enough. Let her go." The words dropped, flat and final.

The bikers froze. Heads snapped toward the diner.

Kingfish stepped out, red bandana stood out against sun-leathered skin. He didn't raise his voice. He didn't need to. His presence shifted the air. "Back off," he snapped.

They obeyed, hands falling away. Babe staggered, clutching the torn remains of her shirt, breath coming fast. Her eyes locked onto the man who'd stopped it all.

Kingfish spat into the dirt. "You know who this is?" he growled, then flashed a grin. "This is Ariana Barbeau."

The name hit like a jolt. Babe kept her face unreadable, realizing Ariana's fame might be her only lifeline. It wasn't the first time she'd been mistaken for her, especially since one of Ariana's cult films had blown up.

The bikers exchanged murmurs, their stance softening, admiration replacing menace.

Kingfish's grin widened. "We're your biggest fans. Loved *The Big Reveal*, ain't that right, boys?"

Grunts and nods rippled through the group.

Babe forced a smile. If they wanted Ariana, then fine, she'd play the role. What choice did she have? "Well, I'm delighted to meet my fans," she said smoothly, pulse hammering.

"Name's Kingfish." His tone softened. "It's an honour."

"The pleasure's mine, Mr. Kingfish." She clutched the coat around her tighter. "Looks like I've gotten myself into a bit of a jam. But it seems your boys have problems of their own." She gestured toward the wrecked bikes.

Kingfish's smile darkened. "Boys need to learn some manners." He shot a glare at Pete, the one who grabbed her first.

Pete fidgeted, then pulled a pen and scrap of paper from his vest. "Miss Barbeau, uh… could I get your autograph?"

"Show some damn respect!" Kingfish snarled. "And get the lady a drink. Can't you see she's about to melt?"

Someone shoved a cold beer into her hand.

"Appreciate it," Babe said, taking a swig. The icy rush cut through the heat like mercy. She wiped her mouth and scribbled a messy signature on Pete's scrap of paper.

Kingfish stepped closer. "Could you do one for me? Make it out to Orville."

More bikers crowded forward with pens and paper.

"Relax, boys. I'll take care of you." Babe signed as fast as she could, masking the fear still coiled in her gut. She handed Orville's autograph back with a tight-lipped smile.

Kingfish studied the autograph, pleased. "Say, Miss Barbeau, could you do something for us? Maybe perform that ugly stick scene?"

Babe froze. Pretending to be Ariana was one thing. Reenacting one of her scenes? That was another. She'd helped Ariana rehearse for hours, sure, but under pressure? Still, the expectant stares left no room to decline.

"Okay, fellas," she said. "Might need to improvise without a director or cameras." She turned to Pete, voice firm. "What's your name?"

"That's Pete!" Kingfish called. "Use him. He'll be up for it."

Pete paled. "I, um, I'm not really—"

"Shut up, fool," Kingfish said. Pete looked away.

Babe tilted her head. "Afterward, can you do me a solid?"

Kingfish nodded. "Whatever you need." He snapped his fingers. "Coat!"

A lean biker peeled off a long brown duster and draped it across her shoulders.

Ariana's voice echoed in her head: "Go big or stay home." This was the moment to live it. Babe took a breath and advanced on Pete. "You've been treated like a redheaded stepchild and beaten with the ugly stick, but nobody cares about pretty here." She grabbed his collar, eyes blazing. "When we claw our way out of this soul-sucking abyss, and make no mistake, we will, everyone will know the best of us stood shoulder to shoulder, united against the forces of evil, ready to fight to the death!"

The backhand cracked across Pete's face. The bikers gasped. Awe thickened the air.

"Will you be that man?" she roared. Another slap landed, harder. Pete's lip trembled. His eyes welled with tears.

"Please, don't… I can't take it," he whimpered.

The gang erupted into cheers and laughter. Reverence bloomed on their faces. Kingfish roared, slapping his thigh. "That was beautiful! Pete may never wash his face again!" The others jostled him, clapping his back, teasing him mercilessly.

Babe adjusted the coat. "Gentlemen, it's been a pleasure. But I need to be somewhere."

Kingfish's grin faded. His eyes narrowed, studying her. "Hold on a second," he said, voice cooling.

Babe's stomach dropped. *Had he just discovered she was an impostor?*

Chapter 27

Mama Kaye's storage shed told a story of grit and secrets. Shovels, hoes, and rakes leaned in one corner, their handles smoothed by years of use. A wooden table bore the scars of countless canning sessions, with jars, lids, and pots arranged in quiet testimony. In the far corner, rows of marijuana plants hung drying above bales of straw, their pungent aroma saturating the air. The mingled scents of earth, wood, and weed created a strange cocktail of vice and labour.

One detail shattered the shed's rustic order: Mechanic Joe, bound and gagged inside a rusted freezer. Bailing twine cinched him tight, the knots clean and unforgiving. Lieutenant Choi had piled bags of weed labelled Holy Smokes on top to keep him in place.

"You better hope Mama Kaye knows something about Yankees around here if you want out," Choi muttered, her voice sluggish. Her eyes were glassy from the joint she'd smoked with her eccentric host. Joe's muffled protests registered as little more than background noise as she slammed the lid, the metallic clang echoing in the shed.

Outside, sunlight pierced the canopy. Choi squinted against the glare and spotted Mama Kaye fussing with her frizzy hair in the Jeep's side mirror. A lit joint dangled from her lips, a lazy curl of smoke rising as she offered it to Choi. She took a pull and exhaled, the smoke catching in her throat. A cough slipped out, followed by a weak laugh. "Mellow," she rasped.

Mama Kaye let out a throaty chuckle. "I add my special touch. Makes the plants hit just right," she said.

They stood quietly for a moment, birdsong and rustling leaves filling the stillness.

Choi tilted her head, refocusing. "Your fiancé," she said, keeping her tone light. "He's not from here, is he?"

Mama Kaye's lips curled into a sly grin. "Oh, Muncie? Between us girls, I reckon he'll pop the question any day now. Men can't resist a good thing when they see it." She laughed, pleased with herself. "Surprised he ain't here already with my firewood. Him, Klarence, and his niece—they'll all be showin' up soon enough."

Choi stiffened. "His niece?"

Mama Kaye shrugged, her eyes drifting to the dwindling joint. "Yeah, she be visitin' for a spell. Scatterbrained little thing. Always runnin' around in the sun without a hat. Them redheads shouldn't do that."

Choi nodded, masking her disappointment. A redhead meant it wasn't Molly, but Muncie's connection to Klarence still didn't sit right. Maybe he was just another oddball, like most folks around here. Still, her instincts told her not to let it go. "You said earlier I reminded you of your husband," Choi said, watching her carefully. "What did you mean? About secrets too heavy to bear?"

Mama Kaye's grin faltered. Her face hardened. She stared toward the trees, her voice dropping to a near whisper. "He carried secrets. Heavy ones. The kind that weigh a man down 'til he can't carry 'em no more."

Choi's chest tightened. "Sometimes secrets spill out."

Mama Kaye's sharp eyes snapped back to her. "They spill out, if you don't bury 'em deep enough. When secrets are buried proper, they stay where they belong. Outta sight. Outta mind." She studied Choi. "You understand, don't ya?"

Choi's voice stayed steady. "I understand."

Mama Kaye's smile returned, slow and knowing. "Good. Diggin' gets messy. And not everyone comes back from it."

The weight of her words lingered as Choi climbed into the Jeep. There was no doubt Mama Kaye loved her sons. Choi had seen it in her reaction to that photograph. There was also no doubt this woman was a force to be reckoned with. Whatever secrets she guarded ran deeper than expected. It wasn't just the marijuana crop or her eccentric charm. Something darker lingered, something buried, both figuratively and literally. Mess with her, and you'd regret it.

She started the engine, the low rumble momentarily grounding her. Mama Kaye's words stirred something uneasy inside. Choi hadn't mentioned Klarence, much less what had transpired between them. She knew she'd never unpack the gritty details, but the basics maybe. In time. Just not now. "Best to keep my visit quiet, Mama Kaye. Don't want unnecessary attention while I wrap things up here."

"Gotcha. Now, you gonna tell me why you stuffed that fella in my freezer?"

Choi managed a faint smile. "He's a material witness in a kidnapping."

Mama Kaye raised an eyebrow. "Who got kidnapped?"

"He did."

"Can't say he'd be much use in a freezer."

"Justice is complicated," Choi replied. "Keep an eye on him for me, would you? If I don't return in a few hours, I've solved the case, and you can decide what to do with him. You have my trust."

A sly grin spread across Mama Kaye's face. "Well, I could use me a yard boy. Seen him in town. He's a bit sensitive. A little hard labour might toughen him up." Shielding the joint from a breeze, she relit it with a wooden match.

Choi shifted into gear. "Thanks, Mama Kaye. I appreciate it."

Mama Kaye waved her off, the joint balanced between her fingers. Her squint followed Choi as if weighing whether she'd ever return.

The Jeep jolted against a tree as Choi reversed. She cursed under her breath, corrected the wheel, and sped off. Muncie's potential return loomed like a countdown, pressing her to stay sharp. If she could reach this so-called Embassy while he was still tied up here, maybe she could confirm Molly had never been there at all.

Then she could finally close this chaotic case and move forward with Klarence.

The thought steadied her as she headed to retrieve her cruiser. With New York plates, she'd have the official credibility to avoid unnecessary questions, especially if locals or embassy staff decided to poke around.

She'd left a note tucked under the windshield wiper, asking the mechanic to fix the flat. If he'd found it and followed through, maybe, just maybe, the rest of her plan would unfold without a hitch.

At least that was the hope. Around here, every plan came with complications.

Chapter 28

Detective Slim Meekins wasn't supposed to be anywhere near this part of town. He'd told the chief he was taking a few days off, maybe hit the dog park, lay low. Brisk had laughed it off, but if the boss found out where Slim was, there'd be hell to pay. There was no way of explaining this detour. Not with a ball-buster like Brisk.

He adjusted the black cat cradled in his arms, its tail twitching against his jacket. Slim approached the mayor's sleek limousine, parked outside Lollypops, one of the city's most infamous strip joints. He'd already dropped the Molly Darnell evidence box at the station. But keeping his name clear of everything else? That was going to take finesse. His gut told him this wasn't the kind of case that stayed clean.

A flickering neon sign bathed the sidewalk in pulsing pinks and reds. Graffiti curled around the building's base, creeping toward broken security lights. The brick façade sagged with age, its mortar flaking like dead skin. Beneath a buckled awning, a knot of women in heels and too-tight skirts smoked in a huddle, their laughter brittle as glass.

The place smelled like stale beer, cheap perfume, and wet asphalt. Slim flinched. He recognized two of the women. He just hoped they didn't recognize him. Awkward wouldn't even scratch the surface.

The limousine's tinted windows reflected his approach, the glossy black paint shimmering in the sunlight. The cat squirmed in his arms, letting out an irritated meow as its claws snagged his lapel. Slim shifted his grip, muttering under his breath. He reached for the door handle. Cold metal met his fingers, sending a shiver up his arm. He pulled.

Locked. A silent refusal.

Inside the limo, Mayor Dickie Darnell sat cloaked in the persona of Delilah Darnell. Soft curls of his golden wig framed a powdered face, while a cobalt-blue sequined dress shimmered in the dim interior. Miss Horn had chosen crimson lipstick to complete the look in a bold, dramatic flourish.

The name Delilah carried meaning for Dickie, evoking cunning and control, qualities he admired in both politics and drag. But tonight wasn't just a performance. This was Miss Horn's strategy. The talk about Chief Brisk's after-hours escapades had reached dangerous heights, and Dickie felt confident this ploy could shift things in his direction. Or at least Miss Horn was convinced.

His painted lips tightened as he watched Slim through the tinted glass. Relief flickered when Miss Horn's voice broke the silence.

"Showing off your softer side, Detective? Careful, or the firefighters will accuse you of stealing their tree-rescue gigs."

Slim turned, the black cat shifting restlessly in his arms.

Miss Horn approached, her horn-rimmed glasses catching the faint neon glow. Disapproval sharpened her tone, though her expression remained unreadable. Amid the grime and decay of the area, she stood poised, immaculate, unflinching, almost porcelain. "Care to explain why you're here?" she asked, her words as precise as the tilt of her head.

Slim slid off his signature red sunglasses and narrowed his eyes. The iPad tucked under her arm caught his attention, though he knew better than to ask about it. He let a trace of sarcasm bleed into his voice. "And you? Still keeping Dopey Darnell under wraps? Or does he just prefer avoiding the locals these days?"

Her expression sharpened. "Detective, you will refer to His Honour as the Honourable Richard Darnell. Or has decorum slipped completely from your vocabulary?"

Slim's irritation boiled beneath the surface. "Right. Is the Honourable Richard Darnell available?"

"His Honour is otherwise engaged."

Slim maintained a level tone. Every attempt to meet with Dickie felt like chasing smoke. He pulled a flash drive from his jacket and extended it toward her. "I have an update on—"

"A bouquet. Yes, understood." Miss Horn intercepted it with practiced ease, her manicured nails clicking against the metal casing as she pocketed the device. "The centrepiece must demand attention," she murmured, already scribbling a note on her iPad. "Perhaps you could focus on faster results that satisfy our head botanist's expectations."

Slim stepped back, irritation tightening in his chest. Miss Horn's euphemisms always grated. "I thought he wanted this update," Slim said, trying not to sound combative.

Miss Horn raised the iPad, tilting the screen so he could read the bold message: *U.S. Marshal Investigating*. Her tone softened, though a note of condescension remained. "Something feels off, Detective. You can't drag your feet forever. Expedite progress while conditions allow." She withdrew a green envelope from her Kate Spade bag and handed it to him with a brittle smile. "Consider this an incentive."

Slim shifted the cat in his arms, his eyes fixed on the envelope. "Shouldn't I speak to him directly?"

Miss Horn sighed. "The mayor is addressing a delicate matter and cannot be disturbed. Rest assured, your update will reach him. We know where to find you."

Inside the limo, Dickie tapped a rhythm against his thigh, watching the exchange from behind the tinted glass. Curiosity tugged at him, but stepping out wasn't an option. Plausible deniability remained his most reliable shield. It would be disastrous if the public caught wind of his private proclivities, not to mention the steady stream of under-the-table money he collected from Big Pharma in exchange for special considerations.

The idea of living on a city official's salary? Unthinkable.

No, he would stay right where he was. Miss Horn could handle anything. She always did. Just thinking about her composure, her precision, how she stripped every interaction down to its most useful form, sent a charge through him.

He'd pictured her onstage more than once, peeling back layers with the same deliberate flair she brought to every meeting. He'd long since stopped pretending he wasn't enthralled. And if the opportunity ever arose to see what lay beneath her veil, well, there were few things he wouldn't trade for that. A voice cut through his thoughts.

"Make sure he gets that flash drive," Slim said, nodding toward Miss Horn's pocket.

Miss Horn's smile didn't budge. "Keep up the good work, detective. Progress benefits us all." Without waiting for a response, she slipped into the limo. The door closed with a final click.

Slim stared at the glossy surface, his reflection glaring back. He slid his sunglasses into place and strode off, frustration burning hotter with every step. "Someday," he muttered to the cat, "they'll wish they treated me better than I'm about to treat you."

"Slim!" Miss Horn's voice rang out.

He froze, half-turning, bracing for another dig.

Her face appeared behind the half-lowered window. "I won't be home for dinner tonight."

Chapter 29

Molly eyed the forest beyond the pickup truck parked outside Mama Kaye's dilapidated shack. Ginger wrestled with a faded blue tarp, yanking it off the firewood and letting it crumple near the woodpile. Birdsong floated through the humid air, a cheerful melody at odds with the turmoil in Molly's mind. She fixated on the trees, where shadows and distance suggested unvoiced possibilities.

Perched on the outhouse roof, Risqué watched as Muncie emerged from the bushes, adjusting his overalls with a smug tug.

"Molly, lend Ginger a hand, or you'll regret it when we get back home!"

"No more games, Muncie," Molly snapped. "You've taken me for ransom. Time you started showing some respect."

Muncie's laugh was harsh. "We'll find a use for that sharp tongue later."

Molly spat, the glob landing squarely on the brim of his Sentinels Mall cap.

Muncie froze, a muscle twitching near his eye. Molly braced for retaliation, but none came. Instead, he removed the cap with forced calm, shaking it off with deliberate precision. His eyes darted toward Mama Kaye's shack, then back to her.

Then it clicked. Muncie didn't want a scene. Not here. His exaggerated nonchalance, the way he placed the cap back on his head with theatrical care, only confirmed it. Whatever control he had over her relied on keeping things quiet, for now. His puffed-up stride resumed as he stalked toward the shack, boots crunching against the dirt.

The realization emboldened Molly. He might be playing a sick game, but she had no intention of being on the team.

"Come on, Molly," Ginger whispered, hefting a burlap sack of firewood. "Help me."

Molly set her cap down and grabbed the end of the bag of wood.

The door creaked as Muncie stepped inside, trading the crisp forest air for the thick, starchy heat of the shack. The scent of burnt potato stew hit him first, blended with clinging weed smoke and the tang of stale cooking grease. He wrinkled his nose as Mama Kaye ladled the charred remnants into a yellowing Tupperware container.

"You never take no money for that firewood, so at least have some nourishment," Mama Kaye said, her voice light despite the glaze in her eyes. "We all know the connection between good vittles and healthy thoughts."

"Not necessary," he replied, setting his Sentinels Mall cap and red controller onto the cluttered counter. He rummaged in a pocket and produced a box of wooden matches. "Here's a little something for you," he said, tossing it onto the counter.

"Thanks, Muncie. Them are me duckies," Mama Kaye said, tucking the matches into an empty cupboard with a missing door. "Did my handsome Constable Karl ever figure out who stole that store-bought hooch from your place?"

He waved a dismissive hand. "Told him to drop it."

"Smart of ya. Karl's as unpredictable as a squirrel on roller skates some days. I'm surprised me Klarence didn't hear nothin'." Her attention shifted to the window framing Molly and Ginger struggling with the burlap sacks. "Where's that boy of mine today?"

"Probably out swimming, kayaking or wandering the woods. You know how much he loves nature."

"Who's that girl?" Mama Kaye asked, wiping her hands on a dish towel.

"That's my other niece visiting for a spell," Muncie said, checking the soles of his boots for chicken shit.

Risqué swooped through the open window, landing on the lip of the battered stew pot, eyes darting, wings twitching. He flicked his tail feathers and let loose a massive dump into the bubbling stew. Satisfied, the parrot fluttered onto the countertop, unbothered.

Muncie straightened. "Any luck finding a yard boy for your chores?"

"Who knows? The Lord works in mysterious ways." Mama Kaye squinted outside. "Look at that! Purdy things doing a happy dance. Bless their poor souls."

Muncie looked out at Molly and Ginger flailing under the awkward weight of the sacks, their efforts more slapstick than coordinated, like a vaudeville audition gone wrong. He turned back just in time to see Risqué pecking at the red controller's activation switch. He shooed the bird away and stuffed the device into his pocket.

Mama Kaye licked the pot ladle and smacked her lips. "I call that a wink and a promise."

Behind the woodpile, Molly ripped a strip off the blue tarp and wedged it between her ankle and the security bracelet. "I'm out of here. Coming?"

Ginger's face drained of colour. "Molly, think this through. Please, don't do this."

"Last chance." Molly grabbed her yellow cap.

Ginger's hands twisted together. "If you think things are strange now, they'll only get worse when he finds out."

"Later." Molly sprinted into the dense forest, shadows swallowing her whole.

Ginger hesitated, then turned toward the shack, breath short and fast. "Muncie! Muncie!"

Muncie stiffened at the sound of her voice. His eyes snapped to the window. Ginger stood outside, pointing frantically at the trees. He moved toward the door.

Mama Kaye stepped into his path, calm and unhurried, wrapping the Tupperware container in foil. Her presence carried a quiet authority. "My clothes need tendin'. A storm's brewin'," she murmured.

Muncie forced a smile. Shoving her aside would only stir up trouble. "Yes, of course. I should be on my way."

Mama Kaye handed him the container and stepped into her worn-out work boots, the laces long gone. She buckled a tool belt around her waist, hoisted a full laundry basket, and walked outside without a backward glance.

Muncie followed, leaving the container on the counter.

Chickens scattered as Mama Kaye reached the corner of the shack. She paused and called sweetly, "Muncie, dear!"

He stopped, irritation flashing in his eyes. "Yes, Mama Kaye?"

"Remember, it don't matter if them hens lay brown eggs or white ones, it don't change how ya handle 'em."

"Of course," he said tightly, then strode toward the panicked Ginger.

Molly ran, her breath ragged, lungs burning. The forest closed in, shadows twisting into clawed shapes that seemed to reach for her. Muncie's threats echoed in her mind, spurring her forward.

Branches tore at her clothes, scratched her arms, but she didn't stop. She vaulted a rotting log, and her foot caught on a root. She crashed to her knees, pain lancing through her leg. Gritting her teeth, she forced herself up.

Then she saw it.

A figure stood in the trees ahead. Still. Not quite hidden, not entirely visible. It blended with the shadows, but something about its posture was wrong. Intentional.

Molly froze, heart pounding. The air turned dense around her, pressing against her chest like a weight. For the first time since being taken, doubt coiled tight. Would she make it out alive?

Chapter 30

"I've got to be honest with you all," Babe said. Kingfish and the bikers leaned in, hanging on every word. The air thickened with anticipation as she accepted a joint from Kingfish and drew in a deep breath. The smoke steadied her, sharp, grounding, familiar. She exhaled slowly, her voice warm, mischievous, and lined with practiced ease.

"So the psychiatrist addresses the group," she continued. "To the first mother, he says, 'You're obsessed with food. You even named your daughter Candy.'

"He turns to the second. 'You're fixated on money, hence your daughter's name, Penny.'

"Then he looks at the third. 'You've got a drinking problem. Your daughter's name? Brandy.' At that point, the fourth mother quietly stands, takes her little boy's hand, and whispers, 'Come on, Dick, we're leaving.'"

The roadside diner's parking lot erupted in raucous laughter and rough-edged banter. Cigarette smoke mingled with weed and the clink of beer bottles, thickening the humid air with electric energy.

Babe smiled, keeping her face loose, her tone light, but the tension in her chest clung like static.

She'd been wrong about Kingfish. He hadn't discovered her ruse, only wanted her to keep the duster, given the buttons missing from her shirt. Babe knew better than to confuse the kind gesture with safety. With the long duster on her back, the skull-and-crossbones kerchief another biker had handed her, and the gang's rowdy approval still echoing in her ears, this was the moment. "Boys, it's been a slice!"

Kingfish grinned, gesturing at his Harley. "Climb on!"

The gang whooped in approval. Babe hesitated, then nodded, her pulse hammering but her movements composed.

Pete shuffled forward, his swollen eye a vivid reminder of their earlier confrontation. He held up his phone with a hopeful smile. "Miss Barbeau, I'm real sorry about earlier. Could I, uh, get a picture?"

"Of course." She posed with a pout, just like Ariana always did. Pete's face lit up like he'd just met a childhood hero.

She approached the Harley, adjusting the long duster as she swung her leg over the seat. The polished chrome caught the sun's glare, the machine exuding power and menace.

Kingfish looked amused. "You sure you can handle her, Miss Barbeau?"

Babe tied the kerchief around her forehead. "Watch me." She slammed her boot down onto the kick-start lever. The Harley roared to life, its growl vibrating straight through her spine.

The gang erupted in whistles and cheers.

Babe leaned back, tightening her grip on the handlebars. "Hop on, Kingfish," she said, voice cool with a hint of challenge. "You're riding bitch."

The gang froze. Her audacity hung in the air a beat before Kingfish adjusted his red bandana and let out a booming laugh. "Well, ain't that something!"

Laughter exploded around them, raw and delighted. A biker darted forward, offering a pair of mirrored aviators. "For the road."

Babe winked. "Thanks." She slipped them on and shifted back on the seat.

Kingfish climbed on, his weight tipping the bike slightly. "Hold on tight," he said, voice low beneath the engine's growl. The Harley snarled as he twisted the throttle. Dust kicked up behind them like smoke from a fuse as they roared down Terminal Road, the gang's hollers fading in their wake.

The wind tore at her scalp, ruffling the short spikes of her blonde hair. Adrenaline surged—hotter than fear, sharper than doubt. If kicking ass was the price of finding Molly, so be it.

They carved through the countryside like a bullet through paper, the Harley's engine thrumming between her legs. The two-lane blacktop stretched out ahead, cracked, sun-bleached, and indifferent. Ditches overflowed with weeds and trash. Rusted mailboxes leaned like drunk old men. Cornfields blurred by, dry and rattling. Power lines sagged in the heat, ticking like time bombs. The air reeked of sunbaked gravel, cattle maybe, or the rot of forgotten things.

Babe pressed herself tighter to Kingfish's back, the long duster snapping behind her like a war banner. She turned into the wind, letting it strip the sweat from her neck and the doubt from her bones. For a fleeting mile, the road belonged to her. Not Brisk. Not Choi. Not the men who thought they could use her up and forget her.

She thought of Molly, her voice, her laugh, and the way she'd once traced a map across Babe's belly when they were little. That ghost of a touch still burned. This wasn't about justice. This was a retrieval mission. To pull her back from whatever hole she'd been swallowed in.

A crow lifted from a fencepost ahead, its wings slicing the sky. Warning or omen, she didn't care. Let the world come. She was ready.

The Harley rumbled into Moosetown, heat rising from the pavement in warped, shimmering waves. Babe tightened her grip around Kingfish's waist. The ride had been fast, loud, and lawless, exactly how the gang liked it. But now, the high was thinning. Ahead loomed a washed-out building with sagging siding and a sun-faded sign: Moosetown Auto Repairs and Rentals. If the outside was any hint, the rentals probably came with a tetanus shot.

Then her eyes snagged on something else. Even from a distance, Babe knew that silhouette.

Choi, squatting beside a jacked-up unmarked police cruiser.

A jolt hit her gut. Of all the people to run into.

The Harley rolled to a stop, gravel crunching under its tires. Dust floated like ash around them. Babe swung her leg off the bike, the duster flaring as she steadied her boots on the hot blacktop. She adjusted the skull-and-crossbones bandana and kept her sunglasses on. Just long enough to assess the danger.

Choi stood, wrench in hand, her eyes locking on her like crosshairs. "The law just a suggestion to you?" Choi said, voice flat, clipped.

Kingfish didn't flinch. He glanced at Choi's badge on her belt, then turned back to Babe. "You need me to stay?"

Babe tugged the duster into place and gave him a casual half-smile. "It's all good. Thanks, Orville. It's been a blast."

He nodded. "Any time." They slapped hands, quick and tight. Kingfish revved the Harley, then peeled away, trailing a rooster tail of dust before hitting the road.

Babe took a steady breath. Her pulse was drumming. Maybe the bandana and shades had bought her time given Choi didn't seem to recognize her. Babe pushed her voice into neutral. "Is the car rental open?"

Choi's eyes flicked over her. "Does it look open?"

Babe swallowed the rising heat in her throat. *Keep it cool. Don't take the bait.* Then she noticed something: one of Choi's shirt buttons was missing. A fleur-de-lis design. Small detail, but off. The cop was always sharp. Always put together. Today? She looked frayed. Babe shrugged. "Worth a shot." She kept her voice even. Unbothered. But her fingers flexed, just in case.

Choi glowered. "Where's your old man gone? Off fetching more dimwit pills? Or are biker chicks like you too dumb to know helmets are required by law?"

Babe eyed the garage and rental area. The place was deserted.

Choi grabbed a coat from the Jeep parked next to her and threw it over her shoulder. "What's wrong? Cat got your tongue? Or do biker chicks like you just grunt and rev engines?"

"You working the helmet squad now?" Babe snapped.

Choi pulled a pair of cuffs from her coat and spun them once around her finger. The metal flashed in the sun. "Keep mouthing off, sweetheart, and you'll find out where it gets you. Capiche?"

It should've rolled off Babe. But it didn't. The memory hit like a jolt to the chest. Trashing Molly. That stink-finger comment. Holier-than-thou attitude.

Babe moved fast. She reached into the open trunk and drew Choi's sawed-off shotgun from its custom leather holster. The weight of it steadied her as she levelled the barrel. "Hand over the cuffs," Babe said, voice low, unshaking. Then she yanked off the bandana and sunglasses. "And if you think I'm bluffing," she added, "go ahead and test me. Capiche?"

Choi froze. The recognition hit fast. "Lincoln?" she hissed. "What the hell are you—"

"Turn around. I won't say it twice."

Choi raised her hands. Slow. Rigid. "Easy. Let's not make this worse. Tell me what you want, no one gets hurt, and we walk away from this."

Walk away? As if that had ever been an option. "Handcuffs," Babe repeated, finger snug against the trigger.

Choi's voice dropped. "You'll regret this."

"Maybe," Babe said. "But not today."

Chapter 31

Sunlight knifed through the forest canopy, stabbing at Muncie's sweat-slicked brow. Each beam seared his skin, carving heat through the grime that caked his face. His Sentinels Mall cap clung damp to his scalp as he stumbled toward the bags of firewood, lungs straining, the thicket behind him rustling with movement.

Ginger burst through seconds later, red hair plastered to her temples, eyes wild and frantic. Her chest heaved as she scanned the shadows like Molly might spring from them.

Neither of them noticed Risqué, a blur diving from the canopy, wings slicing the heavy air. The parrot veered toward the truck and slipped through the open side window without a sound.

A knot twisted in Muncie's gut. Ginger's panic infected him like a virus. "She couldn't have gotten far," he panted, trying to sound sure. But the fire in his lungs made the words feel hollow. "We'll find her."

Ginger knelt by the blue tarp near the truck, trying to fold it. Her fingers fumbled, the plastic slipping through her grip like water. "If only we had a German Shepherd like the one my cousin had—"

"Drop it," he snapped. "You said she'd pull this tonight. What the hell happened to that?"

"I—I thought she would."

"Yeah? You don't know shit." The words bit hard. He spun toward the old well, boots kicking up dry earth. Every step felt like an unravelling thread.

Ginger froze, hugging the tarp like it might shield her. "What if Molly wandered into quicksand?"

A bitter laugh tore from his throat. "Quicksand? Jesus, Ginger. That's over a mile out."

"Or maybe a wild animal got her—"

He whirled, eyes burning. "Will you shut the hell up and let me think?" He yanked the cap from his head and slapped it against the rusty hand pump. The fabric made a smacking sound. He grabbed the bucket, filled it, and splashed cold water over his face. It ran down his neck in rivulets, but did nothing to cool his boiling rage.

Ginger's voice came softly now. "Aren't you going to say goodbye to Mama Kaye?"

He froze. Water dripped from his chin in uneven streaks. "Forget it," he muttered. He swiped his sleeve across his face and turned toward the truck. "Where's that damn bird?"

Ginger opened the passenger door. Inside, Risqué sat slumped on the seat, feathers puffed, beak slightly open in a lazy snore. "Looks like he's napping."

"Great," Muncie snapped. "Wake his feathered ass up. Maybe he'll sniff her out like a damn parrot bloodhound."

Ginger blinked. "You think he could?"

He glared at her. "Are you actually that stupid? Get in the truck."

Her shoulders sank as she climbed into the back seat.

Muncie stomped to the driver's side, yanked open the creaking door, and threw himself into the cab. The door slammed shut behind him, rattling the frame.

For a moment, he sat still, hands locked on the sun-baked steering wheel, jaw tight, eyes fixed on the trees. The shadows there didn't move, they slithered. They watched. They waited.

Molly wasn't just a runaway. She a live wire with no off switch. And the longer she stayed out there, the closer everything got to blowing sky high.

And he had no idea if he'd ever get her back.

Chapter 32

Babe maneuvered Choi's unmarked cruiser through the deserted streets of Moosetown, her fingers pressed hard into the seams of the steering wheel. The town unfolded in eerie stillness, faded storefronts, boarded windows, the slow crumble of somewhere long past its prime. Every corner, every alley drew her eyes scanning for any sign of Molly or Ariana in the red Corvette. If Ariana had already reached Bear Lake Campground, Babe hoped that's where she'd find her.

A buzz rattled the console, breaking the silence. A signal, finally. Her phone lit up. Hope surged. Molly? But the screen told a different story: News 4 Human Resources. She sighed and hit play. "Ms. Lincoln," chirped an overly cheery voice, "just a friendly reminder that News 4 prioritizes mental health! Remember, we offer stress-management resources if you're feeling overwhelmed—" Babe let out a dry laugh and disconnected. "Oh, I'm not the one overwhelmed," she muttered, picturing Choi locked in the trunk, bouncing with every bump in the road. The joint she'd smoked earlier had taken the edge off, but the second one in her pocket promised more peace than any HR pep talk. She slid the phone into her pocket.

A sudden stench clawed its way into the car. She cringed and rolled up the window just as two hulking machines lumbered up the street, kicking up thick clouds of dust and grime. She blinked. Zambonis? For a second, it almost made sense. Canadians loved their hockey. Then it clicked: just street sweepers. The absurdity tugged a chuckle from her, but it didn't last.

A few pedestrians meandered along the sidewalk, faces tilted toward the hazy sky. No phones. No rush. Moosetown seemed to move at its own glacial pace.

Her eyes drifted to the crumpled map she'd lifted from Choi's pocket, now half-unfolded on the seat beside two baggies of marijuana, with one labelled Holy Smokes. The map was a mess of crooked lines and scribbled notes: Nine Mile Road, White Church, and Look Out near Lingus Lane. At the edge, a jagged X marked something ominous. It looked like a puzzle piece from a game she didn't know the rules for. But now wasn't the time to solve it.

As Babe rounded the corner, she spotted a uniformed officer swapping out a magnetic pizza delivery sign on his car for a police logo. She swung the cruiser into a sharp turn, tires screeching as she clipped a trash can. It skidded across the sidewalk with a metallic rattle. She grimaced.

Stepping out of the cruiser, she adjusted the duster draped across her shoulders, the fabric fluttering like a cape.

The officer, a handsome man with Constable Karl Broom stitched on his uniform, looked her over. "You got a driver's license on ya?" he asked.

"Afternoon, officer," Babe said, voice smooth with faux politeness. She cracked her coat just enough to flash Choi's badge beside the Glock on her belt. "Special assignment with the New York Attorney General's Office," she said, all business. "I'm tracking a fugitive linked to an international case. But I've got to say, your town smells like hell."

Karl squinted at the badge, then at her. His mouth twisted like he was chewing on a thought. "Yeah, well, you'd stink too if a whole damn sewage pipe blew its guts under the square. Old pipe, I guess. Or maybe it was the rain. Or them farms." He scratched his head. "Had to call the fire department to hose everything down. Them boys get things done. Sent trucks loaded with the crap down Terminal Road. Surprised you didn't see 'em."

Babe arched a brow, remembering the reek while riding behind Kingfish. "Sounds like quite the operation."

Karl nodded. "Sure is. Still stinks like a cow barn after chili night, don't it?"

Babe's mouth curled into a dry smile. "That's quite a metaphor, Constable Karl."

"Meta what?" Karl blinked. "Anyway, we're still cleanin' up. Think your fugitive did this? Wouldn't shock me. Criminals always got somethin' nasty up their sleeve."

Babe sighed, pulling out her phone. "Not unless plumbing mishaps are trending in organized crime." She held up a photo of Molly. "Have you seen her?"

Karl circled the car, opened the trunk, and tossed the pizza sign inside, revealing bandoliers loaded with ammo.

Babe's stomach growled. Her eyes flicked to the discarded pizza sign. "You deliver pizzas?"

Karl tapped his patrol car's misery lights. "Throw these babies on, pies get there in record time."

"You're a real credit to the community," Babe said. "I'm starving. Got snacks in the car?"

"This ain't a buffet. You want food, you order it."

"Fine." She changed gears. "What about Bear Lake? You deliver to the campground? I heard it's a circus on weekends."

Karl frowned. "Don't recall no circus. Sure you're in the right place?"

Babe rolled her eyes. "I bet there's a dog and pony show."

"Don't bet on it. We don't," Karl said flatly.

She tried another angle. "This girl likes yellow caps. Heard she's staying at the campground. You sure she's not one of your... customers?"

Karl adjusted his belt, then scratched his crotch. "She some porn star hooking up with a politician? They payin' a reward?"

"I'm not a bounty hunter. I'm bringing her back to the States. That's it."

He shrugged. "You ask her mama? That's where I'd start. Your mama usually has the answers."

"Her mother isn't part of this."

"Then I got nothin'."

"Maybe I'll check with the RCMP. Or the sheriff?"

Karl puffed up. "I am the sheriff. We just don't call it that here. Close enough."

"And the Mounties?"

"Right church, wrong pew."

"I don't follow."

"Means I run the show. My papa used to be chief until he suffered from a massive stroke."

Babe softened slightly. "Sorry. Heart attacks are no joke."

"Heart attack? Hell no. My mama took an axe to him for doin' what shall not be mentioned in polite company."

That stopped her cold. "Right. Thanks for your help." She turned, then paused. "One more thing: ever hear of an American Embassy on Bear Lake?"

Karl squinted. "I ain't violating no Vienna laws. Last thing I need is the Viennese showin' up. Heard they don't even allow pizza where they're from."

"God forbid," Babe muttered, heading back to the cruiser.

"If I see that girl, who do I call?" Karl shouted after her.

"That dog doesn't hunt anymore," Babe said over her shoulder, tossing a mock salute as she climbed in.

Karl popped the trunk again and pulled out a girly magazine. "Hunt? It ain't even hunting season, you dummy," he muttered.

Babe exhaled. Molly was out there, but she couldn't tell if she was closing the gap or losing ground. She slammed the door shut, hoping the smell couldn't follow her in, then hit the gas.

Chapter 33

Time thinned as Molly crouched beneath the dense bracken. Every crackle of leaves cut through the silence, sharp and intrusive. Her knee throbbed from the earlier fall, pain rooting her in place. Her eyes locked on the foreboding silhouette ahead. It hadn't moved. Cold sweat prickled her skin. The greasy burger she'd forced down earlier soured in her stomach.

A sharp crack to her right shattered the fragile quiet. Molly froze. She twisted toward the sound. Then, an explosion of motion as a jackrabbit bolted from the underbrush, its wide eyes locking onto hers before vanishing into the shadows. A tremor rippled through her as the tension drained. She dug her fingers into the damp earth, grounding herself. The adrenaline refused to fade.

Far off, the faint hum of an engine rippled through the stillness. Molly's stomach tightened. Maybe Muncie had given up? Maybe he'd circled ahead? Doubt crept into her fragile hope, gnawing at the edges of her resolve. This nightmare felt endless. But first, she had to confront the shadow blocking her path.

Her thoughts flashed to Babe. She always found a way. Clever and resourceful, she could rig solutions from scraps and talk circles around anyone. That ingenuity had bonded them through years of reckless escapades. Molly clung to that memory like a lifeline. If she could reach a phone, Babe would come for her. Babe would know what to do.

A cold sensation slid over her ankle. Her breath hitched. She looked down.

Snake.

A green coil slithered across her skin. A violent shiver shot through her, and she yanked her leg back, heel tearing into the dirt. The snake vanished into the undergrowth, leaving her gasping. Fear cinched her ribs, shoving her forward in a burst of energy.

Her stride faltered as pain knifed through her knee. As the silhouette loomed closer, its true nature revealed itself.

A tattered scarecrow drooped on a crooked wooden post, straw-stuffed arms sagging, its hollowed-out smile seemingly mocking her.

A brittle laugh clawed from her throat, sharp and unsteady. She doubled over, hands on her thighs, relief and absurdity colliding. Shaking off the remnants of panic, Molly looked past the scarecrow. The forest thinned, revealing a narrow strip of asphalt shimmering in the distance. A road. A lifeline cutting through the wilderness. She straightened, ignoring the throb in her leg, and pushed toward the clearing.

The low rumble of an engine shattered her focus, dread crashing down. Molly's stomach twisted. Muncie. He'd outmaneuvered her, cutting her off before she could escape. Pain stabbed her knee, but she pushed forward.

A dark blue sedan rolled into view. She exhaled seeing the police insignia gleamed on its door. Scrambling onto the embankment, she waved her arms.

The patrol car stopped, engine settling into a steady idle. Constable Karl stepped out, the brim of his Stetson shading sharp features. His calm, deliberate movements exuded authority, enough to pierce the last edge of her fear.

Molly sagged against the car's fender, shoulders heavy with exhaustion. "This man," she gasped. "This maniac, he's after me."

Karl's expression didn't change. His voice was low, measured. "All right now. Old Karl's here to help."

Her voice cracked. "The guy at the embassy. He… he wanted me to do disgusting things."

Karl pulled out a notepad, pen clicking open. "What kind of things?"

"Nasty things. He's a pervert, okay?" Molly's voice rose. "He expected me to—" Her throat closed. "Do we have to get into detail? He's coming for me. Please, we need to leave!"

Karl raised a hand. "Settle down. You'll ride in the back, out of sight."

Molly hesitated, pulse still pounding. The forest loomed behind her, every shadow a threat. Karl's calm gave her pause, but the sound of an approaching vehicle snapped her into motion.

"Fine," she said, forcing herself to believe it was the right call.

Chapter 34

Babe chewed as the salt burned her lips from the soggy mess of fries, cheese curds, and congealed gravy. She'd ordered what the owner of the converted school bus turned food stand called the specialty of the house on a whim, not knowing what to expect. The poutine looked more like a dare than a meal.

A faded wooden sign dangled from rusted chains: Stay Chipper. She thought it should read Mind Over Matter.

She sighed and glanced toward the cruiser parked a few yards away. Choi was still stewing in the trunk, silent and stubborn as ever. Earlier, Babe had cracked it open just enough to let the greasy aroma waft in, hoping hunger might loosen her tongue about Molly or the cryptic map. No such luck. When asked about the weed, she insisted it was evidence. The lieutenant clearly thought Babe was a simpleton.

Babe popped another fry into her mouth and grimaced at the oversalted bite. Mr. Stay Chipper hadn't been any more helpful. When she asked about Molly, the owner shrugged. His gruff monotone was about as welcoming as his food.

When she mentioned the salt, he shot her a sour glare, wiped his hands on a grease-stained rag, and told her to watch where she stepped. Said there were landmines everywhere.

When pressed, he nodded at the seagulls circling overhead. "Bird shit, lady. The gulls. They're relentless. Watch you don't step in it."

"Right. Bird crap," she'd muttered, laughing under her breath. For one absurd moment, she'd pictured actual explosives littering the parking lot.

Babe decided her next move was to stop by the campground, pick up Ariana, and see if the proprietor knew anything about Molly. If that didn't pan out, she'd follow up on the so-called Embassy Molly had mentioned on Facebook. The trail couldn't go cold now.

She strolled to the cruiser and popped the trunk. Choi glared up at her, the spare tire digging into her back. Her wrists were cuffed behind her, ankles zip-tied, and a skull-and-crossbones gag muffled her furious protests. Her head rested against the red toolbox, and the fire in her eyes screamed defiance.

Babe slid a gravy-soaked fry under Choi's nose. "Could be yours if you're ready to talk."

Choi's silence held fast.

"Suit yourself." Babe shrugged, slammed the trunk, and tossed the leftover poutine into a garbage barrel.

She dropped into the driver's seat, fished a joint and wooden match from the Holy Smokes baggie, and sparked it up like it was communion. The first drag settled her nerves and kicked her grin into gear. The cruiser rumbled to life and peeled away. She aimed straight for a patch of potholes ugly enough to void a warranty. The car bucked like a drunk bull, each jolt a small revenge. She laughed aloud, picturing Choi bouncing in the trunk like a marble in a tin can.

The cruiser rolled onto Nine Mile Road, the worn asphalt giving way to smoother pavement as the route curved toward Bear Lake Campground. Babe noted the white church along the way, its weathered facade standing like a lone sentinel against the trees. She wondered if the sideroad beside it was Lingus Lane, the ominous marker scrawled across Choi's map. She dismissed the thought. No time for detours.

The cruiser rattled over a steel bridge, tires clanging against the uneven slats like a heavy drumbeat. The road ahead twisted into a narrow coil, snaking toward the campground, each bend winding her nerves tighter. By the time she pulled up outside the campground office, unease had already taken root in her chest. Gone was the buzz of weekend campers experienced when arriving with Molly, of music, voices, and fires crackling. In its place an unnatural hush blanketed the grounds. Empty fire pits and abandoned picnic tables dotted the space like relics of a vanished crowd. Even the air felt heavier, thick with quiet.

Babe's eyes swept the grounds, scanning for Ariana or the Corvette.

No sign of either.

She exhaled, pushing down a flicker of frustration. With any luck, Ariana was off getting a mani-pedi instead of walking straight into trouble.

But luck wasn't something Babe counted on. Wherever Ariana was, Babe needed to stay sharp.

She strapped the holster holding Choi's sawed-off shotgun to her thigh. Taking a deep drag from the joint, she let the potent weed steady her nerves. Beyond a scrub of bushes, Bear Lake shimmered under the midday sun. For a fleeting moment, she imagined diving in, letting the cool depths swallow her whole.

Then she remembered. She couldn't swim.

She thumped the cruiser's trunk as she walked by. "Don't miss me too much, Lieutenant." Not that Choi could respond with a gag in her mouth.

Babe stepped inside the office, where clutter and kitsch collided in chaotic disarray. Shelves sagged under the weight of mosquito repellent, plastic tent pegs, and canned goods haphazardly stacked. A mannequin draped in a rhinestone jacket sparkled under flickering fluorescent lights, casting an eerie shimmer across the room.

She blinked hard. *This weed hits differently.* There was little doubt the stash was laced with something extra. The rhinestones on the jacket seemed to shimmer a little too much, like tiny, twinkling eyes watching her from the dim corners of the room.

A rack of cowboy hats caught her eye. She plucked a brown one and pulled it on, checking her reflection in a slightly warped wall mirror. Her image seemed to lag for a fraction of a second before snapping back into place.

Weird.

With the duster, shotgun, and hat, she looked like some gunslinger straight out of a spaghetti Western. Ariana would've rolled her eyes, Babe thought, tipping the brim slightly.

She strode to the counter and tapped the little silver bell beside a plaque that read: Whitey Whiteside, Proprietor. A framed photo of Michelangelo's David stood awkwardly between cans of bear spray and a stack of folding knives. The absurdity made her snort. A goofball with a bad haircut is what Molly had called him when she registered for her trailer. Babe leaned an elbow on the counter and waited.

Whitey emerged from the back room, a half-eaten red Popsicle clenched between his teeth. His shirt hung unevenly over his belt, and his thinning hair stuck out like he'd been electrocuted. He paused mid-step, giving her a long, appraising look that lasted a second too long. Or maybe it just felt that way. "You feeling okay?" His tone was flat, annoyed.

Babe quirked an eyebrow. "Never better." She held up her phone, displaying a photo of Molly. The screen felt absurdly bright for a second, the light making her pupils contract. "She stayed here recently. Angelic face, body built for sin. Like that girl in the song who was smooth as Tennessee whiskey, sweet as strawberry wine. Ringing any bells?"

Whitey's eyes flickered, darting to the shotgun strapped to her leg. For a beat, Babe thought she saw his pupils expand, like a cornered rat sizing up a way out.

"You're not gonna, uh, threaten me with shoving that thing up my ass, are you?"

Babe sighed, the joint's buzz still thick. "I don't roll that way." She let the words settle. "Let's stick to the topic. Girl in the photo. Molly. She was talking about a party after her sensible companion bailed. Any idea where she ended up?"

"You mean the girl in the red car?"

Babe tapped the bell lightly. "Winner, winner, chicken dinner."

Whitey's lips moved, but for a split second, his voice sounded slightly distant, like a radio station fading in and out. Babe blinked again, pushing through the sensation. Focus.

"I already told that crazy policewoman, I don't know," he grumbled.

Babe's patience frayed. She placed the cowboy hat on the counter and leaned in. "Start by telling me about this policewoman. Then we'll discuss why I'm getting the friends-and-family discount on this hat. Deal?"

"Why would I do that?"

Her hand dropped to the shotgun grip. "You mentioned something about jamming this up your ass?"

Whitey raised both hands, a nervous chuckle escaping. "Settle down. She was Asian. Young, maybe, but you know, hard to guess. Flashed a badge and asked about the same girl."

"And what'd you tell her?"

"Same thing I'm telling you," he snapped. "I don't keep tabs on every kid passing through. This isn't a daycare."

Babe leaned in. "You're sure that's all? No memory lapses you'd like to share?"

Whitey shifted. "Look, after our midnight curfew, some of the campers wander over to Klarence-with-a-K's place. That's all I know."

"Klarence-with-a-K?" Babe arched an eyebrow. "Quite a mouthful."

Whitey's mouth twitched, eyes turning wistful. "Oh, you have no idea."

"And what kind of place are we talking about?"

He scratched the back of his neck. "Not the kind that draws cops. But… strange stuff happens there."

"Define strange."

Whitey fidgeted. "Couple of nights ago, some woman was screaming about a bone doctor. Loud enough to shatter the windows."

Before Babe could respond, a tinny nursery rhyme blared from the back—someone singing along, off-key, dragging every note with drama: "Lost my partner, what'll I do? Lost my partner, what'll I do? Lost my partner, what'll I do? Skip to my Lou, my dar—"

Whitey spun and slammed the door shut, cutting it off mid-verse. His face flushed red.

A muffled voice barked from behind it. "Excuse me for trying to bring a little joy into this godforsaken place! Maybe you'd like me to disappear, huh? Well, poof! Wish granted!" Stomping followed. Then a clang. A crash. Silence.

Babe tilted her head. The quiet felt thicker than before. "That guy gonna be okay?"

"Don't worry about it," Whitey muttered, grabbing a rag to scrub the counter. "That's all I know about the girl."

Babe narrowed her eyes. His voice was off, like it didn't sync with his lips. *Damn. What was in that weed?* She shook it off. Not the time to spiral. "My friend wins a free camping getaway, and that's all you've got? That stretches credibility."

Whitey hesitated, then sighed. "Oh, right. Someone dropped off a VIP invitation for her to check out that new ice cream joint in town. She never came back. I still have one of her knapsacks. Toiletries and junk. Don't know where the rest went, probably stolen."

Babe's focus sharpened. "Now we're getting somewhere. What else?"

"Other than the girl being… pernicious?"

"Skip the character assassinations." She crossed her arms. "What else?"

"Nothing. She probably hitched a ride with one of the degenerates she was partying with. I rented the trailer after her time ran out. That's it."

Her gut said he wasn't lying, but he wasn't spilling everything either.

She tossed a few crumpled bills onto the counter and tipped the hat low over her brow. "I'll take the hat. Friends-and-family discount, as discussed. Now, how do I find this Klarence?"

Chapter 35

The blacktop of Nine Mile Road wound through rolling hills, its sharp bends and blind corners, the perfect spot for a speed trap with lazy law enforcement. Behind a scrubby stand of bushes, Moosetown's lone patrol car crouched, ready to pounce.

Inside the cruiser, a glossy girlie magazine sprawled across the dash, a big-breasted blonde on its page tweaking a nipple with a provocative smile. Constable Karl leaned back in his seat, choking the chicken like a man without shame. A flicker of movement outside the window snapped him upright.

"Shit." He jerked forward, fumbling with his zipper. The magazine slid off the dash, thudding to the floor as he yanked his pants closed, hands clumsy with panic.

Across the road, Muncie sat in his truck, parked on the far shoulder. He didn't move. Just watched. His eyes gleamed with quiet amusement.

Karl scrambled out of the cruiser, his Stetson askew, face flushed. "Mr. Muncie," he called, voice cracking. He cleared his throat and tried again. "Been out making a wood run to Mama's place?"

Muncie climbed out, unbothered. A faint smirk tugged at his mouth. "Alone we can do so little. Together we can do so much." He paused. "Helen Keller."

Karl adjusted his hat, nudging it into place with unsteady hands. "She at Mama's place?"

"Not today, Karl," Muncie said.

Risqué perched on the passenger seat, tilting his head with a wink at Karl, who was peering into the back seat. "Afternoon, Miss Ginger," he said, tipping his hat with forced politeness.

Ginger leaned forward, her smile sharp. "Afternoon, Karl. Didn't know the local speed trap came with… added attractions." She let the words hang, enjoying Karl's squirm. "We're off to buy some fresh farm eggs."

"Sure," Karl muttered, already eyeing Risqué.

"Egg represents the beginning of life," the parrot announced, nodding solemnly.

"Retard," Karl mumbled before slamming the door and turning to Muncie. "Where's the big fella today?"

"Klarence? Probably out diving the lake. You've seen him in that kayak, smooth as a heron across the water. And those woods? Klarence can wander for hours. Always comes back smiling, cheeks flushed like the sun kissed him."

Karl frowned. "Mama said he hit his head when he was little. Explains a lot."

"How are things with you, Karl? Everything running smooth?"

Karl hesitated. "Got an allegation. Some camper's been tear-assin' through here." He pointed toward the bend. "Split tails are the worst, always mouthing off. By the way, seen a car like your brother's in town."

"Already? Made good time getting here."

"Big city detectives. Always bending the needle."

"Yes. They act with impunity," Muncie said, watching him closely.

"That's the truth right there. Do what they want, too!" Karl added. "Some broad was driving." He cupped his hands in front of his chest. "Nice little rack on her."

Muncie said, gesturing toward Karl's still half-zipped pants.

Karl zipped up fast. "Appreciate the heads-up, Mr. Muncie. Don't want bait hanging out. Got enough trouble with these sluts."

"Heavy lies the head."

Karl scratched his scalp, confused. "Got me another allegation." He pulled a notepad from his pocket, voice lowering. "Young lady says you were… maybe thinking about putting your Johnson where it don't belong."

"Quite a story, Karl. Where's this young lady now?"

Karl thumbed toward his cruiser. "Take a look."

He led Muncie to the trunk and popped it open.

Inside, Molly lay crammed in the tight space, wrists bound, mouth gagged. Sunlight hit her face, and she flinched, jerking into the corner. Her eyes blinked rapidly. Scratches covered her arms and legs, and a strip of blue tarp peeked from beneath her ankle bracelet.

The stench hit Muncie like a slap. He recoiled, covering his nose. "Christ, Karl. You driving around with a dead skunk back here?"

Karl slammed the trunk shut with a clang. "What was I supposed to do? She's been like this since I found her."

"Open it back up. Let some fresh air in there."

Karl sighed and complied, reopening it with a creak. Molly trembled, blinking against the sudden light.

Satisfied the stench had dissipated, Muncie sat on the edge of the trunk, his voice soft but precise. "Poor thing's had herself a day," he said, studying her. "These woods are ruthless. Fear makes people run blind, and she's been running scared. See that bite on her ankle? Tried patching it with tarp. Girl might even be rabid, so that gag's smart, Karl. You wouldn't want her sinking those teeth into you. You'd be down at the clinic for shots, dealing with fever, vomiting, maybe worse. Nobody wants shit running down their leg at the worst moment."

Karl winced, rubbing the back of his neck.

"Wouldn't surprise me," Muncie went on, "if she's an orphan. Carrying that deep-down ache. No one to turn to, nowhere to go."

Karl's brow knitted. "That's a lot to think about."

Muncie clapped him on the shoulder. "Tell you what. As an ambassador, let me take her off your hands. I'll get her where she needs to go. You've done your part. Now let's work out something fair for you."

Karl nodded. "Whatever you think's right. You've always treated me square."

"Good man," Muncie said. "Help me get her in the truck. What were you saying about town?"

Karl snorted. "You talkin' about the goddamn disaster or the girl with the nice little titties?"

Chapter 36

The eerie tune of *Skip to My Lou* looped in Babe's mind like an unwelcome guest. She adjusted her new cowboy hat, taking some comfort in the fact that most of the Holy Smokes buzz had faded. She squinted at a crooked placard nailed to a weathered post near the Cape Cod-style cottage. Its bold warning about trespassing and international law jogged her memory, especially the local cop's cryptic mention of Vienna. Maybe the truth lay just beyond the thick tangles of underbrush on the property line.

She eyed the fire pit, where scorched black earth and the remnants of reckless revelry told their story. Charred logs formed a crude circle, their jagged edges dulled by soot, like splintered bones from a forgotten pyre. Beer cans and shattered liquor bottles littered the dirt like a constellation of neglect. The tang of old ash clung to the air, laced with the sharp scent of pine. Nearby, a lopsided mound of dry kindling leaned in wait for the next blaze. A sudden movement from behind snapped her attention.

Klarence emerged from the shadows without a sound, his looming frame unnervingly light on its feet. Babe tensed, her hand brushing instinctively toward her hip, pulse spiking as she sized him up. Garish green lederhosen clung to his thick legs, paired with a checkered shirt stretched tight across his barrel chest. His mismatched outfit might've been comical, if the sight of him didn't send a ripple through her gut. The resemblance to the Moosetown cop struck her immediately. Were they related? Why hadn't the campground owner mentioned this? The back of her neck prickled.

Klarence's lips contorted, caught between a grin and a grimace. His eyes flitted over her wide-brimmed hat, the holstered shotgun strapped to her thigh, the long brown duster sweeping around her legs. His grin widened. "You some kinda jail bite dressed up for Halloween?" His voice pitched high and thin, cracking slightly.

Babe's eyes narrowed. "Did you mean jailbait, or are you just fucking with me?"

Klarence flinched, lips trembling as he clapped both hands over his ears and danced in a frantic circle. "Potty mouth, potty mouth, potty mou—" His voice climbed into a shrill whine as Babe veered toward the cabin. "You can't go there!" He spun like a top and stumbled forward into an awkward sprint, bolting ahead of her.

Babe followed, watching him trip over a garden hose sprawled across the dirt. His jerky movements were as disjointed as his outburst, panic unfolding like bad theatre. What the hell is he hiding? Could Molly be in there?

The moment she stepped inside, the stench hit her. Mildew. Sweat. Rot. Thick and suffocating. Flies hovered over pizza boxes piled in corners, their greasy lids curling like wilted petals. Her stomach twisted. This was the kind of place where bad things festered. The thought of Molly ever being here set her teeth on edge.

Klarence snatched a plush monkey from the shelf crammed with stuffed animals and dog-eared comic books, hugging it tight to his chest. His darting eyes screamed guilt or fear, as he tracked her every step.

Babe scanned the room. A framed photograph wedged between a stack of yellowed newspapers and a chipped ceramic mug caught

127

her eye. She snatched it up, considering the wild-haired woman flanked by two men, Klarence and the Moosetown cop, Karl. She tilted the photo toward him. "Who's this?"

"My mama," Klarence murmured, voice barely a whisper. His grip on the monkey tightened.

Babe shoved the frame under her arm and pulled her phone from her pocket. She tapped the screen, bringing up a photo of Molly, her yellow cap tilted at a mischievous angle. She held it toward Klarence. "Who is this?"

"Your mama?" he said, blinking like he'd missed a step.

She bit back her frustration, voice sharpening. "Listen carefully." She tapped her phone's screen again, pulling up a video of Chief Brisk. She held it up, angling the screen so his mouth aligned with hers. The top cop's gravelly voice filled the room. "We'll investigate this case backward, forward, upside down, and inside out until we find the kid."

Klarence's eyes widened. "Yikes!" he squealed, darting across the room. He dove into a closet and yanked the door shut, rattling the frame. From behind the thin wood, his ragged breaths rasped out, sharp and uneven.

Babe tucked her phone away and folded her arms. "We've got a lot to talk about, Klarence," she said, tone firm but even. "Let's start with a story."

The closet door creaked open, just enough for the monkey's plush face to peek through the crack. "Story time!?" Klarence whispered, voice quivering with excitement. His face slowly appeared beside the monkey, wide eyes brimming with childlike anticipation.

"That's right," Babe said, her tone softening. "Once upon a time, a boy shared some secrets about his mama, papa, and the people living next door. Now it's your turn."

Klarence edged out of the closet, clutching the filthy plush monkey to his chest. "K-Klarence feels tired now," he whispered, voice too high, too sweet.

She thought he sounded like a child waiting for a bedtime story.

His hand hovered at the bulge in his shorts, fingers twitching. "Muncie always plays with his favourite dwarf before naptime." He looked hopeful. Expectant. "Will you get naked and give Klarence a treat? Like that lady who looks like Kamala Khan in the comics."

Babe's stomach turned, bile rising like acid. Instinct took over. Her hand yanked the shotgun from its holster. For a flicker of a second, she considered blasting him into silence. Or knocking him out cold.

Klarence's face crumpled, fear twisting him into something barely human. He stumbled back, the monkey slipping from his grasp as he bolted outside. "Mama, Mama, Mama!" he wailed, cries echoing as he vanished into the forest.

Babe holstered the shotgun and steadied her breathing, swallowing the nausea. Her pulse slowed as she moved through the cabin, scanning for clues about Molly.

The bathroom was a horror show. Cracked tiles, grime, and the stench of mildew. The bedroom wasn't better. Tangled sheets on an unmade bed, clothes and used towels strewn about. The stink of sweat and unwashed bodies clung to the space.

Back in the main room, Babe spotted the monkey where Klarence had dropped it. As she crouched to pick it up, something shiny caught her eye. Beneath the matted fur, a fleur-de-lis button gleamed in the dim light. Her chest tightened. It matched the buttons on Choi's shirt.

The lieutenant had been here.

Babe exhaled, mind racing. Klarence had bolted, but the answers weren't with him. They were with the people pulling the strings.

She stepped outside, breathing in the crisp air. Bear Lake stretched before her, its glassy surface shimmering under the sun. The beauty mocked the questions swirling around inside her.

Who the hell was Muncie? How did Klarence's family fit into this? She thought of the Moosetown cop's words: "Talk to their mothers if you want the truth." The tangled connections gnawed at her like a splinter under the skin. She needed answers. Now. Then she remembered Choi's map with the ominous X. Marking what? A body? A knot twisted in her gut. Was it Molly's grave?

But how was she going to make the lieutenant talk?

The answer was at her feet.

She headed to the cruiser and popped the trunk. Choi lay slumped, still wedged between the spare tire and the back seat. Sweat slicked her face and darkened her collar. Strands of damp hair clung to her flushed skin as her chest rose and fell in shallow breaths. Glassy eyes squinted up at Babe, defiance smouldering beneath exhaustion.

Her muffled protests faltered when Babe held up the fleur-de-lis button. Babe said nothing, letting the silence do the talking.

Moments passed before she broke it. "Two choices, Lieutenant. Tell me where Klarence's mother is or regret it with your last breath."

Choi blinked, lips dry, cracked. Her glare burned with resistance, but the shallow rise and fall of her chest betrayed her nerves.

Without a word, Babe grabbed the garden hose and threaded it from the exhaust pipe into the trunk.

Choi's breath turned to gasps. Her arms strained against the cuffs. Panic surged across her face as Babe tapped the free end of the hose against the bumper.

Babe's tone was almost casual. "You know, Lieutenant, I've had enough. So let's make this simple. Burial or cremation? Or should I just leave you for the gulls?"

Choi talked.

Chapter 37

The dirt road unspooled ahead, each bend curled in quiet threat. Choi had insisted the X on the map marked Klarence's mother's house, Mama Kaye, she called her, and Babe believed that much. But the lieutenant's denials about Molly's whereabouts still stuck in her craw. Another stall. If Choi thought she could keep playing for time, she'd eventually find out otherwise.

The cruiser sat cloaked beneath a tangle of trees, swallowed in shadow. Babe stepped out and knocked on the trunk with two quick raps. "Don't miss me too much."

Silence.

She turned into the underbrush, boots snapping twigs beneath her. Branches knitted a dense canopy overhead, choking the light and striping the forest floor in broken shadow. The air clung heavily. Pine needles and dry leaves crunched underfoot, crisp and unforgiving. A thistle snagged her arm, leaving a thin line of blood.

Her fingers brushed the Glock at her hip, not from fear, but to stay centred. Trust didn't belong here, not with Choi, not with the map, and not in this silence pressing in on all sides. She'd ditched the shotgun, hat, and duster.

Babe pulled up short where the trees fell back into a clearing.

At the centre of the clearing, a woman stapled a shirt bearing the Holy Smokes logo to a sagging clothesline running between a dilapidated shack and a spruce tree. The stapler snapped sharply. The chickens surrounding her kept pecking, unfazed. Babe recognized her from the photo, Mama Kaye. Who else could it be?

Mama Kaye moved toward a patch of soil, carrying a battered blue watering can. She tipped it slowly. "There you go," she murmured. "Have yourself a nice drink."

Something twisted in Babe's gut. The knotted fabric of her shirt dug into her sternum, damp and clinging. Sweat slicked the back of her neck and slid along her temple. She stared at the patch of earth, a sick thought rising fast. *Was that Molly's grave?* "Goddamn," she blurted.

The word sent the chickens into a flapping, clucking frenzy.

Mama Kaye's attention snapped to Babe and the badge clipped to her belt. She raised the stapler like a weapon. "What brings you? Snoopin' on me plants? Get outta here!"

Babe's pulse kicked, but her voice held. She raised her hands. "Take it easy, Mama Kaye. I'm not here for that."

The older woman squinted. "How you know me name? And what the hell you doin' creepin' around me woods?"

Babe forced a dry smile. "I'm filling in for someone you already met. She's… tied up right now, so I'm handling things."

Mama Kaye's fingers tensed around the stapler.

Babe displayed her scratched wrist. "Could use a bandage. Wouldn't want it festering."

"You sure you ain't spyin' on me plants?"

"I swear I'm not." Babe shifted her stance thinking of a way to bullshit the woman. "I work with the Food and Drug Administration.

We regulate medicine, including marijuana. Weed's a Schedule I federally, but I'm just gathering information. I'm not here to shut you down."

A raspy laugh broke the tension. Mama Kaye lowered the stapler and pulled a joint from her apron. With a flick of her fingernail, she lit a wooden match, and took a slow drag. Smoke curled up into the heavy air. "You sure do talk fancy. Come on, then."

Babe followed her inside.

The shack hit like a slap. Musty and close, laced with weed smoke, soured stew, and something deeper clinging to the wood. Wallpaper, thick with grease and something darker, peeled like shed skin. A pot of stew on a wood stove gurgled in the corner. But most important, it was clear Molly wasn't here.

An open Bible lay between two chipped Jesus figurines on a rickety table. A photo leaned against a stack of yellowed newspapers: Klarence and the Moosetown cop flanking Mama Kaye, her grin stretched wide like a warning.

"That there's me boys," Mama Kaye said, cutting through the quiet. She passed the joint to Babe. "Hit this."

Same punchy scent as Choi's.

Babe took it, inhaled lightly. Just enough. The smoke coated her throat, acrid, earthy. She passed it back, thinking of the mound of dirt outside. She needed to find out if Molly was buried there. "The U.S. government thinks someone using the alias Molly is stirring up trouble," she said.

Mama Kaye poured water from a stained jug into a cracked cup. "Drink while I fetch that bandage."

Babe drained the cup. The cool water cut through the smoke's aftertaste. "My job is to investigate. This is a top secret project."

Mama Kaye handed her a bandage, expression unreadable.

"She's clever," Babe continued. "Manipulative. Might be using another name." Babe held up a photo of Molly on her phone. "Usually wears a yellow cap. Have you seen her?"

Mama Kaye studied the screen. "Nope. Don't recall no one wearin' no yellow cap." She hesitated. "That other woman, your partner, that was here. Ask'n about Americans. In case she didn't tell ya."

"I didn't see her report," Babe said. "Did she get anywhere?"

"Not so I know."

As Babe wrapped the bandage around her wrist, she studied Mama Kaye's face. Calm. Too calm. No tells, but her phrasing? Careful. "The government's offering a reward." Babe pushed further. "Maybe a statue for a reward." *Why'd she offer that? Must be the weed.*

Mama Kaye grinned. "Maybe me with an axe? Chopped up my husband once, 'course he be outside there now. Just gave him a little drink, not that he'd be tellin' anyone what went on."

Babe blinked, relieved to know it wasn't Molly buried out in that plot. "Maybe something more subtle," she replied, trying not to laugh. "Though it'd tell a hell of a story. Why'd you do it?"

Mama Kaye's voice flattened. "Things with me Klarence."

The Moosetown cop's voice echoed in Babe's mind: "My mama took an axe to him for doing that which may not be spoken of in polite company." Babe coughed lightly, stalling for time, weighing how to tell Mama Kaye her boy Klarence might've been molested by this Muncie character. The woman had the look of someone who wouldn't think twice about killing the messenger, and Babe had dealt with enough unhinged people to know when to tread carefully. Best to keep it veiled, wrap the message in scripture and suggestion. Her eyes flicked to the Bible. "You a friend of Jesus?"

"He's my saviour," Mama Kaye replied, lighting a roach with the same pliers she used for God knew what else. She exhaled slowly, watching Babe.

"I got a message from him once," Babe said, keeping her tone light while unable to recall any of Johnson's sermons. She chalked it up to the haze from the weed.

"You're pullin' me leg?"

"He told me this parable," she said, "About wrestling with pigs. You get filthy, and only the pig enjoys it."

"Ain't never read that in my Bible."

"I'm paraphrasing. Probably in the back pages." Babe took the blunt and drew slowly. The smoke curled through her lungs and back out again. Her attention returned to the photo. "Might be wise for your boys to reconnect with Jesus, if they haven't already," she said. "Once someone starts rollin' around with the brown it takes more than soap and Sunday to scrub clean."

Mama Kaye shrugged. "We had cousin Brownie, but he be dead now. Lots of folks visited him in the patch." She nodded toward the horizon. "Pumpkin patch by the white church, Nine Mile Road. Big, cracked one in the middle, like it just gave up. That place gone to rot now. Shame, truth be told."

"Noted," Babe said, cataloging it.

Gravel crunched outside.

Mama Kaye moved to the window, her face lighting up. "That's my beau, Muncie. Forgot his hat again. Klarence'll probably be best man, seein' as they be livin' next to each other."

The connection hit hard. Klarence. Muncie. The Embassy.

"My visit stays between us," Babe snapped, slicing through the warmth in Mama Kaye's voice. "Not a word. Not to him. No one."

Mama Kaye's smile thinned. She tapped her temple. "Ain't nobody home but me. Mouth shut, key turned, thrown in the crick." She pulled a baggie from her apron labelled Holy Smokes. "Special recipe. Might come in handy. Doctor's orders."

"Thanks," Babe said, tucking it into her shirt.

She moved through the back room, out the window, boots hitting the ground in a blur. Branches clawed at her arms as she plunged into the woods, breath tearing from her lungs. The Embassy rose in her mind like a warning bell.

If Molly were there, the fuse had already been struck.

Chapter 38

Detective Slim Meekins leaned against the fender of his unmarked cruiser, slicked-back hair reflecting the sunshine. His red-framed sunglasses perched low on his nose as he took in the scene. Bear Lake shimmered, just enough ripple to set the bowrider rocking at the dock. The Cape Cod-style cottage sat tucked against a wall of forest, its secrets steeped in silence, too vile to name. His life was under siege in the city with bosses grinding him down, coworkers smiling while they figured where to stick the knife, and a home life that bled him slowly. But out here? Clean air, no eyes on him, and the kind of extracurriculars Muncie delivered that turned punishment into pleasure. Slim could smell the sweat and sin in the air. And that was exactly how he liked it.

A pickup roared down the gravel lane, spitting a thick cloud of dust into the air that drew his attention.

Muncie climbed out and yanked open the rear door. Molly stumbled from the truck, pale and bruised, dishevelled hair clinging to her damp neck as she limped toward the cottage. Behind her, Ginger emerged, ducking as Risqué soared into the air.

Slim's lips curled into a predatory grin as he watched Molly. When she glanced back, he raised his hand, forming a crude circle with his fingers and wiggled his tongue through it.

Molly didn't break stride. She threw up her middle finger and jabbed it toward her backside before disappearing into the cottage.

Slim chuckled. "Still full of piss and vinegar, that one," he said as Muncie approached. He handed over the green envelope Miss Horn had given him. "Incentive inside. They want that video fast. And keep an eye out for any nosy parkers."

"With our new star, maybe we'll get a bonus," Muncie replied. "Once the boss sees the preview, he'll realize we'll have things squared away in the end."

Slim laughed. "Aren't we clever with our words?" He nodded toward the cottage. "Molly looks rough. You sure she can handle the pressure?"

Muncie exhaled, rubbing the back of his neck. "Had to put her through a few paces," he lied. "Nothing she won't bounce back from. She knows the deal."

"We both know the boss doesn't like sloppy work." Slim turned back to Muncie. "No surprises. You caught my warning about onlookers, yeah?"

"I'm not deaf." Muncie dug a flash drive labelled Molly from his pocket and slipped it into Slim's shirt.

Slim frowned. "What's that for? I already dropped off the drive."

"That one's for you to polish up your diva act."

Slim snorted, his laugh like gravel on concrete. "Yeah, screw you."

A hundred yards away branches clawed at Babe's tied-up shirt as she pushed through the dense underbrush. Every step dragged her pace to a crawl, each snagging branch a fresh insult. Sweat stung her eyes, but she pressed on, tension winding tighter with every inch gained.

The campground flashed in her mind. The empty lot where Ariana was supposed to be waiting. No sign of her. *Where the hell had she gone?*

Focus. One problem at a time.

Then she saw it.

The pickup from Mama Kaye's sat parked at the so-called American Embassy.

The realization twisted in her gut.

Her eyes locked onto Slim and Muncie. Their postures were too casual, their grins too smug. The one with the rooster strut had to be Muncie. And Slim being in Canada made her head spin. First Choi, now this detective? This wasn't a coincidence.

A redheaded woman stood naked in a plastic kiddie pool, her pale skin gleaming with soap suds. The woman smiled lazily, basking in the men's attention as they leered.

Babe dropped low, crawling through thinning foliage until she found cover at the edge of the forest. Her ears strained to catch the men's conversation, catching just enough to sense something dark unfolding.

Slim gestured to Ginger. "Those perky nipples could make a grown man cry like a starving baby."

"Slim! Ginger looks like a pubescent child!" Muncie snapped.

"Hell, I'd make her scream it until she lost her damn voice," Slim sneered. He popped the trunk of his cruiser, his Rolex glinting in the late afternoon sun. He pulled out a folded blue towel and handed it to Muncie. "I gotta jet. Need to pick up the old lady's cat. Took the little bastard to get his nuts clipped."

Muncie's laugh was flat. "Castration, the final solution."

"Speaking of solutions, I found a nice oil-based lube."

Muncie's voice dropped. "She'll squeal no matter what you use."

Babe's pulse pounded in her ears. Each word struck like a blow. These weren't just corrupt men; they were predators oozing entitlement and revelling in filth. This stain wasn't confined to Bear Lake; it spread like rot, infecting everything and everyone it touched.

But at least it looked like Molly wasn't caught in their web. The universe couldn't have that kind of twisted sense of humour.

Her disgust hardened into resolve. If these two thought they were untouchable, she'd make sure they learned just how wrong they were.

Babe had learned that playing nice wasn't the way to get results.

Chapter 39

Lieutenant Choi writhed in the suffocating darkness of the cruiser's trunk, the filthy spare tire grinding into her spine, its coarse rubber pressing deep into her skin. The acrid stench clung to the stale air, seeping into her lungs with every shallow breath. The gag turned each inhale into a struggle, choking her. Her wrists throbbed where the cuffs bit into raw skin. Movement brought no relief, only the burn of futility. She went still. A faint creak shattered the silence—the car door. Choi tensed, pulse spiking as the vehicle dipped under the driver's weight. Then the loud slam reverberated through the metal shell of her prison. The engine roared to life, its vibrations rattling through her ribs, shaking her resolve.

The cruiser lurched forward. Her back hit the spare. Pain lanced through her kidney. Jaw clenched, she swallowed a cry. Not one sound. Not from her.

The road turned rough, every bump jarring her battered body. The gag cut into the corners of her mouth, a constant, mocking presence. She bit down harder. Crying out wouldn't change anything. It would hand the skinny reporter exactly what she wanted.

Babe Lincoln.

Her voice echoed in Choi's mind, sharp, smug. Klarence this. Klarence that. The audacity of that grin. The way Babe thought she could crack her. Amateur. Choi spat the name in her head, bitter and venomous. Babe Lincoln. The reckless, self-righteous fraud parading around like some kind of hero. A scavenger treating danger like a thrill ride. Babe wasn't a cop. Not even close. Just a hack who thought she could play the game and win.

But why?

Brisk.

No doubt the chief was behind her swagger. The thought made Choi's skin crawl. That patronizing old bastard, undermining her investigation after everything she'd done for him. When she got out of this nightmare, she'd sue his sorry ass. The city, too. A million-dollar settlement sounded nice. Hell, there was always money for the illegals destroying the cities. The whole country was going to hell in a handbasket. Why not grab a tidy sum on the way out?

Brisk would deny the affair, but she'd been around enough shysters in courtrooms to know the truth would come out during what they called discovery. Too many florist receipts. Too many hotel rooms. Those conventions. The writing would be on the wall. The power brokers would pony up the cash. Scandals were to be avoided those at all costs.

A pothole yanked her back to reality. The impact slammed her into the trunk's unyielding frame. Pain flared through her body. She hissed through her nose, muffling the sound.

Her thoughts flickered to Klarence. Their future. She'd refurbish his cabin. Perhaps take him on a little getaway to Mexico while the work is done. The Mazatlán Carnival. A walk along the Malecón. Klarence would love the towering, multicoloured figurines the locals call monigotes.

The vibrations drilling into her hip turned merciless. Her cuffed wrists screamed for relief, steel biting deep into bruised flesh. Ally Oops, the derringer strapped to her ankle, might as well have been on the moon. Even if she could reach it, the confines of the trunk turned it into a cruel joke.

Babe's duster.

She'd placed it there earlier with a smirk, letting Choi use it as a makeshift pillow against the hard toolbox. But it was gone now.

Snatched back. Her skull pressed against the red metal. *I'm Lieutenant Choi. Not some helpless victim tossed into a trunk like stolen goods.*

The cruiser swerved. Choi let out a muffled grunt as her body slammed into the tire. Then another jarring bounce. The car bottomed out. Her skull struck the lid. Pain detonated behind her eyes. Black spots danced across her vision. Nausea surged. *This isn't how it ends.* She took slow, shallow breaths, fighting the dizziness.

Years on the street had taught her one thing: survival wasn't about strength, it was about will. Pain. Humiliation. Fear. They were obstacles, nothing more. She needed to stay sharp. Wait for the trunk to open. When it did, she'd make it count.

The tires crunched over gravel, distinct after miles of asphalt. Her senses sharpened. The vehicle veered off-road, dirt and debris pinging against the undercarriage. She braced, angling her body. Each bounce drove the spare deeper into her spine, but she clenched her teeth. She'd taken worse.

A deep rut.

Her body jerked upward. Her head cracked against the lid with a sickening thud. Pain exploded. Breath stolen. A strangled gasp tore from her throat as stars burst behind her eyes. Her thoughts shattered like glass. Darkness pressed in, thick and inescapable.

The struggle faded to black.

Less than a mile away, Detective Slim Meekins paused his cruiser beside the bald eagle statue clutching the No Trespassing sign at the edge of the embassy's laneway. He checked for oncoming traffic, then turned onto Nine Mile Road, where the forest loomed in shadow and low clouds stretched across the horizon.

Leaving the cottage gnawed at him, but the thought of home was worse. His wife's endless nagging and wordplay had become a daily test of his patience.

"Well, detective, I suppose logic's not your strong suit either," she'd said a couple of nights earlier, cutting into her tofu.

Slim clenched the wheel tighter, thinking of Molly with her defiant glare and sharp tongue. The way she'd flipped him off had only stoked the fire. He didn't understand Muncie's obsession with head games.

Slim preferred direct methods. Simple. Brutal. Effective. A dark curl pulled at his lips. Breaking her would be easy. It was only a matter of time.

A shadowed figure emerged ahead, pulling Slim from his thoughts. A wide-brimmed hat and long coat gave the silhouette an eerie presence.

Slim scowled, irritation flaring. He eased off the gas, rolling down the window as he pulled alongside. "Get off the road," he barked.

The figure straightened and stepped closer. Recognition landed like a punch to the ribs.

Babe Lincoln.

"Detective Slime," Babe said, tone cool and sharp. "Far from your jurisdiction, aren't you? Or maybe you've got insights you're dying to share with us commonfolk?"

Slim kept his expression flat, though his pulse jumped. "I'm on a case. Move along."

Babe didn't budge. Her hand brushed the duster. "Looking for Molly Darnell?" she asked.

"Never heard of her," Slim said.

Babe's hand drifted to the shotgun strapped to her thigh. "Maybe this will make you more talkative," she said.

Slim's smirk faltered for a beat. "What do you want, Lincoln?"

"For starters…" Babe leaned in, eyes locked on his. "How can you claim not to know Molly when you delivered an evidence box with her name on it to Choi's office?"

Slim's hand jerked toward his sidearm, but the motion was too fast and too sloppy. A flash drive labelled Molly slipped from his pocket and landed on his lap.

Before he could recover, the shotgun was inches from his face, rock-steady. Slim swallowed. He had baited the beast, and she looked ready to devour.

Chapter 40

Grey daylight filtered into the spacious kitchen of Muncie's cottage. The eating area, a mix of rustic charm and modern touches, felt suffocating under the flat, colourless light. Cuts and bruises throbbed on Molly's body, her knee a constant reminder of the failed escape. She gripped the counter's edge, fighting the exhaustion pressing down. The knot in her stomach refused to ease, no matter how much water she drank.

From her spot at the kitchen window, she saw the yard clearly. Muncie sprayed Ginger with the hose, rinsing suds from her pale skin. The redhead arched her back, posing, her movements exaggerated in the inflatable pool. Molly's lip curled. *Why had Ginger bought into this twisted circus?* It soured her stomach.

A loud belch broke her focus. Molly turned to see Risqué perched on the back of a chair, head cocked as if mocking her.

"Fly off," she muttered, "or you'll end up in a cage."

The door slammed, shaking the cabinets and jolting her nerves. Muncie strode into the kitchen, his presence filling the space like a storm cloud. He set his cap, green envelope, and blue towel on the counter. "Why is someone from America looking for you?"

"Gee, I don't know, Einstein. Would it have anything to do with you kidnapping me?"

"You should start taking this seriously," he said, voice dropping. "If you don't shape up, my report will say someone matching your description tried stealing classified documents."

Molly snorted. "Classified documents? That's rich. I wanted booze, not your imaginary secrets. Go ahead, spin your crap. It clears up any doubts about how clueless you are."

"Maybe it's time you stopped running your mouth and started cooperating. We've got a movie to watch."

Her lip curled. "How romantic. What is it? A dark room with sticky floors full of perverts in raincoats?"

"Enough of your sass," Muncie snapped, herding her into the main room.

The walls bore posters for *One Flew Over the Cuckoo's Nest* and *The Departed*. Risqué followed, perched on a tripod, his beady eyes tracking Muncie as he pointed to two metal folding chairs set before a large-screen computer. "Sit," he ordered.

Molly plopped down. "This your idea of a timeout?"

"Since you refuse to focus, we'll do it this way." He grabbed a sheet from the desk and shoved it at her. "Before we start, sign this."

Molly snatched the paper and scanned it. Her brow furrowed, then shot up. "Back Door Bonanza? Isn't that—"

"Something Slim cooked up," Muncie cut in, waving a hand. "Just sign it."

Molly scoffed and tossed it back. "As if I'd sign anything you bozos shove at me."

"I'm on your side," he said. "But you should consider the alternative. There's this guy I heard about. Paid a fortune to watch someone take a dump on a glass table while he lay underneath. Imagine the millions a video like that could rake in."

"Are you planning to demonstrate?"

Muncie laughed flatly. "Me? Dropping a deuce? Hate to disappoint your twisted expectations."

She bit back a reply. His wild comments and bizarre directives confirmed it. He was unhinged.

"Consider this a tutorial," Muncie continued. "Time you learned the world isn't all rainbows and unicorns." He tapped a key. The monitor flickered to life. "Let's revisit last night's debacle."

Molly braced.

The video rolled: Ginger striking a pose in pink satin shorts and an unbuttoned blouse, her push-up bra struggling to accentuate what little cleavage she had. The camera lingered on her as she batted her lashes and flirted with the lens.

Slim entered the frame, combing his slicked-back hair, eyes locked on Ginger. "How old are you, baby doll?" he asked, voice oozing sleaze.

"Fifteen," Ginger purred. "Mommy always said I was big for my age."

From off-screen came Molly's incredulous voice. "Fifteen? Who are you kidding?"

The camera wobbled, panning to Molly, standing stiffly near the edge of the room in a white hazmat suit and feathery angel wings.

Muncie's voice barked, "Stay in character, Molly. We turned you into an angel. What more do you want?"

The camera returned to Ginger. Muncie directed her: "Stir up some desire. Make us believe, Ginger."

She rolled her eyes and forced a smile. "Mommy always said I was big for my age."

"Cut! Cut!" Muncie stormed into frame. "You already used that line!"

Ginger threw up her hands. "Can't you fix it in post?"

"Let's just move on," Muncie snapped. "Slim, where are you? Slim!"

Slim's face lunged into frame.

"Don't look at the camera!" Muncie barked.

Slim recoiled, mumbling an apology.

"Slim," Muncie growled, "this is your cue. Give Ginger a lascivious look while you unbuckle your pants."

Slim blinked. "What kind of look?"

"Lustful. Lewd. Depraved."

Ginger shifted. "My better profile's on this side."

"No one cares," Muncie snapped. "Slim, do your part. Ginger, say your lines."

"Care for a taste, sugarplum?" Slim drawled.

Ginger screamed theatrically. "You bone doctor!"

"Cut!" Muncie roared. "Ginger, tone it down or you'll wake the dead. Slim, give us your line."

The screen shifted to Slim mooning the camera, his bare ass filling the frame.

"Ready to be my brown-eye girl?" he said.

Molly darted out of frame, face twisted in revulsion.

"What exactly are you doing now, Molly?" Muncie demanded. "You're acting edgier than a virgin with a puckered asshole on prom night!"

Slim leaned toward the lens. "Isn't this where she puts her tongue—"

Muncie slammed the pause button.

Molly glanced at the movie posters. "Are these supposed to mean something?" she asked, grasping at something, anything, that didn't make her skin crawl.

Muncie leaned back, drumming his fingers. "You've seen what I put up with," he said, nodding toward the frozen screen. Then he sniffed the air, face twisting. "What the hell is that smell?" He glanced at Molly. "Did you fart?"

Molly's head snapped around. "Excuse me?"

"Cut the cheese. Break wind. Let one rip."

"You just skip right past creepy into clinical, don't you?"

"Just an observation."

She looked at the ceiling. "It wasn't me."

"Then who was it?"

She pointed to Risqué. "Maybe it was him?"

The bird gave a sharp shake of its head, feathers ruffling in protest.

"Okay… not the bird." Molly's eyes snapped back to Muncie. "Then it must've been you. Maybe you shit yourself watching that train wreck of a video."

Muncie grabbed her chin. "Enough," he growled. "It's time for you to focus."

Molly slapped his hand away.

"Don't touch me."

"You want to play rough?"

Chapter 41

Shadows stretched like restless spirits, spilling across Lingus Lane in the fading sunlight. Wildflowers lined the roadside, their colours muted under the dying light, shivering in the wind. The forest loomed on either side, its gnarled branches clawing at the air like doomed hands. Somewhere distant, a tractor groaned, its rasp carrying through the stillness like the lament of an unseen beast.

Babe shrugged off her duster and draped it over a weathered fence post. According to Choi's hastily drawn map, this spot was marked Look Out. The name didn't fit. No cliffs. No scenic vistas. Just sparse vegetation, damp sand, and an eerie silence heavy enough to crush bone. A prickle ran up her spine. The feeling of unseen eyes.

Lingus Lane carried a dark history. It was a legend that refused to die. Decades ago, Annie, the town's infamous seductress, and her young lover had driven out here, drunk and reckless, and vanished. No car. No bodies. Just a fading trail and whispered stories about restless spirits. Locals avoided this stretch after dark, calling it cursed ground. Even skeptics tread lightly, unnerved by tales of strange whispers and shadows shifting where they shouldn't.

Babe knew none of that. All she felt now was the pressure of the quiet, thick and unnatural. A twig snapped. She spun toward the sound. Nothing. The forest had swallowed most of the daylight. She took a long drag from a joint she'd rolled from Mama Kaye's stash, letting the burn steady her pulse.

Slim groaned from where he lay, his muffled cries slicing the silence. Babe turned, lips curling at the pitiful sight. He was twisted upside down on his back, his legs wedged through the open passenger window of the cruiser. The glass pinned his ankles, locking him in place as effectively as the cuffs biting into his wrists. Gagged and drenched in sweat, the shirtless Slim writhed, his pale face contorted with fear.

Babe approached the cruiser, placing the flash drive on the hood next to Slim's Glock, badge, and Choi's shield, symbols of authority turned useless. She flipped the badges into the ditch and hurled the Glock into the open field beyond the fence.

Sliding on Slim's red sunglasses, she crouched beside him, Ariana's scissors glinting in her hand. The blades felt heavy, not physically, but with the weight of what she was about to do. She twirled them, voice calm, almost conversational. "You know what feels downright sinful, Slime?" She exhaled a slow plume of smoke, the haze twisting heavenward like a forsaken prayer. Her voice dropped, cold and deliberate. "Liars. I can't abide them. And you? You reek of deception."

Slim groaned, his protests swallowed by the gag. Babe shook her head, exhaling slowly through her nose. "Protests won't save you now. Remember that evidence box with Molly's name on it? You delivered it to Choi's office, didn't you?" Her tone hardened. "Don't play dumb. It's insulting."

She snapped the scissors open and snipped through his pants, the blades whispering against the fabric. His pale flesh twitched in the cool air. A muffled cry. Babe flicked a finger against a testicle, drawing a strangled noise that was half scream, half sob.

"Yup," she murmured, her lips curling. "That's gotta hurt. But trust me, Slime, it's nothing compared to what's coming." She pulled out her iPhone, its glow washing over her face as she scrolled.

"Good news: I've got three bars," she said with mock cheerfulness. "Let me read this to you. Forgive me if I botch the pronunciation. It's been a day." She squinted at the screen and began, "Scrotal orchiectomy involves removing a testicle through an incision in the scrotum."

Slim's subdued screams rose to a fever pitch. He thrashed, jerking against the restraints. Babe smiled slightly.

"Oh, don't worry. We're looking at a bilateral orchiectomy," she mused. "That means both of them, in case you're wondering. Thought you'd appreciate the distinction."

The scissors hovered near his groin, the blades glinting like fangs in the dying light. Revulsion coiled in her gut, thick and suffocating. Every instinct screamed that Slim deserved this. But justice shouldn't feel this heavy. She crossed herself, whispering, "Father Jay said confession is good for the soul. When you face judgment, the angels will know your true ugliness. But don't worry, I'll be waiting for you at the gates of hell."

A sudden rustling made her freeze. She straightened, eyes narrowing at the treeline. Birds exploded from the foliage, slicing through the sky in frantic flight. Babe turned back to Slim, voice cold. "Got something to say?"

Slim nodded violently. She yanked the gag from his mouth, and he gasped, choking on the cool air. "Molly's with Muncie and Ginger," he croaked. "At the Embassy."

Babe tilted her head, studying him like a cat sizing up a wounded mouse. "See? That wasn't so hard. But I need more." She pressed the scissors against his nostril, the sharp tip drawing a bead of blood. "Talk."

Slim's voice cracked. "I'm gonna faint. Just let my feet go!" he begged, words tumbling over each other. His eyes rolled back, and he slumped, unconscious.

Babe exhaled sharply, rolling her neck. Releasing his ankles seemed harmless enough, what could go wrong? She circled the car, started the engine, and hit the passenger window switch. The glass lowered, freeing Slim's legs.

She stood still, letting the cool air settle on her skin. Weighing. Deciding. A sudden shuffle.

Slim grabbed the flash drive off the hood and bolted. His pale, naked form lurched into the field, sobs choking his breath. His eyes locked on where the Glock had landed.

He didn't get far.

His scream tore through the dusk until swallowed by a wet, sucking noise as the ground devoured him whole.

Babe stared. The earth was still again, eerily silent. A slow exhale left her lips. Slim deserved this. But justice shouldn't feel like dragging a blade across her soul.

She stepped forward. Then she saw it: a faded sign, half-buried in the weeds, its weathered letters warning, Look Out: Danger Quicksand.

Babe ran a hand down her face. "Fucking hell."

The legend of Lingus Lane had claimed another soul.

Chapter 42

The bright red scarf jammed into Molly's mouth muffled her cries as classical music flooded the kitchen. Duct tape lashed her wrists and ankles to the chair, and each struggle met cold, unyielding resistance. The ever-present ankle bracelet pressed into her skin, a silent reminder of the cage she couldn't escape.

Sweat trickled down her temples, stinging her eyes. Muncie loomed in a black tailcoat and bow tie, the picture of deranged sophistication.

He wielded a knife like a conductor's baton, each gesture sharp and deliberate, slicing the air in time with the swelling tempo. His face twisted in manic concentration, commanding an invisible symphony.

Violins surged, crescendos stabbing into Molly's nerves, the sound conspiring to hold her down. She yanked against the tape, wrists raw, the bindings biting deep. The chair creaked as she twisted, her stomach knotting tighter with every swell of the orchestra. Her gaze darted around the kitchen, frantic, searching for any escape from this waking nightmare.

The violins peaked in a furious crescendo.

With a theatrical flourish, Muncie slashed the knife through the air one final time, then slapped the stop button on the CD player. Silence snapped down like a trap.

He turned to Molly, eyes gleaming. "Music can be therapeutic, don't you think?" His tone was light and casual as if discussing the weather. He tilted his head, considering. "That piece, quite *à propos*, wouldn't you say?"

Molly glared at him, the scarf gagging any response.

Risqué watched from his perch, head tilting in mock sympathy. He studied the terror in Molly's eyes and the madness bubbling behind Muncie's grin.

Muncie turned to a black Kit-Kat clock mounted on the wall, its eyes and tail swaying in hypnotic unison. The hour and minute hands had been ripped away, leaving only the ticking. He pointed the knife at it. "You see, Molly, time here belongs to me." He traced the blade along the frame. "And we'll use that time wisely… to teach you how to stay focused."

Molly's heart jackhammered in her chest. Her eyes flicked to the clock. She needed time. Time to think. Time to escape. This wasn't happening. This couldn't be real.

Her stomach gurgled. A short, explosive fart cut through the silence.

Muncie froze. His nose wrinkled in exaggerated disgust. He snapped his head toward her, expression twisting like she'd committed some cardinal sin. "Whoa, that's ripe!"

Risqué fanned his beak with a wing, echoing Muncie's disgust.

Heat flared in Molly's cheeks. Shame pricked behind her eyes, but she held his gaze. Don't look away. Don't give him the satisfaction. He wanted her humiliated, small, broken. She clenched her fists. No. She wouldn't give him that.

Muncie rushed to the window and shoved it open with a gasp. "God almighty!" He stuck his head out, gulping air.

When the smell finally cleared, he turned back and crouched in front of her. The knife glinted under the kitchen light. The polished steel brushed her cheek, reflecting her wide, terrified eyes.

Molly held her breath. The cold bite of the blade against her skin sent a shiver through her. Her heart pounded in her ears. Sweat clung to her neck, hot and sticky, and the bindings dug into her wrists. She wouldn't give him the tears he wanted. She would endure this. If she survived, she would burn the memory from her mind and leave nothing behind.

"When I was a boy," Muncie continued, his voice low, "one of my chores was getting rid of the barn cat's new litter. Raggedy little things, tolerated only because they kept the rats away."

He slid the knife under Molly's shirt, pinching the fabric between the blade and his fingers. He gave it a quick jerk upward, but the blade snagged. "Once, I kept a kitten for myself," Muncie muttered. "Who would know?" He yanked harder. Nothing. "Who can resist a little pussy so desperate for love?" With a growl, he hurled the knife across the room.

Risqué squawked and ducked as it swooshed over his head and buried itself in the wall with a dull thunk.

Molly's eyes tracked him as he stormed to the counter, muttering under his breath. He grabbed the knife stuck in the wooden block, but it wouldn't budge. Frustrated, he yanked open a drawer and snatched a pair of scissors. "My old man found out about that kitten," he said, slamming the drawer shut on his fingers. "Son of a bitch!" He stomped, sucked the wound, still muttering. "I can still feel the thrashing he gave me."

Scissors in hand, he knelt beside her, his earlier rage replaced with cold focus. Each snip cracked through the silence as he sliced away her buttons. "You've got to be tough, boy," he muttered. "No room for sentimental malarkey if you want to make it in this world."

He flicked her shirt open.

Molly grunted. Her eyes burned, but she refused to cry. Not here. Not now. She clenched her teeth so hard her jaw ached.

Risqué let out a low whistle as Muncie's beady eyes locked on her breast, framed in sleek black lingerie. He drank in the sight like a revelation. "Big, round eyes…" His fingers trembled as he slid the scissors under the center seam of her bra. "Just begging to be loved."

Molly recoiled. *Was he lost in memory? Or had his focus drifted back to her? Was this how it ended? Trapped in a madman's kitchen, stripped like an animal for slaughter?* She forced her eyes to the window. Look for the sky. The sky. There's always the sky. If she could survive this, she could survive anything.

The answer came fast and brutal. Muncie's eyes didn't even see her. He was somewhere else entirely. "I was six years old," he said quietly. "Standing on that dock, the salty air whipping through my hair. He handed me a brick tied to a noose around her tiny neck. 'Hold it for an hour,' he said, 'and she's yours.' You know what happened?"

He turned sharply and pointed the scissors at Risqué. "I ended up with this reject instead!"

Risqué mimicked the wailing cry of a baby. The surreal sound sharpened the madness.

Molly's stomach gurgled again. Her muscles tensed. Another fart ripped through the silence, loud and unapologetic.

Muncie gagged, dropping the scissors as he staggered toward the door, eyes watering. "That is just so wrong!" he gasped, struggling to breathe.

Risqué toppled off his perch, claws splayed skyward, beak agape in a dramatic, wheezing coughing fit.

"You might've dreamed of something better," Muncie choked out, flinging an arm toward the room. "But this…this is your reality!"

Molly didn't look away or flinch. She realized the expression flickering across his face wasn't defeat. It was recognition that he couldn't break her.

He flung open the door and leaned outside. "Ginger, where are you? I want this wench locked up! Now!"

Chapter 43

The bald eagle statue's No Trespassing sign cast a long shadow across the entrance to the gravel lane off Nine Mile Road. Babe kept moving. Every step toward the Cape Cod cottage was steady and sure. No more creeping through the trees, this was a straight-up march to battle. Nothing off the table. The fog of Mama Kaye's weed still clung to her thoughts, and Slim's fate gnawed at her. Brutal. Flawed or not, no one deserved to die like that.

She'd ditched the duster and shotgun, too conspicuous. Instead, she tucked the Glock into her waistband and pulled Slim's oversized shirt over it. The sleeves swallowed her arms, but it beat walking in wearing her own shirt, half-buttonless and tied off like she'd stepped out of a moonshine commercial.

At the cottage door, her pulse spiked. She grabbed the latch. Locked. Molly's face flashed behind her eyes. Was she just on the other side of this door? Babe pounded on the wood. The silence that answered twisted her gut.

She scanned the property. Beyond the sagging inflatable kiddie pool with its colours sun-faded and cracked, stood a squat, two-door structure that looked like a rundown motel. But it was the woodshed by the treeline that caught her eye. She moved toward it, heart drumming, muscles coiling, a plan forming. Break in. Find Molly. End this. Her fingers closed around a solid piece of firewood.

The cottage door creaked open.

She turned. A man stood in the doorway, holding a blue towel. Muncie. The same bastard she'd seen with Slim. Recognition hit, but too late to matter. He pulled a stun gun from the towel and jammed it into her neck.

Electricity tore through her. Her muscles seized. The log dropped from her hand.

Blackness.

When she awoke, her skull throbbed. Recognition of her fuck-up hit like a sledgehammer.

Leather restraints pinned her naked body to a bed, her hiking boots the only thing left. A gag filled her mouth, reducing her voice to guttural panic. Every twitch tightened the straps; the leather bit into her skin with cruel precision.

Her eyes swept the room, frantic.

Stark white walls. Fluorescent lighting. No windows. It felt less like a bedroom and more like a treatment chamber, cold and clinical, stripped of humanity. A stainless-steel cart stood against the far wall, its surface lined with scissors, clamps, and syringes. Everything was arranged with chilling neatness.

The air smelled of disinfectant, but beneath it lingered a faint, greasy note of oil. The clash of antiseptic with her exposed body made her feel less like a captive and more like a subject in someone's private experiment.

A parrot brushed her cheek with its feathers. Its warmth was fleeting. Its claws clicked softly against the frame as it perched beside her, head tilting with eerie curiosity. The bird's glassy eyes studied her in silence. It let out a low, guttural squawk.

Babe flinched as Muncie's hands moved over her body with slow, practiced intention. The oil's thick scent clung to her nostrils. Her stomach lurched. He wore a pristine white shirt and slacks, the outfit of a man playing doctor in a delusion of civility.

She squeezed her eyes shut. Focus on anything else. She tried conjuring a safe place, but the illusion shattered. Resisting only fed his performance. She swallowed down bile.

"You won't tell me your name, where you're from, or who sent you." Muncie's voice was sharp. "Why the Glock? Were you planning to use it on me?"

Her teeth clenched against the gag. She wouldn't give him the satisfaction.

Silence stretched. His composure cracked.

"The Glock already told me everything I need to know. And you still think keeping your mouth shut is an option?" His fingers pressed into her thigh, cold and invasive. "Your silence is saying more than you realize."

She twisted against the restraints, but it only encouraged him. His sneer deepened, and something darker flared behind his eyes. Her thoughts reeled. *How much of that joint did I smoke? Too much. Not just hazy. Baked. Edge dulled. Instincts fogged. Wide open for this.* Her chest tightened. *Reckless. Stupid. Too late to take it back now.*

She jolted as his fingers slid between her buttocks.

"Hold still," he barked.

She snarled into the gag, panic and rage colliding. *Ignore him. Focus elsewhere. Anywhere but here.* His touch sent shockwaves of humiliation through her. An American degrading her, here, in what was supposed to be a sanctuary. *Was this even an embassy? Was this karma for Choi, for letting fury lead instead of reason? Was this how it ended, strapped down and powerless?* Her mind spiralled.

A sudden pluck of hair, sharp and intentional.

Muncie held it aloft with a grotesque grin. "See this?" He flicked the strand between his fingers. "Just a simple ingrown hair. Nothing, really. But left unchecked? It festers. Becomes a pilonidal cyst. Unbearable. Oozing with pus and blood."

Her stomach churned. *She was listening to the mind of a man coming undone.*

Risqué jumped as Muncie slapped her ass. The crack echoed.

Muncie resumed rubbing oil into her skin. "The fact that you're here tells me everything. You're not in control, I am." His breath hit her ear. "And if this ever gets questioned… who do you think they'll believe?"

A pause.

"The raving lunatic?" His grip tightened. "Or me?"

Babe clenched her fists, every inch of her body burning with fury. This isn't over.

"Oh, and before I forget…" He bared his teeth in a mockery of kindness. "You'll appreciate the oil. Eventually."

Chapter 44

The cot sagged under Molly's weight, the metal mesh beneath the mattress creaking as she massaged her bruised knee. Each press of her fingers sent a jolt through her leg, a vivid echo of her failed escape. Scratches flared red across her skin, layered with deep bruises that told their own story. Her shirt, crudely tied after Muncie's invasive alterations, hung loose from her shoulders, barely covering her chest. She had no idea Babe had been captured. She was so close, just a few hundred yards away in the main cottage, yet still entirely out of reach behind the walls of the bunkie.

Ginger stood in the doorway, folding a navy sweatshirt with painstaking precision. Every motion seemed engineered to impose order, as if tidiness could restore trust. "A little gratitude wouldn't hurt, considering the state of your shirt," Ginger said, patting the garment.

Molly eyed an untouched glass of milk and a plate of cookies under the gooseneck lamp. "Thanks for the little snack. What's next? Tuck me in for the night?"

For a moment, Ginger's expression softened. "It might help," she said.

"Right," Molly said. "You'd think Muncie's lackey could do better. Cheese and wine, maybe. Or a drink with a kick."

"Oh, honey, Muncie would lose it."

Anger flared in Molly's eyes. "Newsflash, Ginger. That's what freaks do. They lose it. All you're doing is enabling him." She leaned forward. "What happened to you? Why are you Muncie's pawn?"

Ginger hesitated. Her hands trembled as she refolded the sweatshirt, smoothing imaginary creases. "It's complicated," she muttered. "Not everyone gets a chance to make the rules, no matter how much they deserve it."

"Spare me the sob story," Molly snapped. "I swiped some booze, gut rot, really, and suddenly I'm Public Enemy Number One? The man's too pathetic to appreciate decent Canadian whisky." Her voice hardened. "What's really going on?"

Unease flickered across Ginger's face. Her eyes darted to the door. Her body tensed, like she expected it to burst open. "This isn't about booze," she said. "To them, you're just a payday."

Molly's stomach twisted. *So that was the game. Keep her locked up until she was worth something to the right buyer, someone looking for a sex slave.*

Ginger's voice dropped to a whisper. "It's not for me to question. But you need to understand, the last thing you want is for anyone to think you're dangerous."

The words hung in the air. *If they thought she was dangerous now, they had no idea what she was capable of.*

A distant roar broke the silence, growing louder by the second. A boat engine. The sound carried across the water, shattering the fragile stillness. Ginger stiffened, dropped the sweatshirt on the cot, and slipped outside, the door locking behind her.

Molly stared at the closed door, mind racing. Her stomach growled, a low, defiant sound against the humiliation she refused to feed. She wouldn't let fear consume her. Becoming Muncie's next disciple wasn't an option.

A fragile idea sparked, faint but insistent, like a match struck in the dark. She didn't need their mercy. All she needed was another chance. And when it came, she'd seize it.

The weight of her next move, and the risks it carried, pressed against her as she lifted the glass, took a slow sip, and let the cold liquid coat her throat.

The waiting game had begun.

Chapter 45

Muncie stood at the helm of the bowrider, dressed in a seafarer's uniform. Gold-trimmed epaulets gleamed on his shoulders, and a nautical cap adorned with crossed anchors sat square on his head. Risqué perched on his shoulder, feathers sleek under the fading light, an unimpressed observer of the spectacle.

As Muncie steered the boat into open water, Ginger sprinted toward the dock. The motor's roar shattered the stillness of Bear Lake. Every motion was precise, his calm exterior masking the pulse of dark exhilaration beneath. He smiled at the burlap-covered figure sprawled on the deck—his proof of power. The boat cut through the glassy water, the lake's serenity at odds with the storm clouds thickening on the horizon.

Risqué squawked, "Hubba-hubba!" at Klarence, who was paddling his kayak near the shore. Muncie barely acknowledged the interruption, brushing the bird aside. Risqué flapped to the compass on the dash and tilted his head, watching with cocked interest.

A mile offshore, Muncie throttled back and turned to the bound figure beside the coiled rope. Gripping the burlap sack, he yanked the headpiece off in one swift motion. Babe's glare burned into him. Though gagged and bound, she remained unbroken. He ran a hand through her spiky hair with mock tenderness, his mouth twisting. "You know," he said, voice low, "no one would believe you if you ever made it out of here to tell this tale. They'd think it was just the desperate rambling of a woman hungry for attention."

He hauled her upright, sour breath brushing her face. "But here's the good news," he went on, his tone cloying. "That lotion I rubbed into your skin? It repels water. Impressive, huh? The bad news? The label didn't say how long it lasts." He tapped the rope coiled at her feet. "So… ready for paddleboarding without a paddle or a board? Or," he added, stepping back, arms crossed, "you could save us the trouble. Last chance. Drop the act and answer my questions."

He ripped the gag from her mouth. She sucked in a ragged breath, jaw aching.

"Tell me the truth. Are you the U.S. Marshal investigating us? Yes or no?"

The question hit like a punch. Suddenly, it all clicked. He email to Mayor Dickie Darnell, the accusations about Molly's disappearance, and his retaliation through News 4. He'd taken it all and twisted it into a weapon.

And again, that voice in her head roared: "Go big or go home." Babe's lips curled. "You pitiful excuse for a man," she said, hoarse but steady. "I'll escape, and there's nothing you can do to stop me. And if fate has other plans? My spirit will haunt you long after they've buried your worthless carcass."

Risqué let out a low whistle, as if impressed. Muncie's jaw twitched. For a moment, something flickered in his eyes. "You'll never leave this place." His voice wavered. "Your dream is nothing but an illusion."

Babe laughed. "When you go down, remember who sent you there, asshole."

His nostrils flared. Without breaking eye contact, he pulled the red-handled scissors from his pocket, their blades catching the last of the light. "You won't be needing these." With a flick of his wrist, he tossed them overboard.

Babe snapped. "Are you insane? Those are Henckels!"

The scissors vanished beneath the surface. Muncie exhaled hard through his nose, muscles tightening. He yanked the burlap sack back over her head.

Then, nature struck back. A sudden gust tore the captain's hat from his head. He spun, arms reaching for it, but the wind had already claimed it. The hat skidded across the water, flipped once, and sank.

The boat lurched.

Babe tumbled overboard. She hit the lake hard. The water clutched her like a fist. The wet burlap sealed over her face, choking her scream.

Risqué shrieked, wings flapping, his cries slicing through the rising wind like the storm's judgment.

Muncie staggered to the gunwale, breath ragged, not from concern, but from the creeping dread that control had slipped from his hands.

The lake boiled, wind and water shredding the last illusion of order. Nature wasn't just indifferent, it was erasing him. The weight of his choices pressed down, heavy and final. And for the first time in his life, something clawed its way up from his chest.

Something dangerously close to fear.

Chapter 46

A shard of light pierced the fractured windshield, casting jagged patterns across Ariana's blood-streaked face. Her body lay in the twisted wreckage of the Corvette, her world reduced to shattered glass and crumpled fibreglass, suspended in cold and indifferent darkness. She stirred, fighting to anchor herself as consciousness returned. Each throb in her skull pounded, a brutal reminder of the impact. The fog of confusion began to lift, giving way to the creeping chill spreading through her limbs, sharpening the silence around her.

The car's interior resembled a war zone. Fibreglass shards, torn upholstery, and scraps of paper were strewn like leaves after a storm. Where the driver's door had been was now a gaping void, exposing her to the overheated, stagnant air outside. Ariana drew a breath and shoved the deflated airbag off her chest.

Her fingers found the rearview mirror. What stared back was a stranger, smeared, hollow-eyed, bleeding, a twisted echo of the polished image she'd spent years perfecting.

A slow exhale. *Don't panic.*

She reached for her backpack: water bottle, lipstick, odds and ends that didn't belong in a crash but somehow anchored her. Tearing off what remained of her shredded shirt, she soaked it and wiped the blood from her face. A sharp sting bloomed near her hairline. A small gash, but deep. A souvenir.

She uncapped the lipstick and dragged a pink stroke across her lips. A reminder she was still her.

Clad in a sweat-drenched white tank top that clung to her skin, she crawled from the wreckage. Pain flared with each movement, sharp and relentless, but the crisp air hit her lungs. It cleared her head and hardened her resolve.

The crash site stretched around her in eerie stillness, obscured by thick brush that shielded it from passing eyes. No rescue. No bystanders. Just her and the wreck.

She looked back at the car. *Where's the shotgun?* It had been under her bag on the passenger seat. Now it was gone. Thrown clear? Buried in the wreck? Then it hit her: it would be useless without shells.

She turned toward the trees and pushed forward. Boots crunched through underbrush, branches clawing at her arms and legs. Pain bloomed with every step, but she kept moving. Instinct overruled everything else. The brush thinned.

Up ahead, the pale gleam of pavement.

Ariana emerged onto Terminal Road. Cracked asphalt stretched in both directions, shimmering under the heat. She paused, breathing hard, trying to focus. Heading into town meant possible help, or a collision with those bikers. The boat rental might lead her to Babe. The thought flickered, fragile, but alive.

She inhaled, expecting dust and heat. Instead, the air was thick with something foul—earthy, sour.

She knelt. A dark, greasy streak marred the road. Oil? No. The smell was wrong.

Crouching, she brought her fingers close to the edge of the slick. Even under this heat, it hadn't dried. The scent was rancid, almost organic, and stuck to the back of her throat. Her gut twisted. *What the hell did I hit?*

A distant hum cracked the stillness.

She froze. Engine. Low. Throaty. Closing fast.

Ariana wiped her hand on her jeans and rose to her feet. No time to dwell on the smear, the wreck, or the blood drying on her neck.

The sound grew, vibrating in her chest, bouncing off the trees like a warning. The forest became a tunnel of echoes. Her pulse surged.

Bikers? She stared at the bend ahead, breath catching. "Fuck," she whispered.

Chapter 47

Mechanic Joe's eyes flickered open, his vision swam as gnarled fingers aimed the spout of a blue watering can just above the freezer's edge. "You need water. Good for the cleansing," Mama Kaye muttered, yanking the lace hankie from his mouth.

Joe coughed, choking as water rushed past his parched lips and down his throat. He spluttered, gasping as it dribbled down his chin and soaked his shirt.

"Quit actin' like a baby and drink," she snapped.

The crunch of tires on gravel pulled her attention. Her lips twisted into a grin as she patted Joe's cheek. "Be a good fella, and I'll be back quicker than a June bug in a henhouse," she said, voice filled with false cheer. She slammed the freezer lid shut, plunging him back into darkness.

Karl stepped out of his cruiser, boots grinding on loose stones. Adjusting his Stetson, he shaded his eyes from streaks of late-afternoon sunlight slanting through the trees. "Hey, Mama," he called, his tone a mix of weariness and affection.

Mama Kaye stepped from the shed, her face lighting up. "Well, aren't you a sight for sore eyes?" She spread her arms wide like she could hug him from across the yard. "Got some stew simmerin' that'll fix you right up."

Karl frowned. "Just stopped by to check on you. Need anything?"

She waved him off. "The good Lord provides, you know that. Come on in."

"Yes, Mama," he said, nodding as he followed her into the shack.

Inside, the creak of the floorboards settled his nerves. He set his Stetson on the counter beside her worn tool belt and dropped onto a wooden crate that doubled as a chair.

Mama Kaye moved with ease, ladling stew into a wooden bowl and setting it before him with a proud smile.

Karl dug in, savouring the aroma. "This has a unique taste, Mama," he said between bites. "You use those pizza spices I got you?"

"Just made it with love, son," she replied, eyes twinkling. She poured water into a tin cup and placed it beside his bowl.

Karl took a long gulp, wiped his mouth with the back of his hand, and leaned back. "You seem to like Muncie. He's been good to you, bringin' wood and all that."

Mama Kaye's lips curled into a dreamy smile as she ladled more stew into his bowl. "I'm hopin' he'll take me out for a boat ride. Imagine that, me and him on the open water, just like one of them romantic novels." She sighed, shaking her head. "Reckon he's the kind of man who knows how to treat a lady."

Karl snorted. "Yeah, he's got that politician's knack for sayin' more than he means. Seen it firsthand. Tips big when orderin' pizzas for him and Klarence."

"Better than a pig in a poke," Mama Kaye chuckled. "You notice anything funny between your brother and Muncie?"

Karl frowned. "Well, he just gets Klarence to do odd jobs and buys him pizza. That's all I know. Oh, and those lederhosen Klarence struts around in."

Mama Kaye squinted. "Lederhosen? What in tarnation are you goin' on about?"

"Leather britches," Karl said. "Dropped by one night, and Klarence was modellin' them for Muncie and his niece."

Mama Kaye's face darkened. "Which niece?"

"The redhead's the only one I know. She was dressed like a nurse. Uniform was so short you could see her unmentionables. Imagine that, paradin' around without underwear."

Mama Kaye sniffed. "Foolish girl doesn't know enough to stay outta the sun, and now she's jonesin' for pneumonia. Young folks these days, no tellin' what's in their heads."

"It's that Internet, Mama. No tellin' what they're watchin'."

Mama Kaye nodded, her attention drifting.

Karl broke the silence. "Met a woman in town earlier. Askin' about some missing girl and huntin' season. Said I was a credit to the community."

"She's playin' you, boy. Probably flirtin', like all those other girls you told me about," Mama Kaye said, her tone edged with skepticism.

Karl studied her. "Why you sayin' that? Something I should know?"

"Just opinionatin', son," she said.

Karl set his spoon down. "Come on, Mama. You gotta tell me. I'm a lawman."

Mama Kaye's lips pressed into a thin line. "Finish yer stew."

A faint thump from the shed. Karl's brow furrowed. He turned toward the window.

Mama Kaye stood quickly. "It's just them possums gettin' into my compost again," she lied.

Karl hesitated, then exhaled and pushed the half-empty bowl aside. He reached for his Stetson. "Gotta get back to work."

"Your eyes were always bigger than yer belly," she said with a soft chuckle.

Karl's expression tightened. "Crime rates are up. We all need to stay alert."

"Maybe they'll build a statue for all your good work," she teased.

Karl shook his head. "Mama, you been smokin' those silly cigarettes again? You know they make people act weird."

"Doctors say them plants can heal, you know," Mama Kaye said.

Karl sighed, adjusting his belt. "Just don't let progress run you over. I already lost Papa. I can't lose you too."

Mama Kaye waved him off. "You be careful out there, and watch your language!"

Karl patted his sidearm. "I speak the language perps understand, Mama." He kissed her cheek and stepped out the door.

Mama Kaye stood still, staring after him a moment too long. Her usual smile faded, replaced by a flicker of worry, or regret.

Whatever storms lay ahead, she hoped her boys were strong enough to weather them.

Chapter 48

Slivers of light pierced the fractured surface of Bear Lake, casting jagged patterns across the burlap sack over Babe's head. Bubbles spiralled upward, chasing the last traces of air in her lungs. Too long. Too deep. Her chest convulsed, instinct screaming for oxygen. She twisted. The sack slipped free.

Darkness unfurled around her, shifting and warping like a fever dream. Glowing pumpkins drifted past, their carved faces twisted into mocking grins, eerie reflections of the General's sneer. A white church loomed ahead, rising solemn from the lakebed, its steeple splitting the surface like a splinter. The current dragged her forward. The double doors creaked open.

Come inside.

She stumbled through the threshold, suddenly dry, her clothes intact. The shotgun rested against her thigh, its weight grounding her. A stark white gift box tied with a red ribbon sat atop the baptismal font. A card tucked beneath the bow read, "Happy Birthday, Molly."

Her pulse thundered.

From the choir stalls, Kingfish and his biker gang chanted Psalm 23, their voices pressing in like a weight. Stained-glass windows twisted in their frames, images of salvation warping into something obscene. A dove burst through the nave, white wings flashing, then vanished into shadow.

A single spotlight snapped on.

Ginger stood at the pulpit, naked except for a pink cone-shaped party hat perched askew. She grinned and blew a party horn, the shrill sound slicing through the silence. "Did you bring Molly a present?" she asked, her voice soaked in mockery.

Babe's hands trembled as she lifted the lid. Inside: a carved pumpkin with Slim's face grotesquely recreated in waxy orange flesh. Horror surged through her as the pumpkin tumbled from the box, rolling down the aisle.

Muncie rose from the pews, watching her with cold amusement. "No confession?" he sneered. "Many would kill for this opportunity."

From the shadows, Father Johnson emerged, his orange chasuble glowing faintly. He stopped the rolling pumpkin with one foot, studying Babe with a mix of pity and resignation. "The wages of sin are always paid in full."

The pumpkin's mouth twisted open. Its carved grin moved like lips. A hollow voice rasped, "Beware of those bearing gifts." The words slithered through the air.

Father Johnson dipped his fingers into the baptismal font. "What sins weigh on your soul today, my child?"

Babe's breath came ragged. "This isn't how it ends," she snarled.

Muncie's laughter cracked like a whip. "Time your cupcake had some icing, you saucy little beefeater."

Father Johnson retrieved a stoneware jug from the aumbry. "Merlot. An excellent choice." He poured crimson wine into a gold chalice engraved with the word Sacrifice. "Now, who seeks absolution?"

Babe seized her shotgun and fired. The blast shattered the air, rattling the stained glass windows. Muncie's chest erupted in a spray of blood and fluttering bills.

Father Johnson stepped through the carnage, unshaken. He anointed Babe's forehead with holy water. "Persevere," he whispered. "God walks with you."

From the choir stalls, the bikers rose, voices in unison: "Surely goodness and mercy shall follow you all the days of your life, and you shall dwell in the house of the Lord forever."

The scene fractured.

Reality slammed into her like a fist to the chest.

Babe lay on the lake bed, the burlap sack still tangled around her. Her chest heaved. Each second tighter. The world dimmed. Then, hands. Strong. Yanking her upward.

Klarence's face appeared inches from hers, eyes dark, unreadable.

Her thoughts spun. *Why was he here?*

His arms locked around her, dragging her from the depths.

She fought. Panic flared. *Who the hell…*

The lake swallowed her scream as he kicked for the surface.

And then, daylight.

Chapter 49

Ariana's world narrowed to one thought: survival. Each step along Terminal Road sent jolts of pain through her battered body, every motion a brutal reminder of the crash. The sun dipped lower, humid air clinging to her like a shroud. Pain gnawed at her ribs, but she kept moving. The boat rental lay miles ahead, a mirage offering the barest flicker of hope. Still, dread churned beneath the surface. How would Babe react to the Corvette, wrecked beyond recognition? The memory of its mangled frame twisted her stomach.

Earlier, the roar of an engine had stopped her heart, but it was only a farming combine rounding the bend before disappearing down a dirt path. Relief had flooded her… but it hadn't lasted. Now, the Roadside Diner loomed ahead.

She froze.

The motorcycle gang was in the lot, loading their ruined choppers onto pickup trucks. Shouts and curses cracked through the air. Panic seized her chest.

Ariana dropped into a ditch, landing in muck and rotting leaves. Grit scraped her raw, but she didn't move. She lay there, unmoving, barely breathing. The towering 4x4s gave drivers a clear view of the ditch, if they happened to look. She couldn't risk staying there.

Dragging herself forward, inch by inch, sent fire through her limbs. But she kept going. When the diner finally vanished behind her, she clawed her way out, filthy and trembling.

The road ahead stretched empty. She set her jaw and pressed on. Whatever came next, she had to find Babe. Exhaustion had hollowed her out when she reached the boat rental. Each step dragged like dead weight. When she stumbled onto the sandy path by the lake, relief flickered at seeing a man working beside an empty boat trailer.

Rusty's eyes widened as he spotted her. He dropped his tools and rushed over just as Ariana collapsed to her knees, trembling. "Whoa, easy now," he said, crouching beside her. Concern flickered in his freckled face. "What happened to you?"

Between gasps, she told him about the bikers, the catcalls, the explosions, the crash, the crawl. With every word, Rusty's expression darkened.

"Those guys are bad news," he muttered. "You're lucky to be alive. Let's get you cleaned up." He helped her to the porch of the rental office and gestured to a wicker chair. "Sit. I'll grab some water."

"Wait." Ariana caught his arm. "My girlfriend, she came to rent a boat. Did you see her?"

Rusty frowned. "She left on foot."

"Did she say where?"

"Said something about exploring the lake. That's all I caught. Hang tight. I'll be right back."

Ariana sank into the chair as Rusty disappeared inside. Her gut twisted. If Babe had gone toward the campground, a boat might be her only shot at catching up.

Rusty returned with a dented mug of water and two white pills. "For the pain," he said, dropping them into her palm. He smiled a little too easily.

"What are these?" she asked. Something about his smile didn't match the concern in his eyes.

"Something from the first-aid kit," he said. "Should help with the aches."

Ariana nodded, shifting her weight as she adjusted her waistband. She raised the mug with one hand, the other brushing her lips. The water cooled her throat as she took a long sip. "Thanks," she murmured.

"Don't mention it." He glanced toward the road. "You should come inside, just in case those bikers swing back. Never know who might show up."

"I need to get to Bear Lake Campground," she said, firmer now. "Can you help me or not?"

He hesitated. "Might be safer to stay here. You could rest. Relax a little."

The way he said it sent alarm bells ringing in her head. "No," she snapped. "I need to cross the lake. Now."

"Better safe than sorry." He brushed dirt from her hair, his hand lingering just a moment too long.

She recoiled. "Don't touch me."

Rusty raised his hands in mock surrender, a grin tugging at his lips. "Chill. No need to bite my head off. Follow me." He grabbed a wooden oar from his ATV and led her to the battered aluminum boat. "Your future awaits," he said with mock drama. "Like you were never here."

Ariana stared at it. "This? Are you serious?"

"Think of it as rustic charm," Rusty said, pressing the oar into her hands. "It'll float."

As her fingers closed around the handle, her stomach knotted. He wasn't trying to help. This was a game to him. She was the mouse.

Before she could react, something moved at the edge of the lake.

A figure rose from the water, silhouetted in fading light. A burlap poncho clung to the soaked frame, giving it a ghostlike shimmer.

"Babe?" Ariana's voice cracked, equal parts disbelief and joy. "What the hell?"

Babe's eyes widened, taking in Ariana's bruises and grime. "Never mind me. What happened to you?"

"Long story. I'm fine. This guy gave me some pills." Ariana nodded toward Rusty.

Babe turned, her expression sharp. "What did you give her?"

Rusty shrugged and jerked his chin toward Klarence paddling away in a kayak. "Now that ain't even a real boat."

"Don't change the subject." Babe stepped closer. "Did you drug her?"

Rusty backed off, hands up. "Just a little pick-me-upper. Codeine, hydrocodone, tramadol, maybe aspirin. Think of it as a pharmaceutical potluck. She looked like she needed it."

The words barely left his mouth before Babe snatched the oar from Ariana's hands and cracked it against Rusty's shin.

He yelped and fled into the trees.

Babe tossed the oar into the boat. "Unbelievable. Second guy today to run off screaming."

Ariana let out a shaky laugh. "You really do have that effect on men. But seriously, what was that for?"

"You don't hand out mystery pills and walk away unscathed."

"Oh, I thought… never mind." Ariana stroked the burlap. "What's with the outfit?"

Babe sighed, adjusting the soggy poncho. "I'll explain later."

"Why are you even here? Weren't we meeting at the campground?"

"Why, aren't you happy to see me?" Babe chided.

"What? No, sweetie, never. Don't even say such a thing. I just meant—"

"Hey," Babe said with a laugh. "I'm just teasing. The guy who paddled me over said the owner gave him what he called the heebie-jeebies. Flat-out refused to go near the place."

"This place is like a magnet for creeps," Ariana muttered, her throat tightening. "Did you see Molly?"

Babe shook her head, silent tears slipping free.

Ariana pulled her into a hug. The warmth between them steadied her. Babe pulled back just enough to look her in the eye. "How many pills did you take?"

Ariana reached into the waistband of her jeans and pulled out two tablets. "Zero."

Babe blinked, then grinned. "That's my girl."

"Wasn't gonna swallow a pharmaceutical grab bag."

"Smart."

"I wrecked your car," Ariana whispered. "I'm sorry."

Babe pressed a finger to her lips. "Forget the car," she said softly. "You're alive. That's all that matters."

"You're not pissed?"

"Honey, it wasn't exactly my car."

"The fuck?"

"I borrowed it. People on an extended vacation."

"You what? I thought—"

"You're adorable," Babe said, brushing mud from her cheek. "Even if you look like something the cat dragged in."

Ariana chuckled. "Thanks for the vote of confidence."

Babe leaned in and kissed her. When they finally broke apart, Ariana frowned. "Wait. We don't even have a cat."

"We have each other," Babe said, brushing hair from her eyes. "That's all we need."

Ariana glanced at the wide, empty lake. "True. But we're still stranded."

Chapter 50

The late afternoon sun painted the sky in ominous shades of crimson as Constable Karl doubled over, vomiting onto the roadside beside his cruiser. He wiped his mouth with the back of his hand and groaned, his gut still churning. "Damn, Mama, what've you been puttin' in your stew?" he muttered, working to steady his breath.

A high-pitched whine cut through the air, wrenching him from his misery. Karl's bloodshot eyes snapped toward the sound.

A red ATV tore past, kicking up a cloud of dust. Two women clung to the quad as it zipped across the steel bridge and disappeared around a bend.

Karl straightened, duty flaring through him. This wasn't about some runaway waif, a so-called orphan, as Mr. Muncie had claimed. Nor were these women joyriders. No, they might be suspects in a robbery. And Karl was the man to handle it.

The thrill of enforcement lit him up. He pictured the confrontation in perfect detail: approaching the ATV with calm authority, spinning a cockamamie story about a gas station holdup. Whatever their truth, he'd extract it. He imagined their wide eyes as he snapped on the cuffs, their feeble attempts to wriggle free. He could already hear the women's protests: *We didn't do anything! You've got the wrong people!*

Heard it all before. Excuses. Sob stories. Lies. Oh yes, they'd learn. They all did. Karl called the shots, a lawman restoring order.

His stomach twisted again. He bent over, retching until nothing remained. Wiping his mouth on his sleeve, he pushed himself upright. Serving and protecting came first, no matter how bad he felt.

Karl climbed into the cruiser and started the engine. The low rumble calmed him. As he pulled onto the road, anticipation dulled the ache in his gut.

Rounding the final bend, his imagined triumph shattered. The red quad was nowhere in sight.

His jaw tightened. He scanned the landscape. Then he saw it: an abandoned ATV at the water's edge near the campground's office.

Karl hit the brakes and leapt out, boots crunching on the pebbled shore. He stormed toward the vehicle, then stopped.

No women. Just an empty quad, its engine ticking as it cooled.

His fists clenched. This wasn't how it was supposed to end. Not with him standing alone beside a deserted ATV while two suspects slipped away.

Movement flickered in the campground office window. His gut said they were inside. *God help them if they have alcohol or drugs.*

Karl took a breath. Justice didn't always come with fanfare, but tonight felt different. *What were they doing in there? Plotting their next move?*

He could see it: the women cornered, their escape plan falling apart. A grim smile tugged at his lips. He stepped toward the door.

Then it hit.

A violent cramp stabbed his gut. He doubled over, staggering back, clutching his stomach as bile surged up his throat. Sweat dripped from his brow as he gasped for air. He fought to keep his insides in.

Through blurred vision, Karl glared at the door. It loomed, mocking his weakness. *You're Constable Karl. Lawman to the core. No sickness, no setback keeps you down.* With a spit to clear his throat, he straightened. The night wasn't over. And neither was he.

He stepped forward, hand dropping to his holster. But as his fingers brushed the door handle, his gut twisted again. The pain hit like a bastard. This wasn't just nausea.

Not now. Not here.

Karl stumbled away, fumbling with his belt. Muncie's words rang in his skull: "Nobody wants shit running down their leg at the worst moment."

Cursing, he veered into a patch of bushes. Yanking down his pants, he crouched. This wasn't the triumphant scene he'd envisioned. It was just him squatting in the dark, pants around his ankles. If anyone saw him like this, they'd drag his name through the dirt and laugh him straight out of town.

His mother, too. *Mama Kaye might say he was never the son she'd hoped for. That was Klarence, always Klarence.*

Karl gritted his teeth, cursing the cramp, the night, and the whole damn world.

A hundred feet away, the tiny silver bell's metallic clink cut through the stagnant air of the Bear Lake Campground office. Ariana struck it again, fingers trembling with impatience. "Jesus H., where is this guy? We should've gone into town. This place is pathetic," she muttered, dropping her backpack onto the counter beside a sun-faded plaque: Whitey Whiteside, Proprietor. She rolled her eyes at the photo of Michelangelo's David above rows of tacky trinkets. The gaudy displays and cheap souvenirs felt like a personal insult. She tapped the bell again, frustration rising.

Behind her, Babe lingered near a mannequin wearing a rhinestone-studded jacket. Ariana cringed at the thought of wearing something so garish. Relief flickered when Babe turned to inspect a rack of plain blue coveralls, ugly but functional.

The door to the rear slammed open, the sharp sound echoing in the cramped space. Whiteside appeared, clutching a portable stereo like a shield. His sharp eyes flicked between them, suspicion etched into his features.

Ariana forced a smile. "About time. You must be the man," she said. "Planning on some musical accompaniment while we shop, Mr. Lightside?"

Whiteside's eyes flashed at the insult, though his expression remained neutral. "Folks around here call me Whitey. But you can call me anything, long as it ain't late for dinner."

Ariana ignored his lame attempt to be funny. "You might consider adding valet parking and hiring an interior designer," she suggested. "This place isn't exactly a luxury shopping destination."

Whiteside's polite facade cracked. "Whatever you say." He set the stereo on the counter with a deliberate thud and slid his hands into his pockets. His attention shifted to Babe. "This the girl you were lookin' for?"

"Does she look anything like the girl I was lookin' for?" Babe shot back, voice cold and cutting.

Whiteside's grin widened, his tone mocking. "Got tired of playin' cowboy and decided swamp witch was more your style, huh?"

Ariana's temper flared. "Excuse me, but there's no need for that attitude! How would you feel ending up somewhere, stripped naked, and forced to wear that… that rag?" She gestured toward Babe's burlap poncho.

Whitey let out a low chuckle, leaning against the counter. "Actually, I'd need more details. Who's takin' my clothes off, and where—?"

The front door slammed open.

Constable Karl stormed inside, each step heavy with hostility. Babe and Ariana recoiled as his eyes raked over their bodies. "Where are you two from?" Karl demanded, voice steely and sharp.

"Galoot," Babe said flatly, crossing her arms. "We're researching tree-climbing knuckle-draggers in remote areas."

Karl frowned. "Galoot? Never heard of it. Whitey, you know it?"

Whiteside scratched his head. "Maybe it's one of them frog towns in Quebec?"

Ariana drew in a breath and let out a loud, deliberate ribbit. Then another. The mocking sound echoed through the room. Her expression didn't change, but her eyes stayed locked on Karl's with icy defiance.

Karl sneered. "This one's got a smart mouth."

"Her friend's no crackerjack prize either," Whiteside muttered, trying to ingratiate himself with the constable.

Karl's patience snapped. "Let's see some identification."

Babe stepped forward, defiance burning in her eyes. "You don't have probable cause."

Karl's voice dropped, low and dangerous. "Did I ask for a lawyer? Whitey, did you hear me askin' for a lawyer?"

Whiteside forced a strained laugh, tapping the stereo like a lifeline. "Nope, not a word about lawyers. But hey, this stereo? It's got bass that'll knock your socks off. Great for parties, or interrogations!"

"Shut the fuck up, Whitey," Karl snapped, grabbing Ariana's arm with a crushing grip. He spun her around and snapped cuffs onto her wrists with ruthless efficiency. The cold steel bit into her skin.

Babe lunged. "Let her go, you sick—"

Karl's sucker punch landed squarely on Babe's face, snapping her head back. She crumpled, blood trickling from her nose.

"Babe!" Ariana screamed, voice breaking. She strained against the cuffs, tears blurring her vision. "Get away from her, you fucking monster! Leave her alone!"

Karl ignored her, turning to Whiteside. "Check the bag on the counter. Let's see where these sluts are from!"

Ariana sobbed, her voice raw. "Please, Babe, get up! Don't let him win! I can't do this without you!"

Whiteside hesitated, his hands hovering over the bag. His eyes darted between Karl and the women, fear creeping in.

Karl yanked Ariana closer, sneering. "You're a fucking ten, sweetheart. We're gonna teach Whitey here a little something about proper behaviour. He's got this crazy idea about lettin' folks love whoever they want. Says you can't change people any more than you can turn pigs into cows. Once we strip them filthy clothes off ya, we'll show him some good old-fashioned lovin'."

Ariana's terror froze her. Her wide eyes locked onto Babe stirring on the floor.

"Whitey," Karl barked. "Open that damn bag!"

Whiteside's shaking fingers fumbled with the clasps. He pulled out a gleaming silver .45 automatic. His face turned ashen. "Well, well," he stammered. "Look what we got here."

From the floor, Babe braced a hand against the counter and pushed up, her breath ragged. Her voice came rough and low. "It's my cigarette lighter."

The gunshot cracked like thunder.

Karl's head snapped back, skull erupting in a crimson spray. Blood splattered across Ariana's face, warm and sticky. She stood frozen, trembling.

Whiteside stared at the smoking barrel, mouth opening and closing like a gasping fish.

Babe shoved him aside. The stereo crashed to the floor and snapped on, its nursery rhyme warbling: "Lost my partner, what'll I do? Skip to my Lou, my dar—" She silenced it with a kick and pulled Ariana into her arms, her hands trembling as she stroked Ariana's blood-streaked hair. "Don't look at him, baby. I'm here. I've got you," she whispered, her voice cracking. She nearly asked where the gun had come from, but the gore smeared across Ariana's arms and that thousand-yard stare said it could wait.

Ariana buried her face in Babe's shoulder, sobs breaking free in ragged bursts.

Whiteside stumbled back, pale as a sheet, a dark stain spreading across his pants. "I… I didn't mean to—"

"No one ever does," Babe snapped. "Until everything goes sideways."

"It was an accident," he stammered. "I swear, it was an accident!"

Babe's stare cut through him like a blade. "Sure. And you think anyone's buying that? The guy called you out for accosting his brother, and now he's got no head." Her voice dropped, deadly quiet. "Klarence told me all about you. How you tried to cozy up to him with your wandering hands. You thought offering him candy would get you what you wanted? That kid is terrified to even step onto this property."

She stepped closer, voice low and dangerous. "You think any jury's gonna believe this was an accident?"

Whiteside's eyes darted toward the door, breath shallow. "I—what are you saying?"

"I'm saying you take a little vacation," Babe said. "We'll make it look like this dirtbag interrupted a robbery and got himself shot. Or…" she leaned in, "we tell the cops we overheard you bragging about how you planned to kill the fuck-stick."

"That's blackmail!"

"That's justice," she snapped. "Now decide. I don't have all fucking day."

A beat of hesitation, then Whiteside bolted for the door.

Ariana slumped to the floor, her voice barely above a whisper. "We're so screwed. We need to go home."

Babe crouched beside her, brushing the tears from Ariana's face with unsteady hands. "Sweetie, look at the bright side—"

"Bright side? Are you fucking kidding? We have no clothes and no car. Where exactly is this bright side? Cause I'm not seeing a whole lot of sunshine here!"

Babe tried smiling. "We've got free shopping for starters?"

Ariana let out a hollow laugh. "I can't do this. I can't stay here. We need to go home."

Babe's expression hardened. "We can't."

Ariana narrowed her eyes. "Can't? Or won't?"

"I know where Molly is."

"The fuck!? You knew this whole time?"

"I didn't know how to tell you," Babe said. "I was waiting for the right moment—"

"Oh, great timing! You wait until some guy's missing half his head. Peachy!" Her fists clenched. "You kept this from me?"

"I'm sorry." Babe caressed her cheek. "But if we turn back now, it's over. We've come too far. You need to trust me."

"I'm exhausted. All I want is to feel safe for five minutes. Do you get that?"

Babe nodded. "I do, I do. So will Molly, and that's why we can't stop. We're all she's got."

Ariana closed her eyes. Then: "You swear this isn't some wild guess?"

"I swear."

Ariana's voice steadied. "Then promise me something. You don't leave me behind. No matter what happens. We do this together."

Babe squeezed her hand. "Together."

"And there's one more promise you need to make..."

Chapter 51

Molly pressed her back against the bunkie's icy wall, the chill leaching into her bones despite the thin blanket draped over her shoulders. The cot sagged beneath her, its thin mattress stretched over a loose grid of metal wires that bowed under her weight. Damp wood and mildew choked the air, pressing into her lungs like wet rags. She tried to move, but her limbs felt as though they were detached from her body.

The drug coursing through her veins made thought slippery, like trying to hold water in cupped hands. Shadows twitched across the walls, flickering under the gooseneck lamp like they were alive. She curled her fingers into trembling fists, nails biting into her palms. *Stay awake. Hold on to something real.*

But the pain barely registered, smothered beneath the creeping fog. The milk. A gesture of supposed kindness from Muncie. Compassion wasn't in his DNA. Her chest tightened at the memory of his face: cold, smug, triumphant as he took her yellow cap. A trophy. She wasn't a person to him, just another thing to own.

Anger flared, cutting through the haze, then slipped away. The sedative pressed down harder, scattering her resolve like brittle leaves in a storm.

Where is Molly?

No. I am Molly.

Or maybe she wasn't. Perhaps she was already gone, sinking into the hollow space Muncie had carved out for her.

Fight, you stupid girl. He can never win.

She bit her lip hard. The sting flared. Her breath hitched, every inhale like drowning. She blinked, trying to stay conscious, but her vision blurred, and the edges of the room began to dissolve.

Somewhere beyond the walls, faint vibrations stirred. Metal shifted. A handle turned. The subtle mechanics of a door in motion. Real or imagined? The drug blurred the line. Her thoughts fractured.

The door banged open.

She flinched and forced her head up, vision swimming.

Ginger's keys jingled at her hip, the sound carrying a finality that made Molly's stomach drop. And that slick smile. The bitch knew she'd brought drugged milk and was proud of it. "Still not wearing the sweater? How disappointing," Ginger cooed.

Molly squinted, trying to focus.

"I see you've enjoyed your nightcap," Ginger continued. "Muncie thought you could use help unwinding." She perched on the edge of the cot, pressing the sagging mattress lower.

Molly's tongue was thick, the words slurring. "What… do you want?"

Ginger leaned in, breath sour against her cheek. "What do I want?" she echoed sweetly. "Honey, it's not about me. It's about Muncie. Always dreaming big. Always finding ways to make an impact."

Molly caught a glint of something behind Ginger's eyes. Devotion, maybe. Or delusion.

"And now?" Ginger went on, "We're on the brink of something huge."

Molly's pulse stumbled. Panic threaded through her sluggish veins. She tried to push back against the drug's grip, but it clung like tar. "Muncie… doesn't own me," she rasped.

Ginger's brittle laugh cracked the air. "Oh, honey. You're his latest project. But not just any project. You're valuable. He's got big plans for you." She pulled something burgundy from her bag. Leather. The tails of a flogger swayed like venomous snakes.

"We start simple," Ginger murmured, running it across her palm. "Just a little tease. A hint of skin. Enough to pull them in. Soft lighting, white linens, the illusion of desire. All tied together with a little whack here and there."

Ginger's words coiled around Molly's throat. "You're sick," she spat.

Ginger stood. "This is about power," she said. "Muncie gets it. Soon, you will too. This is your moment to shine." She let the flogger arc lazily through the air. "It's about suggestion, not pain."

She reached down and tugged back the blanket. A rancid odour wafted up. "For fuck's sake!" She bolted outside, gagging, and slammed the door hard enough to rattle the frame.

Silence returned.

Molly lay still, exhausted. They'd tried to break her. Strip her of dignity. But they didn't own her. The drug would wear off. The bruises would heal. And when the time came to run, she'd be ready.

If they tried to stop her… she'd make them choke on it.

Chapter 52

The shower at Whiteside's campground had washed off the grime but not the unease. Babe and Ariana stepped out of Karl's patrol car into a forest clearing thick with shadow. The air smelled damp and metallic, with the promise of rain. Both women wore blue coveralls swiped from the campground office, which, as Ariana put it, made them look like fugitives in a low-budget film.

"If you keep stealing police cars, the cops might have to start using Uber," Ariana said, eyeing the two unmarked cruisers parked nearby.

"Never mind that," Babe said, yanking open the trunk. A sound sliced through the thick canopy. She froze, her gaze fixed on the woods. Something shifted, a whisper of movement in the underbrush. The forest felt too close. Too aware. The trees, dark and gnarled, leaned in as if listening. A prickle crawled up her spine. Her voice dropped. "Did you hear that?"

"There's nothing." Ariana pointed at the deepening bruise on Babe's cheek. "That's twice someone's clocked you. Does it hurt?"

Babe's fingers grazed the tender skin. Her jaw tightened. She'd taken harder hits before and from people who'd meant worse. But it wasn't the welt that lingered; it was the way Ariana had looked at her back at the campground. As if she wasn't sure who Babe was or maybe didn't want to know. "I've had worse," Babe said. She didn't say more. Didn't trust herself to. The pain was simple. It was the stuff underneath that got messy.

Ariana eyed the two bandoliers coiled in the trunk, brass tips catching the dim moonlight filtering through the canopy. "Looks like someone was gearing up for action." She grabbed one and tossed it to Babe. "Here, put this on. You'll look like an action hero saving the world."

Babe caught it one-handed as Ariana lifted a Mossberg 500 from the trunk. Her grip wavered, just slightly, but enough. "We could take down a bear with this thing. Dual extractors, steel-to-steel lockup," she said, forcing confidence into her voice.

Babe raised an eyebrow. "How do you know that?"

Ariana ran a finger along the barrel. "Research for my film, *Barbarian Babes Break Free.*"

Babe caught the slight tremor in Ariana's hand, the way her voice dipped like she was trying too hard to sound casual.

"Damn it," Ariana cried.

"What now?"

"I broke a nail," Ariana complained, holding up her middle finger. "I do some of my best work with this digit. Don't you think?"

Babe ignored her, her attention back to the forest. The underbrush shifted again. A slow, deliberate movement. She flinched. "Did you hear that?"

"If you ask me that again, I'll punch you myself and make it a hat trick."

"Don't you mean a trifecta?"

"Fine, whatever. Call it an owie." Ariana sighed. "But seriously, why would Dopey D turn on Molly like that? She's his daughter." She gestured toward her coveralls. "And for the record, I haven't complained once about that dreadful roll-on deodorant we found in her knapsack."

Babe reached into the trunk and pulled out two pizza signs. "He's a politician." Her voice had gone cold. "They'll do anything to keep slurping at the trough without getting caught. Molly must know something that could ruin him." She didn't say the other part. The part clawing at her ribs. That Molly might already be dead. That there'd be no saving her this time. She had made promises before. And broken them. But this time was different. Failure wasn't an option.

Babe twisted the cap off a tube of red lipstick. "Interrogate Choi. See what she gives up."

Ariana's head snapped up. "Interrogate? You mean like *interrogate* interrogate?"

"I'm tired of her shit. It's our best option." Babe gestured vaguely. "Just improvise. Like I pretended to be you with those bikers. Turned out pretty good, if I do say so myself."

Ariana shook her head. "Who the hell are you? That guy at the campground didn't know whether to shit or wind his watch. He probably thought you'd shoot him."

Babe shrugged. "Who cares? Which reminds me, I'm still waiting for you to address the elephant in the room."

Ariana crossed her arms. "First, you talk about cats being dragged in, and now it's elephants. What room are you even talking about?"

"The gun."

"Oh. Right." Ariana scratched at the fabric of her coveralls. "Well, remember Gomsie, the prop guy who got us that old lady mannequin? He said it could be modified into a lighter. I thought it'd be a nice gift since yours is shot. No pun intended."

Babe snorted. "Sweetheart, you can't believe everything you hear. Besides, that thing's got a hair trigger. We're lucky it didn't go off again." She straightened, flicking her chin toward the cruiser. "Now, off you go and quiz that cougar."

Ariana rolled her eyes. "Stop with the animal references; you're making me crazy." She wiped her sweaty palms on her coveralls and popped the trunk of Choi's cruiser.

Choi's dark eyes snapped up at her.

Ariana smiled. "Evening, sunshine. Rough day? Mine's been a bitch. You're probably thinking this is the moment when everything turns into something very, very bad."

Choi mumbled behind the gag, her body tensing.

Ariana sighed. "Babe, I think she's ready to talk." Without waiting for a reply, she yanked the fabric free.

Choi sucked in the air. Her voice came out thin and shaky. "Who... who are you?"

Ariana tilted her head. "Who do you want me to be?" She turned over her shoulder. "Babe! She wants to know who I am."

Babe crouched by the cruiser, carefully printing on the pizza sign with slow, deliberate strokes of lipstick. "Tell her to use her imagination."

Ariana turned back, flashing Choi a grin. "You heard the lady."

"I heard her," Choi snapped, irritation flickering through the fear.

Ariana wagged a finger. "No need to get testy. We're all friends here. Civil discourse and all that."

"Yes. Sorry. My bad," Choi muttered. She swallowed and shifted her tone. "Look, I'm not gonna fight you. Just take the cuffs off. Shut the trunk, and I won't run. My feet are zip-tied."

Ariana cocked her head, shooting Babe a questioning glance.

"This isn't a negotiation," Babe replied, her voice dry as rustling leaves.

Ariana turned back. "Sorry, Lieutenant. Doesn't look like you're getting the point of this exercise."

"At least take this tire out," Choi blurted, indicating the spare crammed beside her. "I'll tell you everything I know about Molly and the mayor."

Ariana crossed her arms. "Fine. Let's hear it."

Choi drew a steady breath. "The mayor… he has a secret. Word is, he's been dressing in women's clothes for years. Molly must've threatened to expose him. That's probably why he's so desperate to stop her."

Ariana raised an eyebrow. "Dickie Darnell's a cross-dresser? Huh. That hardly qualifies as being a bad guy. I'd even be willing to bet he gets better discounts on outfits than I do."

Choi's lips tightened. "Bad optics. His voter base wouldn't stand for it."

Ariana's grin faded. "People vote for morons and con artists." Her voice sharpened. "What does that tell you? Are you done, or do I slam this trunk shut?"

"Molly was supposed to meet Chief Brisk. He said he had something life-changing to tell her. That's all I know," Choi blurted.

"The police chief is dead."

Choi's eyes widened. "What? No, you're lying!"

Ariana's mouth curled, voice mockingly slow. "Shall I quote the illustrious Mr. Dickens? 'Old Marley was as dead as a doornail.'"

Choi closed her eyes.

Ariana leaned in, voice dropping to a whisper. "Try anything funny, and I'll personally arrange for you to hook up with your boss. Got it?"

Choi nodded stiffly.

Ariana set her gun aside, grabbed the tire, and yanked it from the trunk. It rolled away and toppled over with a dull thud that echoed too loudly in the quiet clearing. "There. Better? Now, promise to keep quiet, and I won't gag you again."

Choi's lips parted—hesitantly.

"Practicing ventriloquism?" Ariana asked. "Because I didn't see your lips move."

"Yes! I promise!" Choi blurted, her voice cracking. She shifted, struggling to sit up.

Ariana yanked down the trunk lid, cracking it against Choi's skull with a brutal thud. The lieutenant slumped sideways into the well of the trunk, eyes rolling back. "Okay… I guess that's a wrap on Choi," Ariana said, pressing the lid down with both hands until it latched. She grabbed the Mossberg and headed back to Babe. "You catch all that?"

Babe, setting the pizza sign on the hood of Karl's cruiser, didn't look up. "Doesn't change anything."

"We should grab a car and go home," Ariana suggested, shifting the shotgun. "This Muncie guy's probably long gone with Molly."

Babe didn't blink. "He's an arrogant prick. Thinks he's untouchable. Plus, he'll never suspect we're coming. He thinks I'm dead."

"Good point. What about the promise you made me?"

Babe tensed. "What? Here? Now?"

"You thought I'd forget?"

Babe scowled, yanked a pack of cigarettes from the sun visor, and turned it over in her palm before chucking it into the bushes. "Happy?"

"Happy isn't listed under cancer warnings."

"Whatever." Babe moaned.

Ariana shifted the shotgun and grabbed one of the pizza signs. "Two fearless women embark on a deadly mission where courage meets anarchy."

Babe snorted. "That from one of your movies?"

"No, it just sounded cool." Ariana shrugged. "I left out the part about our odds of surviving being piss poor."

"Smart move." Babe picked up the other sign, thinking piss poor sounded about right.

They set off through the woods, boots crunching against damp earth, pizza signs swinging like a parody of something noble. Shadows thickened as the trees loomed higher, branches knitting into a canopy that choked out the last traces of moonlight.

Ariana glanced at Babe. "Just so we're clear if this goes sideways, you take the blame."

"Sure. Say it was all me. Wouldn't want to ruin your sterling reputation."

Before Ariana could respond, a branch snapped. Then another. The sound was deliberate, like something big moving through the underbrush.

Ariana's breath caught. "What the hell was that?"

Babe felt the night press in, heavy with the weight of something unseen. "Yeah. I heard it."

Another snap. Closer this time.

Babe glanced at Ariana. Her grip on the gun was rigid, her eyes wide with panic. Babe's voice dropped to a whisper. "Let's keep moving."

The shadows swallowed them as they pressed forward.

Behind them, something followed.

Chapter 53

Molly moved through a lush forest, golden light filtering through the trees. The scent of blooming flowers hung heavy in the air. Her steps made no sound, the moss underfoot thick and slick as flesh. A strange calm settled over her, but unease coiled beneath the surface, tight as wire pulled taut.

Up ahead, a figure shimmered into view, emerging from the radiance. Wings soft, white robes glistening like oil on water.

Babe.

Her voice floated through the trees. "I'm sorry I left," she said. "But I'm here now."

Molly blinked. She wanted to believe her. Needed to. But she didn't.

"We are sisters in pain," Babe continued, her tone too smooth, too knowing. It wrapped around Molly like silk. The light surrounding her pulsed with her heartbeat, a steady thrum syncing with her fear. "Don't be afraid. I'm here to guide you." Babe extended a hand. Her eyes didn't blink. "While you slept, I saw the lines. Threads winding beneath you, pulling toward something greater."

Molly's fingers twitched. She didn't want to reach for them, but she did. Her hand brushed the invisible threads, and everything flared white.

Now, she was on a mountaintop, a golden city sprawled below. Spires glinted. Rivers snaked like molten glass. The air tasted like joy.

But something was wrong.

Dark shapes slithered at the edges of her vision. Limbs where no limbs should be, eyes staring from impossible places. Faint filaments crisscrossed the sky, strung like cords humming with trapped energy. Whispers slid into her ears in a language she didn't know but somehow understood.

Trust what you see.

A shadow swept over the city, tracing railway tracks cutting between the buildings. Molly drew back, her breath catching. The

184

world dissolved, and she stumbled into a room pulsing with light. The walls thrummed, alive with a low, constant vibration. She lurched toward the window. Outside, hydro lines sagged across the sky, dark against a bruised backdrop. Trees shimmered too bright, their leaves sharp as blades. A beauty so sharp it could cut her open.

The door creaked.

Babe stepped in, wearing Molly's discarded coveralls. Her skin was a deep blue, smooth as porcelain. Her eyes shone, backlit with something ancient.

Molly froze.

But Babe smiled. A smile that said, *This is safe. Trust me. Obey.* "You're still afraid," Babe said, moving closer. "It's okay. I'm here to help." Her voice oozed like syrup, slow and heavy, laced with something she couldn't place.

Molly didn't want to believe her. She reached anyway. A jolt of heat surged through her, electric and wrong, sending them running through an alien forest. Grotesque creatures shifted between the trees. Some floated, others crawled. Faint cords of light threaded between branches, twisting into the bodies of the creatures like veins.

They reached a circular tent. At its center pulsed a glowing orb, tendrils of light or roots or cables spilling out, tangled in the dirt.

"Touch it," Babe urged. Her eyes gleamed like glass.

Molly hesitated, then obeyed. Her fingers skimmed the surface, and she rose into a cloud with a golden city spread beneath them, perfect and too clean. Babe hovered beside her, smiling wide.

Then the sky bled red. The buildings twisted. Streets folded like wires coiling into themselves. The city melted into a nightmare. And from the wreckage, it emerged. A thing of mouths. Of hunger. Of him.

Muncie.

Tentacles lashed out. One wrapped around Molly, dragging her down. She screamed, her hands burning with heat she didn't understand. She raised her arms and tried to destroy the creature.

Babe's voice rang out. "That's not what we're here for."

Molly's hands pulsed, a flash of light surging outward as she pushed him away.

Muncie's form flickered like static on an old TV until the vision fractured.

Molly jolted awake, heart hammering, breath tight in her chest. The bunkie's cold wall pressed against her back. The air was heavy, real, and wrong. Her hands didn't glow. The golden city was gone.

But the dream clung to her. Not the images. Not the voices. It was the message.

Don't wait to be saved. You know how to save yourself.

Now, she'd follow through on what the vision revealed.

Chapter 54

Muncie leaned against the kitchen counter, thumbing through the stack of bills stuffed in the green envelope Slim had delivered. Across the room, Ginger stood at the sink, peeling a hard-boiled egg with quick, angry flicks. The shell shattered in her grip, shards clinging to her damp fingers. Tension crackled between them.

"Bonus, incentive, whatever it's supposed to be in Canadian money," Muncie whined. "Why are they screwing with me? Probably Miss Horn is behind it. Always working an angle. She's a real piece of work."

"Planning a shopping spree, Muncie?" Ginger snapped. "It's found money. You're the one with issues respecting people, not her."

"Slim says a marshal might be sniffing around." He kept his tone easy, but his eyes cut toward her, watching.

"A marshal? This is what it's come to? Marshals now? He should've warned us when he was here."

Muncie shrugged tossing the envelope onto the counter. He'd debated whether to tell her. Now that he had, her reaction told him he'd guessed wrong. "Slim's always been passive-aggressive."

Ginger laughed, brittle as the eggshells in her hand. "Passive?" She sucked in a breath through clenched teeth. "He didn't seem too passive when my tongue was—" She caught herself. Her face twisted.

"Enough," Muncie snapped. "We've got ways to handle it."

"Like that explosion in town?" Ginger slammed the egg onto the counter, fragments scattering across the laminate. Her knuckles whitened around the edge of the sink. "That's what you call handling it? You turned Moosetown into a trauma zone."

Muncie sliced the air with a hand. "We were releasing pressure. How the hell was I supposed to know the pipeline would blow?"

"You're missing the point," she said, palm smacking the counter. "We shouldn't have done any of it. And we sure as hell shouldn't have taken her."

He folded his arms. "Oh, right, so your plan was what? Snatch her from the campground while they sat around singing Kumbaya? The ice cream parlour was the perfect lure. The explosion was just a bonus."

"Perfect?" Ginger threw up her hands. Bits of eggshell clung to her fingers. "Slim's not getting us out of this. He's a moron, Muncie. No one's coming."

"Trust me, Ginger. I'll come up with something."

She barked a laugh. No humour in it. "Trust you?" She shook her head, then swept the shells off the counter. "I wasn't born yesterday."

"I'm fifteen; I just look older," squawked Risqué from the windowsill.

Ginger spun, glaring like a blade. "One more word, and I swear—"

"Take it easy," Muncie said, chuckling. "He's just a bird."

"Then deal with him before I do," she snapped, spinning back toward Muncie. "And speaking of distractions, did you get anything out of the one you took boating while I was stuck with Stinky Leroux? Whatever you drugged her with, she smells like a swamp full of dead fish."

His grin faltered. "Let's just say she didn't leave dressed for success." He paused. "But Molly's the real problem. She's a loose end."

"She's Dickie Darnell's kid," Ginger said tightly. "That's not just a loose end."

"She's leverage." Muncie's voice turned hard. "Don't get sentimental."

Ginger's hands clenched. "What happened to us, Muncie? We used to stand for something."

"We still stand for something. Survival. That's all that's left. No wall behind us anymore, just the drop."

"No, Muncie. That's what makes you a coward." Her voice had an edge you could bleed on. "You'd sacrifice anyone." She slammed the counter. "I've had enough. I did what you wanted. I'm done."

The silence thickened.

She turned toward the trash. Her eyes locked on an empty condom box, *Big Boys*, near the bin. Her stomach twisted. "What the hell is this doing here?"

Muncie grinned. "Special order for Klarence."

Her lip curled. She grabbed the box and hurled it at Risqué. It missed by inches. "You're disgusting."

"Was that rhetorical?"

"I swear to God—"

"We're in too deep," Muncie cut in. "There's no turning back. I'm going to chop some wood. Clear my head."

Ginger crossed her arms, voice shaking with fury. "Maybe you're right. Maybe there's no going back. But don't think I'll let you drag me down with you."

Muncie exhaled hard through his nose. "Survival's all that matters, Ginger. The rest?" He sneered. "Fairy tales."

Tears glistened in her eyes. "There has to be more than this."

"Need me to tweak your meds?"

Her hands trembled. "And this bullshit having me load firewood? You treat me like a dog."

Risqué mimicked the screech of tires, followed by a yelp.

Ginger snapped. She grabbed the flogger off the counter and cracked it straight at Risqué. Feathers burst. The bird shrieked and tumbled in a flurry of wings and panic.

Muncie didn't flinch.

"Deal with your only friend," she hissed. "Looks like he finally learned to mimic your conscience." She stormed out, slamming the door hard enough to rattle the windows.

Stillness returned, dense and smothering. Muncie turned to the window, jaw tight. Moonlight cast long shadows across the yard.

Risqué stirred, voice child-like: "K-K-Klarence keeps secret long-long time."

Chapter 55

A light rain pattered against the tinted windows of the black limousine as it prowled through the shadowed streets of the city. Miss Horn sat across from Mayor Dickie, shifting in his seat, wig askew, crimson nails drumming on the thumb drive Slim had delivered. "We're dancing on razors," Dickie said, unease thick in his voice. "One wrong step…"

Miss Horn's eyes gleamed under the dim interior lights. "What's the move, MD?"

Dickie leaned forward, clammy fingers tightening around her arm. "We thought we could silence The Remedy, but after seeing that footage, and now a U.S. Marshal sniffing around, thanks to that meddling reporter, Babe Lincoln…" He slumped back, head dropping to his chest. "It's all unravelling. That video was supposed to be our ace."

"We've weathered worse." Her voice slid through the car, smooth as velvet, a predatory smile curling her lips. She tapped a stylus against her iPad. "Leverage, MD, is more than just a simple scandal."

Dickie groaned, covering his face with a manicured hand. "Angel wings, clown shoes, and that redhead doing things with her tongue that would make a sailor blush. It's a circus of depravity, Miss Horn." His voice rose, sharp and desperate. "We need The Remedy back. Now. You'll go to Canada. Make it happen."

She tilted her head. Feigned regret, paper-thin. "A pity we'll need to postpone my grand debut, but you are correct, as usual. The True North awaits." It took everything not to laugh in his face. Going to Bear Lake had never been part of her plan.

One call to her deadbeat husband could end Molly's captivity, but that was never the point. The girl's abduction orchestrated by Dickie at Miss Horn's subtle urging had been another chess piece in play. Silencing Molly to protect Dickie's political career had never mattered. This was about tightening the noose around his neck.

All he needed was to feel the fear of the unknown.

And now, the man she hired with a camera would deliver the final blow. Soon, the footage of Dickie cross-dressing inside the strip club would become the ultimate leverage. Maybe she'd even make him ride up front in the limo now and then, a little reminder of who held the leash. And while he squirmed under her direction, her ascent to power would continue uninterrupted. Dominance hovered just beyond her grasp, so close she could taste it. After all, one could never have too much ammunition when the opportunity to advance presented itself.

The limo eased to a stop, the traffic having thinned with the late hour. Neon lights from the posters of scantily clad women outside Lollipops cast garish streaks across Dickie's face, deepening the strain etched into his features. "That bastard, Brisk," he muttered, almost to himself. "If ever we needed him in our pocket, it would be tonight."

Miss Horn's placid smile masked her satisfaction. Chief Brisk's untimely death was nothing more than an inconvenience, and Dickie's ignorance of the fact didn't matter. She could have bent him to her will, too, but her plan was already in motion. "Your focus is admirable, MD," she said, her voice a practiced purr.

Dickie tugged at his wig, jaw tight. "This isn't about prevention anymore, Miss Horn. It's survival. Politics is a food chain, and I've clawed my way to the top." His voice dropped to a conspiratorial whisper. "I can only hope you'll forgive me for exposing your husband's... proclivities. But with his brother pulling these stunts, I assumed he'd be the reasonable one. Clearly, I miscalculated—"

"Spare me, MD," Miss Horn cut in, her honeyed tone turning brittle. "Muncie is a stranger to me. Slim's assurances were naïve at best." Her lies flowed with the ease of a seasoned performance. Muncie's incompetence, and her husband's, had never surprised her. They were pawns, perfectly placed in her grand design.

"Your loyalty is priceless, Miss Horn," Dickie murmured, his eyes lingering on the bare skin revealed below the hem of her skirt as she reached for the door. "One more thing. If Chief Brisk asks why I want the police uniforms, what should I say?"

"Simple. You've connected with a couple of girls on stage who are hosting a private party, and they want to do some role-playing. Tell him you'll make sure he gets an invitation once the date is set. He'll eat it up."

"Good plan. Are you sure I look presentable?"

She rested a hand over his, a soft squeeze meant to offer quiet reassurance. "You look better than presentable. I couldn't be more pleased. Take a moment to settle yourself, then make us proud."

Dickie responded with a thumbs-up, his painted nails catching the faint glow of the interior light.

The cool night air swept into the limo as she stepped out, crisp with possibility. She paused, silhouetted against the glowing entrance, where music pulsed, and posters promised fantasies few could afford. "Once again, good luck, MD," she said, shutting the door with quiet finality.

Her heels clicked as she walked, her mind humming with the elegance of a flawless plan. Pulling out her phone, she whispered into the device, "The package has arrived. He should be inside within ten minutes."

Disconnecting, she let the anticipation bloom. Dickie's face when confronted with the photos would be devastating. Christmas morning couldn't compare.

Ahead, a shadow loomed, long and menacing, cutting across the dim alley. "Are you ready for how this is gonna end?" a gruff voice rumbled.

Miss Horn's pulse quickened as she stepped out of the light.

Otis stepped forward, his bulk swallowing the narrow space. Sweat trailed from his temples, glistening under the alley light. "I tipped off News 4 about Dopey Darnell's kid. Where's my money?"

Miss Horn didn't flinch. "And you thought this was the best way to handle it?"

Otis sneered, taking another step. His size filled the alley, his presence oppressive. "I didn't come here for small talk." His voice dropped, thick with threat. "Where's my dough?"

Her fingers brushed the cool metal inside her bag. A flick of the wrist. A silver blur in the darkness.

The jab was swift. Otis lurched back, a strangled groan escaping as his hands shot to his eye. He staggered and dropped like a dead weight, writhing and howling.

Miss Horn watched him, lips curling into a faint smile. "Consider this the end of your story, Otis. You were always a bad investment."

The stylus, its tip streaked with red, vanished into her bag after a quick swipe against his shirt. She stepped over him as if he were nothing more than discarded trash.

The night was far from over.

One thread had been cut, but others were tightening, tangled and just out of sight.

Chapter 56

Babe and Ariana tore from the forest, moon shadows knifing across Nine Mile Road. Ariana's fingers skimmed the bandolier, her eyes sharp, darting. She shot Babe a look, pupils blown wide with fear. "This rescue mission… we could be dead in seconds."

"I think we're beyond that. Not to mention we discussed this already," Babe said. She crouched beside the bald eagle ornament marking Muncie's laneway, passed her shotgun to Ariana, and propped up Constable Karl's pizza signs.

Ariana scowled at the lipstick-scrawled sign, scratching her temple. One read Free, the other Fruit, with a bold arrow pointing in the direction of Muncie's estate. A shadow of doubt crossed her face. "You sure about this?" she whispered.

"Stop with the questions. It's a diversion," Babe replied, scanning the woods. "Around here, people notice every out-of-place thing. When Muncie's forced to deal with that, it'll buy us time."

"Shouldn't it say what kind of fruit?"

"Fantastic idea," Babe deadpanned. "Let's add some doodles. Maybe a neon arrow too. Want to head back to the campground gift shop?"

"Fine! No need to go full psycho." Ariana glanced back to the road. "Do you think someone was following us?"

"They're not here. That's what counts."

"What about that lieutenant? We can't just leave her in the trunk."

"We grab Molly first. Then swing back and cut her loose."

"She'll bust us!"

"Choi's got no authority here. It's our word against hers. The chief's dead with no one to back her up. As they say, fuck her and the horse she rode in on."

"Who even says that?"

"No idea. Enough talking." Babe's whisper turned razor-sharp. "We circle through the woods, hide, and watch. Timing is everything."

Babe's grip on the shotgun was iron, her knuckles pale in the dark.

"Remember," Ariana warned, "those are real bullets. Don't get stupid."

A dangerous flicker lit Babe's eyes. "Don't they say in the movies, 'Kill 'em all and let God sort it out'?"

"Since when is this an action flick?"

An engine growled in the distance. Both women went rigid.

"Down!" Babe ordered.

They hit the tall switchgrass hard, lungs cinched tight.

A battered blue tractor rolled past on Nine Mile Road, its elderly driver in overalls and a straw hat humming a tune.

Babe sighted down the barrel, tracking the farmer like prey.

"Have you lost your damn mind?" Ariana hissed. "He's just a farmer."

"Could be a decoy," Babe whispered, finger twitching near the trigger.

"We're here to save, not slaughter."

The tractor rumbled away.

"Fine. Whatever." Babe lowered the weapon.

Ariana swatted at a mosquito near her ear. "We had a store full of bug spray, but here we are, live bait."

"Let's go," Babe ordered. They bolted into the trees, vanishing into the dark. Thunder rolled like an oncoming war drum, lightning slicing the sky in jagged streaks. Mosquitoes swarmed, their high-pitched whine drilling into Ariana's skull.

"A whole store of bug spray," she muttered, slapping her arm. "And we're the special."

"You said that already," Babe snapped, eyes sweeping the darkness. "Quit whining."

Ariana bent forward, clawing at her backside. "These mosquito bites feel like hell."

"Power through. We're close." The air reeked of rot and pine sap, thick and cloying, coating her throat like oil. Lightning slashed through the canopy, casting shadows that twisted like lurking predators. A rustle snapped to their left. Babe didn't hesitate, shotgun up, eyes locked on the sound.

A pheasant exploded from the shrubs, wings flapping as it vanished into the dark.

Ariana gasped, a cry escaping before she clamped her jaw shut. She dropped to one knee, pain twisting her face. "My ankle again!"

Babe dropped beside her. "Let me see." She helped Ariana up, an arm around her waist. "Can you walk?"

Ariana gritted her teeth, easing pressure onto the joint. "Give me a minute. If I can't, leave me behind."

"I'll carry you before that happens."

Ariana's voice wavered, raw with pain. "I love you. Don't be mad," she said, voice trembling as much from pain as fear. She tried to smile, but it faltered. "If this goes sideways—"

"Not happening," Babe cut in, firm as steel. "Not tonight. Not ever. I've got you. Always."

She studied the sweat beading on Ariana's face. "Is it that bad?"

"No," Ariana said, forcing a weak grin. "I just really need to pee."

They had no way of knowing that just a few hundred yards away, Molly's bloodied fingers trembled as she worked a bent wire against the unyielding lock on the bunkie's steel door. Her mind clawed through the drugged haze, forcing focus. A hysterical giggle threatened to rise as she recalled childhood jokes with Babe about inserting wires where they didn't belong. The cot's wire mesh had yielded the tool she needed, but at a price. Thin red lines etched her palms.

CLICK.

The lock surrendered. Her pulse spiked. She eased the door open, the moon casting treacherous shadows across the grass. Muncie's threats tried to paralyze her, but the siren call of freedom pushed her forward.

Her plan was madness: cut across the estate, plunge into the lake, and swim. No searching for boat keys. No hesitation. Just a life jacket and raw determination.

A memory flickered. Ginger, in the blow-up pool, ankle monitor catching the sun. Molly latched onto the thought: Water disrupts the ankle bracelet's signal. It was a long shot, but it might be her only one.

A porch creak stabbed panic through her ribs as she adjusted the navy sweater Ginger provided. Her yellow cap lay in the Muskoka chair, tempting her to grab it. No. Bright colours meant being seen.

Across the inky stretch of Bear Lake, distant cottage lights flickered like salvation. The ankle monitor, once her shackle, would now be the evidence that could burn them all, if she made it.

Belly to the ground, she crawled. Shadows writhed, warping the landscape into a battlefield of lurking figures. The kitchen window loomed like a glassy, unblinking eye. *What if someone looked out?*

The brush bordering the shoreline promised cover. Mosquitoes descended, their bites burning, but she dared not swat them. Sweat slicked her skin as she crept forward, chest tight, every nerve screaming.

The cottage's back door slammed.

Lightning forked across the sky, illuminating Muncie heading to the woodpile, axe in hand. Molly's stomach hollowed. No alternate route. *I shouldn't have rushed.*

She had miscalculated. Trapped too early in the night, she had only guessed at Muncie's schedule. She should have known that Ginger had mentioned his evening wood-chopping routine, the one where he roped in Klarence, some dim-witted guy living next door. A flicker of absurdity crossed her mind. Klarence, with a K. It sounded made up. But reality had twisted into something more surreal than any lie.

A screech split the air.

Risqué swooped down, claws gripping Muncie's shoulder, giving Molly the slightest crack of opportunity.

She seized it.

Rolling hard, she plunged into the thick foliage.

Then, a figure on the dock.

Ginger.

The flogger dangled from her hand, its leather tails trailing the water's surface like a lazy predator waiting for its moment.

Molly froze. Every nerve screamed. So close. So goddamn close. But now, pinned between a madman with an axe and a woman who enjoyed the suffering of others. Molly had no good options.

Risk everything in a sprint for the water? Or crawl back, surrender, and face whatever horrors awaited? The night thickened, pressing against her skin like a second, suffocating hide. Every second stole another inch of her chances. Her mind clawed for a miracle, but the brutal truth remained: Her escape had led her straight into a trap of her own making. And there might be no way out.

Chapter 57

Candlelight flickered, casting elongated shadows across Mama Kaye's weathered face, reflected in the cracked wall mirror. She yanked her stained dentures from a nearby jar and snapped them into place before dragging a comb through her mullet. "Slo-Joe!" she barked, glaring at Mechanic Joe, slumped in the corner of the bedroom. His vacant eyes and sagging posture bore the cruel evidence of the freezer's toll. "You been listenin' to me?"

After a moment of scrutiny, Mama Kaye frowned and smoothed the front of her white party dress with rough hands. His mind had likely buckled under the strain, and the odds of his recovering seemed nonexistent. But Mama Kaye had more urgent worries. The day's events spun in her thoughts, refusing to quiet even under the influence of homegrown weed. Two strange women had appeared asking about Americans. Slo-Joe had ended up in her freezer. And Muncie's nieces had performed that crazed dance. Worst of all, the nagging uncertainty surrounding Klarence, the apple of her eye, gnawed at her.

She paced across the creaking floorboards, her bare feet pressing into the cool wood. The blonde waif's words lingered, pulling her focus back to Muncie. "What's your game, Muncie?" she muttered under her breath, her voice dropping into a low growl.

She considered the axe resting by the doorframe, a blunt reminder of her capacity for decisive action. The handle had worn smooth from years of use, the blade dull but still effective. Her late husband would attest to that, had he not been buried out in the yard.

She shoved thoughts of him aside and turned her focus to Karl. The boy had always been trouble. Once shot out a deputy's headlights just to watch him swerve. His recklessness had pushed her to the edge more times than she cared to count, and yet here she was, defending him.

"Klarence is family," she reminded herself. That's what mattered. Not what the girl had said. Not the things she'd noticed. He was hers. Her narrowed eyes bored into Mechanic Joe, still slumped on the floor, motionless as a rag doll. "Karl should give a damn."

"Muncie'll face the music tonight," she growled, shoving her feet into battered work boots. "Time for answers." She grabbed the foil-wrapped Tupperware of Muncie's forgotten food—it would serve as her excuse for the visit.

Mechanic Joe wouldn't do for this trip. His usefulness would come later. Yard boy, maybe? She hadn't decided. For now, the man was just furniture.

Mama Kaye hit the gravel. The road stretched ahead. She exhaled, ragged. No turning back. She cut a strange silhouette against the twilight, her tattered white party dress flaring around her legs above steel-toed boots. She looked like a question no one wanted the answer to. A bright red bow perched in her hair completed the off-kilter ensemble. She clung to a fragile hope the night might still turn her way, and if not, the baggie of Holy Smokes in her fanny pack might take the edge off.

The steel bridge loomed cold and indifferent under her boots, each step reverberating through the hollow span. Her breath fogged in pale plumes, vanishing into the night air.

As she approached Bear Lake Campground, a red ATV parked near the roadside caught her attention. The vehicle looked familiar, likely belonging to that boat rental guy. Karl had once made an offhand comment about some university grad running the place, a man with too many degrees and not enough sense to match. Scuttlebutt around town painted him as "light in the loafers." Mama Kaye scowled, the corners of her mouth pulling downward.

Darkness cloaked the office. Any campers hoping for supplies would find more than they bargained for inside, though she had no way of knowing that.

She trudged onward, her grip on the Tupperware tightening as doubt turned to grit. The incline ahead was cruel, the road lined by gnarled trees. The wind slipped through the branches, dragging her thoughts to places she didn't want to go. Shadows flickered at the edges of her vision, threatening to pull her mind into darker places.

The trees leaned in, close as gossiping women. The wind carried something rank. She didn't want to think about what. A girl had to be ready for anything. Even love. Even blood. Sometimes they were the same thing. The Tupperware felt like a stone in her hands. Every step toward Muncie weighed heavier, her doubts growing as the night deepened.

The night pressed in as she reached the pizza sign. Fruit, scrawled in bold pink lipstick and paired with an arrow, pointed down Muncie's laneway. The other word, Free, had blown away, lost now in the tall switchgrass, sometime after the women vanished into the forest.

"Fruit?" she grunted, brow furrowed. Was this a prophecy, a twisted signal forcing her to confront the truths she'd long refused to face?

Thunder rumbled in the distance, the air charged and coiling around her like an unseen predator. The sound mirrored her tangled history with Muncie, a labyrinth of shifting rules and veiled intentions.

She tightened her grip on the foil-wrapped leftovers. Free firewood. Chicken feed. Matches. What once seemed like simple gestures now felt like misdirection, cloaking something far darker.

Was Karl's offhand comment a warning I dismissed? And what about that strange blonde with the short hair? Or is this just the weed dulling my senses? Whatever the truth, there was no turning back now.

The ignorance she'd clung to was unravelling, thread by thread, leaving behind raw truths she wasn't ready to name. Reality had shifted. She stood at the edge of something vast, an abyss that demanded her courage. Mama Kaye squared her shoulders. She'd turn over every rock, even if something under it bit.

The path to Klarence's cabin stretched ahead, each step heavier than the last. She'll listen to her boy's explanation, if he even gives one, and then confront Muncie.

Rain hit without warning, drenching her in seconds. Lightning slashed through the trees, splitting the darkness in jagged bursts. The forest twisted, shadows writhing like living things. The downpour warped the night into something savage and surreal, yet every pounding raindrop sharpened her focus.

No more denial. No more looking away. The truth waited ahead, and Mama Kaye would meet it head-on, no matter what it destroyed.

The gale howling through the trees pushed against her. Her soaked dress clung to her frame, fabric twisting with each step. The foil-wrapped leftovers felt ridiculous in her grip now, but she refused to let go.

Ahead, the cabin loomed, its silhouette barely visible through the rain. She knew every warped board, every rusted hinge, yet something about it felt unfamiliar. Mama Kaye hesitated. Her fingers curled tighter around the Tupperware. Another bolt of lightning lit the porch. The door hung ajar, swaying in the wind. Her stomach knotted. Klarence wouldn't leave the door open in a squall like this.

A breath. Then another. She stepped forward.

The boards groaned as she ascended the steps. Rain dripped from the red bow in her hair, running down her face in cold streaks. One last pause. Then she nudged the door wide with the toe of her boot.

The cabin was dark, save for the glow of a weak, flickering light. The kitchen table stood empty. No sign of Klarence. No movement at all.

Only the shadows reached out.

Her voice came low, rough in the quiet. "Klarence?" No answer. No boots by the mat. No coat on the hook. Her chest tightened. She would check every room, every corner, the attic, even the crawlspace. If he wasn't here, that meant he'd gone out in the storm, or worse, someone had taken him. And if he was hiding, something had scared him bad enough to vanish inside his own home.

Not far off, Klarence trudged through the dense forest, his steps faltering on the slick underbrush. Rain drenched his clothes, chilling him to the bone. The lederhosen had been a terrible mistake, but he'd never imagined he'd be fleeing through the woods in a storm after such a beautiful day. He was glad he'd saved the drowning girl, but it gnawed at him that she looked so much like that shotgun-wielding lunatic dressed like a Wild West woman who'd shown up at his cabin.

He didn't want to dwell on that now.

He'd taken a shortcut after spotting two other women in coveralls, armed to the teeth, and followed them toward the road. He didn't like confrontations, and those two had the look of people who'd shoot first and skip the questions. It was confusing. Didn't hunters usually wear orange? He thought of his mama. *What in tarnation is goin' on here?* he imagined her saying.

Lightning forked through the sky, illuminating the forest in a stark flash of white. Klarence flinched. The charged air felt dense, electric, like everything was holding its breath.

Exhaustion pulled at his limbs. All he wanted was to get back to his stuffed animals and the familiar warmth of his bed. Maybe enough time had passed. Maybe it was safe to return to the clearing where the two unmarked cruisers still sat beside his brother's patrol car.

A crackle from the radio. A dispatcher's voice fizzed through the static. "Karl, are you there? Karl?"

Klarence's relief wavered, wondering why his brother wasn't behind the wheel. Where had he gone for so long? Maybe he met a real woman, a smart woman, but still. He cautiously reached through the open window and grabbed the microphone. "K-Karl's here?" he stammered, his voice nearly lost in the wind.

"Karl? Thank God." Her voice was tight with relief. "We received a report of a murder at Whiteside's campground. Can you confirm your location—" A lightning strike surged through the radio, cutting the transmission in a burst of static.

Klarence froze, his thoughts fracturing. Then, a piercing scream ripped through the downpour, yanking his attention toward one of the cruisers' trunks. He stood motionless, the sound locking him in place. Something cold settled in his stomach. He crept closer, staring at the shut lid, rain pounding against the metal.

Something was alive in there.

Inside the crushing steel confines of the trunk, Choi braced herself for a final, desperate act. The air reeked of sweat and cold metal, clinging to her tongue like dread. Her head throbbed from the earlier concussions, and her breath came in thin, ragged gasps. Time stretched into eternity as the weight of her entrapment pressed in, suffocating. The handcuffs had numbed her wrists. The zip ties around her ankles bit deeper with every futile attempt to wriggle free. She felt like a trapped fox, and the idea of gnawing off her limb to escape felt reasonable.

Her mind circled the same grim thoughts: These women aren't afraid of death, and they are going to kill her when they return. She remembered attending a seminar: *folie à deux*. Shared psychosis—how two people could reinforce each other's delusions, twisting reality into something unrecognizable. That's what was happening. These two weren't just dangerous, they fed off each other. Dealing with one behavioural case was bad enough. Two? Twice the unpredictability. Twice the danger. Twice the crazy.

Her derringer was tucked against her ankle. Two bullets. One chance. Maybe, just maybe, she could end this madness, if she timed it right.

Choi's pulse pounded, sweat crawling down her back despite the cold. Her fingers fumbled toward her ankle. "Ally Oops," she whispered, "come through for me, my little darling." Gritting her teeth, she twisted her body, ignoring the burn in her muscles. Her trembling hand angled the tiny gun toward the latch.

The first shot rang out, deafening in the confined space. The acrid stench of gunpowder stung her nostrils as the bullet tore through the trunk lid. A muffled yelp came from outside. Choi's breath caught. Had she shot someone?

A twisted surge of triumph rose inside her. Was it Babe? Or that cheeky friend? The thought of taking one of them down sent a jolt through her battered body.

She fired again. The trunk lid burst upward, lightning slicing across the drenched clearing.

Klarence.

Her eyes widened. A cold weight settled in her chest as she saw his wide, terrified stare. Choi screamed, her voice raw and jagged. Had she killed him? Dread coiled in her gut, tight and unrelenting.

She hooked her fingers over the edge of the trunk and hauled herself out. Shuddering gasps tore from her as she collapsed onto the wet ground, rain plastering her hair to her scalp. The moment she looked up at Klarence's stunned expression, a blinding bolt of lightning split the sky, striking with brutal precision.

Agony. The sharp stench of ozone. The sickening scent of charred flesh.

Choi's body jerked, then crumpled.

Klarence stumbled backward, the flash still searing across his vision. He stood frozen, unable to process what he'd just witnessed.

Then panic flooded him. "Mama, mama, mama!" he screamed, bolting into the forest, his cries lost in the thunder.

The weather shrieked above, unfeeling, unyielding. Lightning flickered in the distance, mirrored in Choi's lifeless eyes, as rain washed the grime from her skin.

Chapter 58

Babe tightened her grip on Ariana's arm, steadying her as they slogged through the rain-soaked forest bordering Muncie's cottage. Mud sucked at their boots. The downpour blurred their vision. Every step dragged heavier, exhaustion clawing at their heels.

Then, through the curtain of rain, they spotted the bunkie. Molly's yellow cap perched on a Muskoka chair, illuminated by a jagged fork of lightning. Both women froze.

"Look." Babe's voice cut through the rainfall, sharp as a blade. "Do you see that?"

Ariana squinted, pain pulsing in her swollen ankle. "Great. What now? Go in guns blazing?" Her voice carried the bite of frayed nerves.

"And risk shooting Molly? Brilliant plan," Babe snapped. "We're almost there. Let's not make this harder than it already is."

Rain swept down in sheets as they crept forward, the wind muffling the brittle snap of deadfalls littering the ground. They moved as one, inching toward the bunkie.

Crack! The unmistakable sound of an axe biting into wood.

They went rigid.

Lightning slashed the sky, revealing Muncie beneath the canopy at the woodpile. The axe rose and fell in a steady rhythm, each swing deliberate, almost hypnotic. He was far from the bunkie, but the sight of him, calm and unaware, sent a shiver through them both.

"The fuck," Ariana whispered, gripping Babe's arm.

"We go now," Babe whispered. "While he's distracted."

Together, they edged toward the bunkie. The porch groaned under their weight, but the storm swallowed the sound. Babe hesitated, eyes on the yellow cap. Its brightness felt out of place, almost mocking in the gloom. She shook the thought away and eased open the door. The hinges creaked as she guided Ariana inside.

The door clicked shut.

Locked.

Their eyes met in the dim glow of the gooseneck lamp, tension thick between them.

The bunkie reeked of mildew and sweat. Babe considered the cramped space. Two cots, bare except for stained mattresses, sat against opposite walls, their metal frames rusted and skeletal. A rickety table stood in the corner, a single chair pushed stiffly against it. The lamp cast warped shadows across the walls.

Silence pressed in. The thunderstorm's onslaught was muted by the thick walls. Only their breathing filled the room.

Ariana slumped onto the cot, cradling her ankle. Babe exhaled, feeling the sting in her cheek. The bruise had darkened, the skin throbbing with a dull heat.

They stared at each other, the weight of what came next heavy in the air.

"Are you ready for this?" Babe whispered, her voice steady, though her heartbeat hammered in her ears.

Outside, the rainstorm raged, a relentless reminder that the hardest part of their journey was still ahead.

Near the edge of the estate, a different kind of storm was gathering.

Mama Kaye stepped away from Klarence's cabin, dread twisting within like a viper. Her boy could be out there, lost, soaked, and shivering in the dark. Exhaustion dragged at her limbs, but she pressed on. The rain-soaked party dress clung to her frame, a tattered banner of determination.

Lightning split the sky, the glare catching Muncie at the woodpile beyond the Vienna Convention sign, posted crooked against the jagged trees.

Mama Kaye drew a breath, a cold, brutal fury tightening in her chest. Granddad's voice echoed in her mind: *It was time to see who had shit in the buckwheat.*

"Muncie, youse and me needs to talk."

Muncie's shoulders jerked, the axe handle wobbling as his eyes snapped to her. His expression shifted, surprise bleeding into apprehension.

"What's this about, Mama Kaye?"

"There'll be no goddamn wedding until you tell me what's going on between you and me Klarence!"

"Okay, whatever that means," he chuckled, tossing a split log onto the pile. It landed with a heavy thud, like a stone in the pit of her stomach.

She stepped closer, her voice low and lethal. "Word's reached me from the woods, Muncie. People say you've been overly familiar with me boy. I want the truth, and I want it now."

Muncie's mouth twitched. The way his gaze darted from her to the ground reminded her of a boy caught filching candy. "Mama Kaye, was it the boogeyman whispering tales? I have been… guiding Klarence, helping him lift his spirits. That's all. Whatever you're thinking, maybe it's best you go home, dry off, lie down. We'll talk tomorrow."

She knew that expression, one where he thought his words were gospel. "Guidin'? Or controllin'? You think I'm blind to what's been happening right under me nose? Don't you sugarcoat nothin', Muncie." She jabbed a finger toward him. "What goes between you and me Klarence in those moonlit hours?"

Risqué screeched from a nearby tree, feathers slick, hopping higher, his beady eyes pinned on the scene.

A deep flush crept up Muncie's neck. "We simply enjoy each other's company. We go skinny-dipping, letting the lake wash away life's burdens. I help him release tension and ease his mind. We take turns opening up to each other, diving deep into our… feelings. Sometimes it's as simple as lending him a hand, offering comfort when he needs it. That's all it is. Support. Male bonding. Connecting with our… primal selves, exploring emotional depths." He leaned in, adjusting a log on the chopping block. His movement was stiff, deliberate. His fingers clenched tighter around the axe. "Isn't that what families are for? After all, Klarence doesn't have a father to look after his needs."

She smiled. "You are one silver-tongued devil." Scripture burned through her mind: *Vengeance is mine; I will repay, saith the Lord.*

But waiting for divine justice felt like waiting for rain in the desert, and that smug look on his face only meant one thing.

She yanked the axe from his grip. Lightning flashed across the blade as it bit through flesh and bone. Muncie crumpled into the dirt, blood spraying warm against the cold rain, soaking into the earth like an unholy baptism.

Risqué shrieked, vanishing into the storm.

Mama Kaye stood over him, breath steady, heart a hard drum in her chest. The wind lashed through the trees, a raw requiem for the man who had thought himself untouchable. She tilted her head toward the heavens and let out a raw, unbroken scream.

It tore across the estate, over sodden lawns and empty woods, slamming into the dock like a hammer strike. The driving rain lashed against Molly as she waited in the water, silent as a shadow, her breath barely breaking the surface. The cold gnawed into her bones, turning her muscles stiff, but she stayed still, watching Ginger on the dock.

The skinny redhead's legs dangled above the dark water, the flogger resting in her lap, coiled like a snake.

That wail from the far side of the estate had been the distraction Molly needed. The moment Ginger's head tilted, searching for the source of the scream, Molly struck. Her hands clamped around Ginger's ankles, yanking hard.

Ginger shrieked, arms flailing as she tumbled backward, the flogger slipping from her fingers and smacking against the dock.

Molly hauled with every ounce of strength, dragging her into the lake. The impact sent water spraying in a burst.

Underwater, limbs tangled. Molly's lungs burned, but she held on, feeling Ginger's nails rake across her neck.

They broke the surface, gasping. Rain lashed their faces. Ginger's hand snagged the flogger floating nearby. Triumph flashed across her bloodied face as she raised it high above her head.

Molly was faster.

She plunged beneath the waves, vanishing into the storm-churned dark. Ginger's wild swings sliced through empty air, her frustration mounting.

Seconds passed.

Molly erupted from the water. She flung her sodden sweater over Ginger's head, the heavy fabric clinging like a shroud.

Ginger thrashed, clawing at the sweater as the storm swallowed her muffled screams. The flogger bobbed nearby.

Molly seized it, her body shaking with exhaustion and fury. Every nerve screamed for vengeance, for justice, for the satisfaction of ending her tormentor once and for all.

Then, a sharp screech split the night.

Molly turned.

Perched on the rope tethering the bowrider, Risqué's feathers glowed like embers in the moonlight, his beady eyes locked on her.

The rain had eased to a steady drizzle, the wind softening. The storm was beginning to fade.

She remembered Ginger's words: Risqué never left Muncie's side. Its presence here could only mean one thing.

She was free.

The weight of her captivity lifted. She tossed the flogger into the dark water and turned to Ginger, who had torn the sweater from her head, wide-eyed, shivering, and cornered.

Molly felt the rage boiling inside her. The bunkie was just yards away. The thought hit like lightning: drag Ginger inside, lock the door, leave her to rot.

But the thought soured.

Molly had lived that nightmare. She wouldn't become the thing she despised. Not even for revenge. She drew a breath, steadying herself.

"Go," she said, her voice low and clear. "Run. If I ever see you again, there won't be a second chance."

Ginger didn't wait. She scrambled onto the dock, slipping, lurching, then vanished into the forest.

The lake's surface calmed, faint ripples trailing the echoes of their struggle. Molly hauled herself onto the dock and sank to her knees, trembling. She looked at Risqué, who tilted his head, eyes gleaming.

A broken laugh escaped her lips. She reached out, and the bird hopped onto her wrist. As she rose, Risqué climbed to her shoulder, claws anchoring her to the moment.

She had endured. She had survived. The yellow cap on the Muskoka chair caught her eye, but she turned away. Some things belonged to the past.

The lake stretched wide before her, dark and unknown. Moonlight skimmed the surface in a pale shimmer, casting a quiet glow over the water.

Molly's gaze followed Risqué as he took flight, the bird's silhouette slicing across the stars. She stood still as the mist washed over her and felt the truth settle in her chest.

She would never be caged again.

Part Two

Chapter 59

The vent hissed, stirring stale air. Ariana sprawled on one of the narrow cots pressed against the wall, fanning herself with an outdated crossword puzzle book.

Babe hunched over a chipped desk beneath a gooseneck lamp, scribbling on a thin paper tray liner. Its teal border framed her tight, hurried script. The stiff collar of her institutional coveralls scratched at her neck, the words State Psychiatric Hospital stamped across her back like a brand. A muscle jumped in her jaw. "Say that again," she said without looking up.

"I said, do you really think General Sedgewick read that sick story you sent him?"

"The General would've devoured it. He was probably too busy enjoying himself to read between the lines," Babe muttered. "You remember what he was like during indoctrination, don't you? Or was I the only one subjected to his psychotic little games?"

Ariana snorted. "I'm still surprised nobody's shanked that prick. If I'd had a pencil sharp enough, I might've."

Babe kept writing. "So why bring it up now?"

Ariana swung her legs over the edge of the cot. The crossword book slipped from her fingers and landed with a dull thud. "It was twisted as hell, Babe. And reckless. You basically laid out the whole plan. If he catches on, we're done."

Babe set down her pen. "If this place isn't hell," she said quietly, "I'd hate to see the real thing."

Ariana stood and began to pace. "I just hope this doesn't blow up in our faces."

"It won't," Babe replied, though her fingers trembled as she folded the tray liner. "General Sedgewick's too arrogant to notice what's right in front of him. He'll probably parade it around, bragging to his lackeys about how delusional I am."

"Is that why you never explained what Chief Brisk wrote on that envelope? With that stupid Number 10 pencil?"

210

"Any loose ends will drive our glorious General straight up the wall. Whatever Brisk scrawled is going to fester in his skull."

Ariana stopped pacing. Her voice dropped. "You pretty much poked everyone in the eye, so let's hope you're right."

"If the truth hurts, not my problem."

Ariana faced her. "And you're sure Molly's gonna come through?"

"If anyone can, it's my sister. She's got the cojones for it." Babe passed her the folded tray liner. "We'll know soon enough. Stay sharp. You remember the plan?"

Ariana rolled her eyes and tucked the paper into her coveralls. "You've made me drill it so many times I could pull it off backward while blindfolded."

"I know. Sorry."

Babe's voice levelled out, but her hands still betrayed the pressure building under her skin. "You know what's at stake."

"I hear you, girlfriend. If this—"

A metallic click sliced through the air. Both women froze as the door creaked open.

Karl stepped into the frame, his crisp blue security uniform stretched tight across his chest. The embroidered Staff label caught the overhead light. "You," he barked, pointing at Ariana. "With me."

Ariana headed out the door, her face unreadable.

Karl's gaze shifted. His lip curled into a smirk that made Babe's stomach knot. "Doctor Muncie wants to see you."

"It's almost lunchtime," Babe said, her voice smaller than she liked.

"Take it up with the doc." His eyes dropped to the faint bruise along her cheek. "And try not to have any more accidents with the walls, yeah?" The door slammed shut. The lock clicked.

Babe sat motionless. Her mind had already left the room, climbing the stairs, slipping into Muncie's office, where he waited with that smug smile curling at the edges.

She closed her eyes and forced herself to breathe. Missing lunch was the least of her problems. It was the hunger that came for you when no one's watching.

Chapter 60

The institution's medical director's office, isolated on the far side of the building from Babe and Ariana, exuded authority. Half-closed louvred blinds veiled the large windows, offering fragmented glimpses of the outside world, a jarring contrast to the carefully arranged interior. Floor-to-ceiling bookshelves lined one wall, packed with psychiatric journals and clinical psychology texts. In contrast, the opposite wall was dominated by diplomas and awards. The only item disrupting the room's sterile order was Salvador Dalí's *The Persistence of Memory*. Its warped landscape of melting clocks draped over bare branches and distorted faces mocked the passage of time. In the background, golden cliffs rose against a barren horizon; in the foreground, ants swarmed a pocket watch, adding a sickly sense of decay as if madness lurked beneath the surface.

The General sat in his wheelchair, tapping bony fingers on the wooden desk, each hollow sound marking his tension. A miniature American flag stood in a pencil holder beside a nameplate engraved with General Sedgewick, Medical Director, in elegant script. Nearby, Newton's cradle sat untouched, its polished spheres holding their silence.

He studied the visitors across from him. Chief Brisk, Tika, and Molly occupied plush armchairs, each radiating a different brand of unease. Brisk's foot jittered beneath him, a sharp, restless rhythm. The man had already voiced his disdain for what he called "invasive security"—the magnetometer, the wanding, the tense elevator ride to this tenth-floor enclave. The General didn't care how it had unsettled him. But Brisk's dissatisfaction didn't end there. He'd gone further, suggesting the institution reeked of paranoia, its pristine surfaces masking something far more sinister.

And then he'd commented on Miss Horn.

It was one thing to deride a medical director, quite another to malign his receptionist. The statuesque, impeccable Miss Horn had tracked their every step, Brisk had claimed, greeting them with a smile more ritual than warmth, as if she ruled the asylum by silent decree. The General allowed himself the faintest smile. Naturally, she had tracked them. And even now, she was no doubt poised at her desk, fingers resting near the phone, ready to respond the instant he rang.

He considered Tika a sad case if ever there was one. The way her eyes darted about the room, furtive and unsteady. No doubt, the idea of her daughter locked in a psychiatric hospital clawed at her pride. She was probably worried about what the bridge club would say. How they'd smile in her face, then whisper behind her back. Every sympathetic glance would come laced with condescension. The shame, that was the true illness here.

Then, there was the other daughter, Molly, slouched in her chair, twisting the brim of her yellow baseball cap. Red smudges stained her denim jacket, evidence of the spilled pasta sauce from the Tupperware container now parked on a side table. The General watched her struggle to maintain a neutral expression, though he could sense her simmering under his gaze. He nearly chuckled. He'd heard just enough from her to suspect she was the sort who'd describe this facility as something pulled straight from the pages of 1984.

Her voice shattered the moment.

"Babe's been spinning wild stories since we were kids, everyone knows that. She even told people I had a phone sex business, for God's sake. Hell, I wouldn't be surprised if she wrote to you, too. But just because she sent letters to the president doesn't make her public enemy number one. Calling him TACO and orange man, joking about carving him like a pumpkin, seriously, who takes that stuff literally?"

The General's smile twitched. He noted, not for the first time, the subtle but unsettling closeness between Brisk and Molly: the way his hand rested just a little too long on her thigh. There was something off about it, something that didn't belong between a father and daughter. And if Babe's account was to be believed, both girls had already endured more than their share of emotional and physical abuse.

Not a bit of wonder she'd killed him off in that outlandish story of hers.

His voice remained measured. "Any threat, real or perceived, toward a sitting or former president is taken seriously. The Secret Service evaluates every potential risk; even offhand remarks can carry consequences."

Brisk leaned in, visibly irritated. "Significant for who, the Secret Service or you? She shouldn't even be in a place like this!"

The General's composure held. "The court ordered her commitment for evaluation after much deliberation, Chief Brisk. This procedure is standard in cases involving potential threats against a president. Until we complete our assessment, Babe will remain—"

"Her name is Bina," Tika snapped. Her frustration cracked through, brittle and loud. "Bina Brisk. B-I-N-A. Bina!" She shoved her hands into her pockets and blew out a breath.

"Yes, of course. Bina," the General replied smoothly, though the faint twitch of his jaw betrayed a flicker of annoyance. Anyone who had spent five minutes with the girl knew she insisted on being called Babe.

Tika turned to Molly, her expression pinched. "I don't understand why your sister insists on doing things like this, Molly. It would be helpful if you could talk to her. Bina never listens to me or your father. We worked our fingers to the bone so she could get her mechanical engineering degree from MIT, and now she's writing… this nonsense. I can't even count the number of cars she's stolen."

"Yes, Mother, we all appreciate your sacrifices," Molly replied, her voice stiff with strained politeness, her fingers tightening on her cap.

Once again, Brisk's hand found Molly's leg.

"Stop that," Tika barked, glaring at him.

The General shifted in his chair, the wheels bumping the desk with a soft clack. "This seems like an ideal time for refreshments." He lifted the phone and pressed a digit with deliberate precision.

Outside his office, Miss Horn didn't blink as the phone buzzed to life. She had anticipated the request before he even made it. The receiver was already at her ear. "Yes, General, he is here now. And I must say, I applaud your thoughtful actions for our guests. Should you require anything else, I'm on standby," she murmured, her eyes narrowing as

Boris approached. "My pleasure, as always." She returned the handset to its cradle.

The reception area rivalled any executive's office, a fact she took personal pride in. The walls were panelled in rich mahogany, the air thick with the scent of polished wood and imported leather. A Persian rug stretched across the marble floor beneath a chandelier, casting a muted golden glow over the meticulously curated space. Every detail, from the fresh-cut orchids in crystal vases to the deep green velvet chairs arranged at precise angles, had been personally overseen by Miss Horn during the recent refurbishment. It was, after all, a reflection of her standards.

"Refreshments for the man," Boris announced, his tone clipped. The phrasing was a deliberate jab crafted to provoke.

Miss Horn folded her arms. "You are here to see whom?" The contempt in her tone was not subtle.

Boris didn't rise to it. He was exhausted by her theatrics, by her hold on the General and by the way he had allowed himself to be led. She pulled strings across every system—payroll, supply lines, internal policy. Nothing moved without her consent.

Boris had given decades to this institution. He knew where the bodies were buried, figuratively or not. And he had plans. But until the opportunity to unseat her came, he'd play the part. "I have these beverages for the esteemed General Sedgewick, our beloved Medical Director," he said flatly.

The door to Sedgewick's office swung open. The General turned as Boris entered with the tray. "Thank you, Boris."

"Of course, sir," Boris replied, placing the tray with exact precision. He nodded toward the stained Tupperware on the table. "Shall I take your offering to the kitchen?" he asked Molly.

Molly stiffened, her fingers tightening on the brim of her cap. "I planned to give it to my sister. Today's her birthday."

"Very thoughtful, miss," Boris said, handing her a damp cloth. "This may help with the spill."

"Thanks," Molly replied, dabbing at her jacket. She kept her tone even though irritation prickled beneath her skin. "I guess the lid wasn't tight. I just wanted to treat my sister. Sorry for the mess."

Boris inclined his head with distant politeness. "Not something to concern yourself with. We have people for that." His eyes lingered a beat too long before shifting to the General as if dismissing her entirely. "Will there be anything else, sir?"

The General waved him off. "No, thank you, Boris."

Boris gave a shallow bow and departed, letting the tension settle again like an uninvited guest.

Molly exhaled. "If I might continue, I think everyone's missing the point." She met the General's eyes. "The last time I talked to Babe, she told me about a woman in here. Married to a film guy. Went nuts after catching him cheating. Gouged out his eyes, castrated him with scissors, strangled him with a sex toy."

The General's brow furrowed. "Was that a question?"

Maybe not, Molly thought, *but it had been a message.* And judging by his reaction, it landed. "My point is simple," she continued. "Are you keeping her here because you think she's like that? Because you're afraid she'll snap?"

The General exhaled through his nose. "Your sister's issues may run deeper than you realize. That, to reiterate, is why she remains our guest."

Our guest. The phrase turned in her stomach. Like Babe was here on some spa retreat instead of locked behind thick walls and cold glass. "Can't she come home while you push some paperwork around?" Her voice stayed taut, controlled, though the fury burned hotter now. "Or does the system only work one way?"

"We don't offer outpatient treatment," the General replied, tone cold, clinical. "Until we determine she poses no threat, she will remain under our care."

Molly pressed her nails into the damp cloth in her lap, bunching the fabric into a knot. There it was again. The wall. The same one she'd been slamming into since she walked in. Bureaucratic, bland, and impenetrable.

Brisk sighed and pinched the bridge of his nose. "Enough with the psychobabble. Can we see my daughter?"

"She's in isolation," the General said smoothly. "COVID-19 precautions."

The lie hit Molly like a slap because she knew it was a lie. Babe had whispered as much three days ago on a borrowed phone. *If I disappear, don't trust them. Especially not the man in the chair.*

Tika gasped, her fingers flying to her pearls. "COVID!?" Her voice wobbled with theatrical horror. "But how could she… She's always been so healthy! Molly, didn't you say she takes vitamins?"

"Mother, that's not how the virus works," Molly muttered through clenched teeth.

Brisk's jaw flexed. "When will we be allowed to see her?"

The General's eyes narrowed. "I wish there was more to tell you," he said. "For now, we must prioritize her well-being."

Brisk leaned back, crossing his arms.

"Well," Tika said lightly, reaching for the teapot as if this were just another afternoon tea, "I suppose we could use a moment to collect ourselves."

To Molly, her mother was either oblivious or determined not to see the tension winding through the room. And that bastard behind the desk, he was lying through his polished teeth.

Every red flag Babe had waved, every paranoid-sounding warning made sense now. The script. The blank civility. This wasn't a psychiatric evaluation. It was an act.

They came here for answers. Not to be worn down.

The General gestured toward the tray. "Please," he said with infuriating ease. "Help yourselves."

Molly didn't move.

She'd done everything Babe told her. Now she waited.

Chapter 61

Down the hall from General Sedgewick's office, an antique elevator gleamed with polished brass panels and stainless-steel trim. Ariana knelt on the herringbone floor, her faded blue coveralls a jarring contrast to the spotless shine. Each careful stroke of her rag worked away the last of the pasta sauce splattered during Molly's chaotic arrival. Details mattered.

The brass walls caught her reflection in warped segments, teeth clenched, and curls clinging to her damp forehead. Behind her, the mop handle she'd used earlier still obstructed the security camera's view. She wiped her brow and kept moving. The stain was gone. Only the faint scent of tomatoes lingered.

Footsteps sounded down the corridor, each footfall measured. She didn't need to look.

Boris.

He turned the corner, spotting Karl lounging in a plastic chair, flicking through photos of naked women on his smartphone. "Well? What's our status?"

Karl chuckled, eyes fixed on the screen. "Shame we can't rent her out. Scrubs that floor like she's trying to erase her sins."

Boris studied Ariana. "She done? Feels like she's been at it all day."

Karl scoffed. "What's your hurry? Had to shut the whole system down for spaghetti cleanup."

Ariana remained silent. Every word reached her, but none touched her face. "I'm finished, sir," she said. Her voice was steady. She wrung the sponge once more and stood slowly, adapting the subservient posture she had spent weeks perfecting.

Karl leaned forward and pointed to the red toolbox beside the bucket. "You got everything packed, Barbeau? Don't want any tools going missing."

"Yes, sir."

Boris tilted his head. "Tools? What tools does it take to clean an elevator?"

Karl shrugged. "You saw the mess, didn't you?"

Boris didn't look at him. "I asked her, not you."

Ariana looked at Karl, who offered a lazy nod. She turned back to Boris. "Some sauce got behind the wall panels, sir. I had to remove them to clean properly."

Karl smirked. "Or maybe she just didn't want the General gagging when this place starts smelling like a dumpster."

Boris exhaled and walked off, shaking his head.

Karl called after him. "That's right, Boris. Next time you play delivery boy for His Majesty, grab a wipe. We wouldn't want you drooling on Miss Horn."

Boris flinched. "Trailer trash," he muttered and continued on his way.

Ariana filed the exchange away. Knowledge is power, Babe always said, although it was probably a moot point now. She handed Karl the toolbox, taking great pains not to let him see the roll of Scotch tape she had tucked into her pocket earlier. She wheeled the bucket into the hall and gave the air a quick spray of deodorizer. "We wouldn't want the General disappointed," she murmured as the scent of lemon filled the air.

Karl barked a laugh. "Image is everything, huh? You'd make a perfect wife if you weren't so damn crazy."

Ariana smiled. Just enough. Let him believe it.

They reached the stairwell, and she paused and looked back. The elevator glowed behind her, polished like an altar. Sanctified.

She said a silent prayer for Babe. Then she turned away.

Behind the polished surfaces and lemon-bright air, something waited. Not in plain view but tucked behind heavy doors and humming lights.

The treatment room wasn't far. Just another hallway. One more locked door.

To the staff, it was nothing. A space on the floorplan. A box to check off on the schedule.

But to Babe, it was a battlefield. Not a war waged in silence, but in sound.

The white walls gleamed under fluorescent lights. Disinfectant clung to the air. Monitors droned a steady note, warning of what was about to begin. In the center of the room stood the Electroconvulsive Therapy machine. Small. Silent. But it held enough power to split a mind.

Its hum buzzed underfoot like a trapped animal waiting to strike. The first time left scars. Some still marked her skin. Others went deeper.

Leather restraints dug into her wrists, ankles, and forehead. A thick mouthguard muted her screams, reduced them to panicked gasps. Her eyes darted overhead, searching for a fixed point.

They found the Kit-Cat clock.

Mounted high on the wall, its black-and-white frame looked absurd in the sterile light. Its eyes shifted side to side. The tail swung. *Tick. Tick. Tick.* That plastic grin never moved. Time still passed, even here. That was the cruelty.

The clock had no second hand. Its ticks dragged, each moment stretching out beyond what the body could bear. Its rhythm matched the deepening hum of the machine. A duet of dread.

Her gaze jumped from a garish macaw in a dollar-store painting to the metal tray of electrodes to the stained padding beneath her spine. Always back to the clock. Its tail. Its stare.

Then, the whine sharpened. The hum thickened, vibrating through her bones. She tensed. The straps tightened. The air shifted.

And then—

The current hit. White static burst behind Babe's eyes. A bitter taste rose in her throat. One thought looped and blurred: don't let them take you.

Colors shattered. Reds. Yellows. Blinding blue. Her muscles jerked. Her spine arched. Her mind unravelled.

Then stillness. Only the clock remained. *Tick. Tick. Tick.* Counting down to next time.

Today, stripped to her bra and underwear, Babe waited again. The name embroidered on his lab coat read Dr. Muncie. Neat black thread. She couldn't stop staring at it. He placed the electrodes with surgical calm. Her heart pounded. Her palms stayed slick. The hum returned. Her body braced.

"Nurse Shepard," he said without looking up, "if you would."

Ginger stepped in, starched and clinical. Her white uniform contrasted sharply with Babe's discarded coveralls. She worked quickly, double-checking the connections. Then she pressed the button.

CLICK.

The electricity surged. Babe's world vanished in a burst of light. Her limbs snapped against the gurney. Her breath vanished. For a moment, she was nowhere. She was nothing.

A sharp beep. Then the power stopped. Her body fell slack.

She reached for a thought—any thought—but they scattered like dry leaves across a highway.

"You're doing fine," Muncie said. His voice sounded distant, clinical. As if he were reading it off a chart. "Just one more step in the process."

Ginger removed the mouthguard, her face unreadable. "I think she's had enough."

"Careful, Nurse Shepard. You always sound concerned."

"Just making an observation." She unfastened the wrist strap.

Muncie checked the wall clock. "Ah, yes. The time. You wouldn't want to explain to Miss Horn why the transfer is late, would you? The escort team is likely already waiting."

Ginger hesitated, then nodded. "Of course, Doctor."

Once the door shut behind her, the air shifted. Muncie turned the lock. He faced Babe with a practiced smile. "That was just a taste," he said. "A little preview of what's ahead."

From a nearby cabinet, he retrieved a stack of paper tray liners. Teal-bordered. Familiar. "Your pathetic little story." He flicked through them like playing cards. "And your colourful commentary about me. Something about a rooster, wasn't it?" He shook his head, almost laughing. "What a damaged little mind."

Babe looked up. A single crack ran across the ceiling. Small. Thin. Still there.

Muncie's voice cut through again. "Did you think General Sedgewick wouldn't show me this? That your twisted fantasies would do anything but make things worse?" He hurled the stack into the cabinet. "By the time I'm done, you won't remember your name. You'll be too far gone to care."

She didn't blink. Didn't move. The crack stayed fixed in her vision. "Do you hear me?"

Babe tried to answer, but her throat was sand.

The slap turned her head. Pain lit her skull. Tears came without sound.

"Still got a shiner from last week. Let's even it out."

The backhand landed hard. Her vision doubled.

Muncie exhaled. Slowly. Deliberately. Then he unfastened his belt. "Now," he whispered. "For the best part." His eyes dragged over her body. "Let's call it something special for your birthday."

Babe stared at the crack. This place would break everything but her will. And the war wasn't over.

Chapter 62

The facility's cafeteria buzzed with tension, a disjointed symphony of shuffling feet, clattering trays, and muttered conversations. Fluorescent lights hummed overhead, their harsh glow casting a sickly yellow pallor over the room. Rows of institutional grey tables with bolted-down chairs stretched across the space, their scratched surfaces worn from years of nervous tapping and mindless fidgeting. The scent of lukewarm, overcooked vegetables and industrial-strength disinfectant clung to the air.

Patients drifted between the serving line and their assigned seats, some clutching their trays with white-knuckled intensity, others staring blankly into nothingness. Some whispered to unseen figures, their mutterings broken by bursts of laughter or sharp warnings.

At one end of the room, Choi and Slim stood guard, dark uniforms crisp, boots planted. Their expressions mixed boredom with contempt. They were here to project authority, but their disdain for the facility's residents was plain to see.

Choi surveyed the room, her mouth twisting into a smirk. "Look at these freaks," she muttered to Slim. "A bunch of animals in hospital gowns. If it were up to me, I'd set up a firing range in the courtyard and turn 'patient discharge' into a whole new experience."

Slim chuckled, folding his arms. He eyeballed Kingfish, straddling an imaginary motorcycle, hands gripping invisible handlebars as he revved a phantom engine. "Hell, I'd give them all lobotomies. And for the ones who can't stop playing with themselves? Snip, snip, problem solved." He made a scissors motion with his fingers. "Look at this one, Harley Davidson over here. And we're the lucky dopes stuck babysitting him."

His eyes shifted to Father Johnson, who stood on a chair in the corner, arms outstretched. "Who's ready for a come-to-Jesus moment?" Johnson called, hopeful but strained. "Anybody? Hello? Anyone at all?"

Slim rolled his eyes. "Or that one. Thinks he's some saint. Put him out of his misery, and we'd all be better off."

Choi patted the baton at her hip, fingers stroking the handle as she watched Klarence cross the room. "Most of them belong in cages," she said, "and some others could use an adjustment to their therapy."

She glanced toward Klarence again, her smirk deepening. "Though I gotta admit, some of 'em are… gifted." She tapped the baton meaningfully, eyes gleaming with amusement.

Slim snorted. "Yeah, Klarence could knock a man out cold just by turning too fast."

Choi laughed, shaking her head. "Damn shame about the wiring upstairs, huh?"

Slim's grin widened as his attention turned to Whiteside, who shoved his way to the front of the food line. "Look at this guy, hustling like it's gonna make a difference. He'll still be nuts when he gets his grub."

Behind the counter, Otis, an orderly in a stained white apron stretched over his belly, handed out hot dogs with a huff of resignation. Each tray held a paper liner with a teal border. Utensils were plastic, counted before and after every meal. Nothing sharp. Nothing weaponizable.

"Am I late for dinner? Am I late?" Whiteside shouted, cutting ahead of Mr. Lincoln, who panted like an eager dog, tongue lolling as he waited behind Klarence.

"Does it look like you're late for dinner?" Choi snapped. "Back of the line, Whiteside. Capiche?"

Klarence glanced at Whiteside's wet pants and danced in a circle. "Pee-pee pants! Pee-pee pants! Pee-pee pants!"

Mr. Lincoln barked and growled, drawing chuckles from nearby patients.

Otis rolled his eyes as he handed Whiteside a tray. "For Christ's sake, take ya goddamn food an' sit down. Ev'ry freakin' day with you people, take what ya get an' move along." He let out a long sigh. "Swear to gawd, this place is gonna be the death of me."

Mama Kaye leaned into Rusty. "Use an axe, save yerself the tomfoolery."

Rusty nodded. "Just the way it is, sister."

Not long after finishing her elevator shift, Ariana stepped into the supply closet, a narrow space stacked with industrial-sized detergent bottles, disinfectant, and bundled mop heads. The air was thick with the acrid scent of bleach. She'd already handed Otis his key, but not before letting herself in to stash the cleaning supplies. Her expression stayed neutral, tuning out the background noise of the guards' smug commentary and the patients' scattered ramblings. She'd heard it all before.

Then the door swung open.

Karl guided Babe into the room, his hand firm between her shoulder blades like he was helping her walk a straight line. She didn't resist, but she didn't respond either. The collar was twisted, fabric creased where someone had gripped it too tight. Her arms shook. Her eyes stared through the room, blank and unreachable. Karl shoved her forward. She stumbled into the daily menu board.

Ariana stepped in fast, brushing past Karl to catch Babe before she collapsed. He recoiled like she was contagious. "Get off me, schizo," he growled, slamming the door behind him.

"Honey, hold on to me," Ariana said, her tone low, calm, laced with fury.

Babe clung to her, fingers digging in. Her lips quivered, her voice frail. "God help us."

Ariana didn't need to ask what had been done. And she knew she'd be next once the novelty of Babe wore off. She pulled a capsule from her pocket, cracked it open, and positioned it under Babe's nostrils. "Sniff. Come on, Babe, I need you!" A sharp snap. Then, fire in her sinuses.

Babe gasped, jerking away from the sudden burn ripping through her. The world snapped into focus in an instant. Her pulse hammered against her ribs, and she choked on the sting of chemicals.

"Good, honey, you're doing good," Ariana whispered. "Stay with me."

Babe nodded slowly. Her muscles ached from the procedure, and her skull throbbed like a clenched fist, but the fog was gone. The heaviness pressing against her mind had somewhat lifted, replaced by raw, buzzing awareness.

She was here. She was awake. And she was still in hell.

A patient in a tattered hospital gown clambered onto one of the sofas, his bare feet sinking into the worn fabric. Swaying, he giggled under his breath, then stretched his arm up and smacked the power button on the television bolted to the wall.

The screen flickered to life with an ad for Dickie's Women's Clothier. The announcer's voice cut through the din as Dickie's smug grin filled the screen. "This programme is brought to you by Dickie's Clothier, on the corner of Meyer and Darnell, proudly serving—"

The earsplitting wail of the fire alarm drowned out the broadcast.

"Dammit!" Slim roared, shoving a patient who lunged at him. His eyes snapped to the red alarm bell mounted high on the wall, where the muffling fabric had been removed, exposing the metal clapper hammering out its piercing warning. "Who the fuck tampered with this, Choi-ski?"

"Who knows? It worked the last two times," she shouted, backing away from the patients, who couldn't process the painful, mind-breaking sound.

The cafeteria erupted into sheer madness.

Choi found herself pinned to the wall by a swarm of wild-eyed patients. She shoved one back, swinging her baton at the hands grasping at her uniform. "Move it! Move it! Outside to the rear courtyard! How hard can it be for you animals to get in line?" But the chaos swallowed her orders.

One patient grabbed another's hair and ripped; the victim's screaming was lost in the frenzy. Another sank his teeth into someone's arm and wouldn't let go.

Otis bellowed, throwing a patient off his back. Another lunged, a cafeteria tray flashing through the air, catching him in the throat. His eyes went wide. His knees buckled. His mouth opened, and the only sound was a strangled wheeze. Blood pulsed through his nose as he dropped, skull to tile. No second chances.

Slim and Choi vanished beneath a wave of fists and fury.

Babe and Ariana slipped into the storage closet and shut the door with pandemonium swallowing everything behind them.

Nine floors above, the alarm still wailed, muffled by distance but no less urgent, as Boris guided the General's wheelchair down the hallway. A new safety measure had been implemented after previous incidents: Boris would accompany the General in case evacuation required him to be carried.

Even in the pandemonium surrounding her, Miss Horn maintained her polished appearance, aside from the jarring contrast of her stark white HOKA running shoes. There was no way she was taking ten flights in designer heels. She ushered Brisk, Tika, and Molly toward the stairwell.

"Why can't we take the elevator?" Tika shouted, panic sharpening her voice.

"Emergency protocol. Restricted access," Miss Horn replied.

"Mother, suck it up," Molly snapped, nudging her toward Brisk at the top of the stairs.

Boris swung the General's chair around the corner, nearly colliding with Muncie as he burst from his office. The trio approached a grim-looking Karl, standing beside the open doors of the General's private elevator.

"Updates, Karl?" the General barked.

"Police and SWAT are on-site with paramedics. Fire should be arriving now." What he didn't say was that he'd reached the cafeteria too late. His coworkers were already gone, swallowed by the riot. He figured his contract didn't include a death sentence. It's better to stay clear of the slaughter and wait for law enforcement than to play hero.

The men filed into the elevator behind Boris, who pressed the control panel after wheeling the General inside. The doors slid shut with a metallic finality, muffling the blaring siren and plunging the cabin into silence.

"How is your patient progressing, Munce? Her family is here today," the General said.

Muncie shrugged. "A sad young lady. Delusional, truth be told. No question she'll need more sessions. Now she's making noise, accusations, actually. Says I've assaulted her using lubricant."

The General snorted. "No doubt she'll write something about that next. I'll be curious if she claims it was silicone or water-based."

The men chuckled.

"General, your key," Boris interrupted, urgency creeping into his voice.

"Karl, you had it last for the cleaning," the General said.

Karl dangled the key in front of Boris, who snatched it and slotted it into the panel. He twisted.

Nothing.

A heavy click. Then... silence.

Boris jabbed the buttons again, sweat beading along his temples. "This beast won't activate!"

"Wait. What's that?" Muncie muttered, spotting something taped to one of the doors near the floor. A teal-bordered paper tray liner, half-peeled and curling at the edges, fluttered from its adhesive.

Muncie ripped it free, eyes narrowing at the jagged handwriting. Confusion flickered across his face, then dread.

"Well, what does it say?" the General demanded, leaning forward in his chair.

Muncie hesitated, gripping the placemat like it might combust in his hands. His voice dropped. "It's... it's the conclusion to that story Lincoln wrote."

"I asked you what it says," the General hissed, composure fracturing.

Muncie swallowed hard. "Sedgewick, you, with your twisted games and fascination with Newton's cradle, should remember your question the first day we met in this shithole. The answer is a reaction. Now you're about to experience what that word means."

"What else? There must be something. Speak, goddamn it!"

Muncie skimmed the lower half of the placemat, dread sinking deeper into his gut with each word. "She's compromised everything, the locks, the brakes. That key triggered it. She signed it, Cheerios, Babe Lincoln."

Karl shoved Boris aside and jabbed the button for the main floor. The elevator jolted, began to descend, then shuddered to a stop. The lights flickered.

"Fucking useless!" Karl growled.

"Call security," the General snapped. "Or maintenance!"

Boris snatched the emergency phone off its hook and pressed it to his ear. A beat passed. His face twisted in fury. "Son of a bitch!" he bellowed, smashing the handset against the wall. The plastic shattered, fragments raining to the floor. "Phone's dead!"

"Of course it's dead," Karl hissed, his speech clipped. He clawed at the middle seam of the doors, yanking with all his might. Nothing. "We're trapped!" He turned, levelling a finger at the General. "This is that little tramp's doing. She set this up! And you, General, you're the one who's responsible."

The General remained still, eyes studying the golden key still lodged in the panel. His fingers curled, then relaxed. His voice, when it came, was a whisper. "Our end."

Boris scoffed. "What?"

The General exhaled, eyes distant. "Our actions, like the cradle, have returned to us."

Boris barked a laugh. "Philosophy? Now?"

"Where the fuck is my phone?!" Karl growled, digging through his pockets.

Silence sealed the elevator as the light overhead flickered once… twice… then dimmed.

Muncie leaned against the wall, closing his eyes as fragments of memory surfaced. When he opened them, the others were still, their eyes fixed on him. His lip curled.

"That little bitch thinks she's won." He rolled his neck, a sick smirk curling at the corner of his mouth. "By the time I'm finished with her, she'll be begging to forget."

No one spoke. The elevator remained still. All through the institution, the fire alarm kept screaming.

Chapter 63

The New York State Psychiatric Hospital loomed like a fortress against the sky. Fire truck lights and ambulance beacons flashed red and blue across its facade, strobing in urgent rhythm. The building seemed to breathe, alive with a sense of madness.

A perimeter of police cars cut into the hum of the city street. Their headlights sliced through the growing crowd. Curious onlookers pressed against the yellow tape, craning their necks for any glimpse of the unrest inside. Officers stood sentinel, their stiff postures and unsmiling faces a silent warning to anyone who thought about stepping closer.

Beyond the barrier, firefighters moved with purpose, their helmets and SCBA masks reflecting the emergency lights. Axes and tools clinked against their heavy suits as the wail of sirens reverberated off the hospital's walls.

Inside, the cafeteria was a war zone. The fire alarm shrieked like a banshee, stabbing at every corner of the room.

The patients' eyes darted in every direction. The hysteria that had consumed them moments ago had ebbed. Like animals sensing their own destruction, some whimpered. Others scratched at their arms or yanked their hair in fragmented confusion.

SWAT officers shouted orders as they seized control. Boots pounded against the linoleum, their rhythmic thuds underscoring the mayhem as they ushered patients toward the doorway.

Teal-bordered paper tray liners lay trampled underfoot, torn and stained with blood and half-eaten food. Crushed trays littered the floor, smeared with the remains of abandoned meals. Blood pooled in broad, sluggish smears beneath the flickering fluorescents.

Order had returned, but only just.

A Rastafarian man wedged between a sofa and the wall stirred from his stupor. His dreadlocks clung to his sweat-dampened face like wet vines. He blinked, head lolling as he took in the wreckage around him. "Hey, man," he mumbled, "Someone answer da phone."

No one responded. The room had been swallowed by madness.

Then, a mechanical click. The fire alarm cut out.

The Rastafarian gave a slow nod. "Cool," he mumbled.

Across the room, the bodies of Choi, Slim, and Otis lay sprawled and broken. Paramedics moved past them without urgency, their focus on the living. The dead would stay where they were until the scene was secured, their presence just another part of the wreckage.

Scattered around them, patients lay still, some twisted at unnatural angles, others slack-jawed, eyes wide open and unblinking. A frail man in a shredded hospital gown had been trampled into the corner, his foot jutting from beneath an overturned table. One woman, face smeared with blood and applesauce, clutched a plush monkey to her chest in frozen rigor mortis, her expression a haunting mix of terror and surprise.

They were casualties not just from the riot but of abandonment, left to fend for themselves in a world that had always kept them locked away and sedated. Now, in death, they were finally still.

Nearby, two firefighters lingered before turning and heading for the exit. Their helmets and SCBA masks hid their faces; reflective visors turned them into mirrors. Unlike the frantic paramedics and officers, they didn't rush. They moved with eerie calm, untouched by the destruction.

The Rastafarian's gaze drifted to the daily menu board hanging askew on the wall. Behind it, the red fire alarm pull station had already been pulled. Just beyond, the supply closet door stood slightly ajar, revealing a dislodged ceiling tile above two empty cardboard boxes. Stencilled letters on the sides read "Buffalo Fire Department." He tilted his head, lips moving as if to voice a thought, but whatever came to mind slipped away into the haze clouding his brain.

Outside, the fire trucks loomed like hulking shadows, their emergency lights dimmed but still pulsing red against the hospital's windows. Engines rumbled low and steady, a bass note beneath the soft shuffle of emergency personnel and the slow dispersal of the crowd beyond the barricades. The sirens had faded, but the tension clung to the air like the echo of something unfinished.

Babe and Ariana emerged from behind a fire truck, helmets tucked under their arms, the weight of their borrowed gear pressing down on sweat-dampened bodies. The cool night air bit at flushed skin, but Babe barely registered it. Her limbs still felt heavy, her pulse lagging behind the rush of adrenaline. She leaned against the cold metal, letting it ground her. Something real. Something solid. Her chest rose and fell in slow, even breaths, the ammonia capsule still burning faintly in her sinuses. It had snapped her awake, but the echo of the ECT still clung to her bones. "That was insane," she murmured, voice rough. "Can you believe it?"

Ariana exhaled, peeling off her gloves and flexing her fingers. "Told you it'd work. Just like in the movies."

Babe blinked at her, her eyes dropping to their gear. "What did you do to get these?"

Winking, Ariana peeled off her jacket. "Let's just say… I made a friend."

Babe straightened. "Ariana—"

Their eyes locked. Ariana's expression was unreadable. "Do you really wanna know?"

A long beat passed before Babe exhaled. "Forget I asked."

Ariana nudged her forward. "Smart choice. Let's move before someone starts asking questions."

They crossed the street and ducked around the corner. In the shadow of a shuttered storefront, they stripped off the firefighter gear, tossing it behind a stack of crates. Sweat soaked their blue coveralls, the fabric clinging to their skin. They peeled the top halves down, knotting the sleeves around their waists to hide the stamped letters across their backs.

Babe turned. "Tell me you've got it."

Ariana pulled a phone from her pocket and handed it over. "You up for this?"

"Watch me."

With a few quick swipes, Babe accessed the hospital's internal security feed. She tilted the phone so Ariana could see. The screen flickered to life, showing grainy footage from inside the elevator. Karl, Muncie, and Boris sat against the brass walls, faces drawn. The General stared straight ahead, unmoving in his chair. There was no sound. Just panic, fury, and the slow bleed of realization. "Hey, Sedgewick. Nice to see you," she muttered. "And Karl, Ariana says thanks for the phone."

Karl exploded. His mouth twisted in a snarl as he slammed his fists against the panel. "Babe, you little—"

"Save it," Babe said.

Muncie lunged toward the camera. "Let us out, you little witch!"

Babe leaned in. Her voice dropped. "Sedgewick, you read my story. I promised you the ride of a lifetime. Enjoy it."

Her thumb hovered over the keypad. For a moment, she hesitated. Not because she doubted what needed to be done. Because of memory. The sterile white ceiling. The sting of the electrodes. The way her voice had broken when she begged him to stop.

Is this who I am now?

She shoved the thought aside. Maybe it didn't matter. No one had ever saved her. No one had stopped them. Her hand trembled. She pressed the sequence.

The screen jolted. The elevator shuddered. Fury twisted into fear. Their mouths opened in silent screams as the car began to fall.

The feed went dark.

Ariana exhaled. "When I think of that story you wrote. . . it feels like we were killing them again."

Babe stared at the screen, her face unreadable. "I thought it would feel different."

"Think of the women who won't have to suffer anymore." She reached out, threading her fingers through Babe's and led her toward the open street.

Ariana stopped short. Her hand tightened on Babe's arm. "You've gotta be kidding me."

Babe followed her line of sight.

Under a sputtering streetlamp sat a black 1967 Corvette Stingray—sleek, low, and gleaming like wet stone. It crouched like a predator, daring them closer. Everything about it screamed run now, ask later.

"You're shitting me," Ariana whispered. "We'll be a fucking billboard leaving town in that."

"You know what I always say."

Ariana groaned. "Oh God. What?"

"Probably something stupid."

They laughed.

As they neared the curb, Ariana blew out a breath. "You sure this isn't a trap?"

"Relax. Molly left us that Corolla behind it."

Ariana blinked, spotting the battered tan Toyota parked a few yards back. Relief softened her features. "Okay. That's more our speed."

She froze mid-step. Her hand snapped out, gripping Babe's wrist. "Babe… do you feel that?"

Babe pointed at two trembling kittens by her foot, their tiny bodies pressed together. She watched them scamper into the street. "We need to keep these darlings safe," she said, ignoring a low, unnatural vibration settling in her ribcage like a warning from something unseen. She stepped forward.

Ariana followed, then stopped. "Wait!"

The vibration spiked. It became a growl, a deep mechanical snarl that rattled the air.

Ariana's breath caught. "Babe!"

The growl erupted into a roar as a fire truck tore through the intersection, sirens off, lights dead, moving like a juggernaut. Steel and death and momentum.

Babe and Ariana spun to face it.

Time stretched. The truck's horn blared.

Ariana lunged. Her fingers brushed Babe's. Locked tight.

Their eyes met, and in that glance lived every word they'd ever shared.

Then—

The world went black.

Epilogue

The elevator opened with a faint chime, revealing a space reborn. Once an antiquated chamber, it now exuded modern elegance. Matte-black walls absorbed the ambient glow of sleek LED strips, casting diffused light across the pristine interior. Beneath the subdued illumination, polished black flooring gleamed like liquid night. A faint scent of cedar and citrus lingered, replacing decades of mechanical grime and musty neglect.

She crossed the threshold. A pair of stiletto heels, matched to a tailored slate-blue suit, clicked across the seamless terrazzo floor, each step measured and precise. The sound echoed briefly, then faded into the hush of the corridor. In her hand, a cream-coloured envelope rested, its edges slightly worn, as though it had travelled far to arrive at this moment. She wasn't sure why it felt important, only that it did.

The hallway stretched ahead, pale grey walls interrupted only by narrow vertical panels of frosted glass that caught the muted gleam. Recessed lighting traced a quiet path toward a single black door at the far end, unmarked except for a discreet silver biometric keypad embedded beside it.

Miss Horn moved through the reception area with fluid precision. She reached the keypad and pressed her thumb to the scanner. A soft chime acknowledged her clearance, and the door opened with a smooth hydraulic hiss.

Inside, the office was a masterclass in modern minimalism. A vast glass desk dominated the space, its surface immaculate save for a closed laptop. Where Newton's cradle once stood, there was now a single orchid in a black ceramic pot and a nameplate in elegant script:

Evangeline Horn, Medical Director

Sunlight slanted through motorized blinds, striping the room with alternating bands of light and shadow. Behind the desk, the walls were slate grey, unbroken except for Dalí's *The Persistence of Memory*, its melting clocks suspended in a world where time had lost its meaning.

Miss Horn crossed the room with purpose, her heels landing softly on the plush charcoal carpet. She stopped at the desk, setting the envelope precisely in its center. A faint reflection of her perfectly coiffed brunette hair gleamed on the glass surface as she stared at it.

She reached for the silver letter opener and, with a clean stroke, slit the envelope open. A single sheet of ivory paper slid free. She unfolded it carefully.

Her eyes moved across the page. Slowly. Once. Then again.

No reaction. Not at first.

But her gaze sharpened. Her mouth tensed at one corner, barely perceptible. Her hand lowered the letter to the desk, though her fingers stayed resting on the page as if reluctant to let it go. The script was unmistakable.

Dear Ms. Horn,

Congratulations on your well-deserved promotion. Stepping into leadership is no small feat, and your commitment to both excellence and discretion has clearly been recognized. You've earned your place as top dog in the kennel, and with it comes the responsibility of ensuring no loose ends remain untied.

In light of this, we must address something that cannot go unacknowledged. It is with a mix of solemnity and quiet admiration that we report the death of the identity known as Babe Lincoln. The woman behind the name lives on. But the persona, the façade, the legend, has fulfilled its purpose.

Babe was more than just a force of nature. She became a beacon for those who had been overlooked, cast aside, or left without a voice. She devoted herself to the weak, the helpless, and the forgotten, always seeking justice where others turned a blind eye. Her defiance was matched only by her compassion. She never backed down from a fight, especially the kind everyone else had already given up on.

Her life was spared in a moment of extraordinary courage by her companion, Ariana Barbeau. When a stolen fire truck came barreling toward them, Ariana pulled her from its path without hesitation. It was a single act of bravery that captured everything Babe once stood for: loyalty, instinct, and the refusal to let the world have the final word.

In the days that followed, the woman who had lived as Babe Lincoln slipped free from the place that tried to erase her. This was not just an escape but the beginning of something new with someone who loved her.

Reports place them somewhere warm, where the weight of what they endured has finally begun to lift. Together, they left behind the chaos and the coveralls, trading it all for sunlit beaches, salt in the breeze, and bare feet in the surf.

They did not vanish without consequence, and the path was never clean. But they are beyond the reach of those who would never understand, and any search now would find only shadows.

Now, side by side, they sip something strong and watch the tide roll in, no longer waiting for the world to break them.

As you step into your new role, Miss Horn, remember that legacies are not always built in boardrooms. Sometimes, they are written in defiance, lived in truth, and sealed in silence. Let hers remind you of what strength can look like.

Congratulations again. The future of this institution lies in capable hands.

Cheerios,
Bina Brisk
P.S.: Remember: we all answer to someone.

Acknowledgements

To the brilliant (and possibly brave) teams at MyPoolitzer, Quantifiction, and Blue Denim Press, along with the panel of judges, for hosting the first AI-judged writing competition. And to my endlessly patient family and friends, who continue to indulge my love of storytelling, humour, and all this glorious foolishness.

Author Bio

After a successful career as a locomotive engineer, Dave studied writing at George Brown College in Toronto before escaping to the quieter shores of Cobourg. Now retired, he splits his time between spoiling his grandchildren, dodging yard work, and conjuring up strange new characters who refuse to leave him alone. He is the author of the novel *Ballet of Deception* and is currently at work on his third novel, another twisted tale sure to draw readers into the shadowy corners of his imagination.